CW00970613

St
in the
Wind

British detective fiction at its best

Carol Cole

THE
BOOK
FOLKS

Published by The Book Folks

London, 2025

ISBN 978-1-80462-311-4

www.thebookfolks.com

STRAW IN THE WIND is the second title in a series of standalone mysteries set in Hampshire featuring Detective Inspector Callum MacLean.

Chapter One

Callum MacLean awoke with a start. The quilt had slipped from his thrashing body during the night and drying sweat tingled on his bare skin. He flung his arm across the other side of the bed. It was empty and cold. 'Grace?' He turned his head, shattering his dream of his late wife and their Kelvinside flat.

He sat up, swung his legs over the edge of the bed, and dropped his head into his hands. His long hair fell forward, and he ran his fingers through it, pushing it back from his face, pushing back the nightmare. This was the third consecutive morning Grace had woken him before the alarm. He raised his arms above his head, stretching his spine, then flexed his neck and shoulders before blinking the sleep from his eyes to look out of the window. He slept with the curtains open. The novelty of viewing the stars sprinkled high above the New Forest was still with him after three months away from Glasgow. Fading pinpricks of glitter and a pale, dead moon remained visible in the predawn grey.

Dressed in running clothes, he slipped out of his cottage on the edge of Hatchet Green, walked down behind the village school, and then up an incline onto Hale

Purlieu. He eased into a run. The dewy mist dampened his face, and familiar smells of dank vegetation and horse dung travelled with him. At this early hour, the turf that was scorched by last summer's sun, was silvered with moisture and his feet beat a steady tattoo as he ran. There was no one else about, save for a solitary van heading in the opposite direction, its headlights turning the birch foliage into flickering lace.

When he reached Stricklands Plantation, he veered to the left and bounded down through the tussocky grass onto the boggy valley floor. He startled a chestnut mare and her colt, who darted from the bushes, heads held high. They trotted a few strides, then dropped their heads to graze. He was still getting used to the herds of wild ponies that ran free in the New Forest. There was a vast chasm between his previous location and this one, but the biggest adjustment was life without Grace.

He leapt over the narrow stream on the valley floor and jogged up the steep climb to the ridge. The gorse bushes stood silent, cloaked in dew-beaded spiderwebs like shawled women standing at a graveside. These first three months in England had changed him. He was not sure if he could still cope with his old life, with the noisy crowds and the constant bustle of the city. He was not sure that he even wanted to try.

The rising sun slashed a knife edge of gold along the horizon. He crested the ridge, brushing through the calf-high heather, and surged onto a gravel trackway. The mist was thinning, and he caught a flash of pink in his peripheral vision. It was the woman he had seen in the distance two mornings before. She was heading away from him along the wide track that ended at the gate to Mays Firs. He knew two things about her; she ran with the conservative actions of a pro and, from a distance, appeared to have no hair on her head. His policeman's curiosity wanted to know more. He was not alone in marking her progress.

In the lee of Millersford Copse, fallow deer paused in their grazing of the lush bog grass and lifted their heads to watch her. The herd leader stamped a hoof as his huge palmate antlers swung back from the retreating woman to watch Callum. When the rut began in a few weeks, opposing bucks would bellow and clash antlers to fight for control of territory and does. That would be a time to maintain a safe distance. Callum did not rate his chances of outrunning an angry buck.

Once on the ridge, he lowered his head and sprinted towards home. Legs pumping, elbows scything, he set a pace that would have left Grace far behind. He wondered if the pink woman was running away from memories, too. The drumbeat of his feet was an overture to the day. The mist bowed and withdrew, a cloud-dotted blue sky appeared above, and he knew that the clear air promised another fine day. In Glasgow, the weather had never really bothered him beyond turning up his collar against the dreich drizzle. Here, good or bad, it seemed to be a preoccupation, at the forefront of every new conversation.

Breathing hard, he slowed, scattering gravel on the path down to the stream. The flow had depleted to a brackish trickle after the hot summer, and he leapt over it in one easy stride, the peaty smell filling his nostrils. Away to his left, a rabbit zigzagged, squealing, through the bracken, then dived into a hole, with a flash of cotton-wool scut. A dog fox gave up the chase and watched Callum. Daisy Donaldson, his animal-loving sergeant, would have shared her thoughts on the food chain and survival of the fittest. He had learnt a lot from her about this formerly alien environment.

He slowed to a walk and took deep lung-filling breaths when he reached the tarmac of Tethering Drove. He turned left, heading for home, but paused to look through the heras fencing into the building site where his new house would stand. The place was silent and still, save for a late-hunting tawny owl ghosting through the old apple orchard. Callum stepped back onto the road and broke into a jog. It would be months before his home would be habitable. Currently, it was just a subterranean maze of trenches that his builder referred to as 'the footprint'. The ribbon of houses on his right was mostly dark, but one or two early risers were flicking on lights and opening doors to let their dogs out into the garden. When he reached Hatchet Green, his phone buzzed. It was Daisy, and he stopped to answer it.

'Morning, sir. We've got a body.'

* * *

Late-September sun stabbed through the conifer trunks, gouging shadows across the busy crime scene. Outside the cordon, Godshill Wood Inclosure sheltered a forest cottage, and the grey smoke from its garden bonfire drifted towards Callum. The smell reminded him of childhood holidays on the Seil Island croft of his grandparents. There was a bite in the air this morning as if the turn of the season had awoken the weather from a summer doze, and it was snapping its teeth in protest.

Crime scene tape surrounded the wide gravel area between the cottage gate and the tarmac road. The uniformed constable guarding the entrance stamped his feet and blew on his cupped hands. When Callum moved towards him, he pulled back his shoulders and stood up straight.

'Morning, sir.' The smell of cigarettes hovered around him as he wrote "DI MacLean" on his clipboard.

Callum's attention was fixed on the blurred outline of a person inside the milky sheeting of the crime tent. He hoped it was Dr Martha Jones. She was a bossy besom, but also a consummate professional. In Glasgow, he had constantly nagged his team to keep up to his high standards and was unconcerned that they had considered him a thirty-four-year-old intolerant misery.

Pushing through the door, his view of the victim was obscured by Martha kneeling beside the body, her back towards him. The Tyvek suit strained in every conceivable direction and appeared, as usual, to be several sizes too small for her. She did not look up when he closed the flap.

'The Miracle Man cometh. Good morning, MacLean.'

'Morning, Martha. What have we got?'

He leaned sideways to peer around her at the body and static electricity in the roof snatched at his hair, making the canopy feel small and claustrophobic.

'What we have not got, MacLean, is room for a giant and a goblin in this pixie house.' She glanced over her left shoulder as he shuffled a little closer. 'Nice boots. Been shopping?'

He had, but asked instead, 'What can you tell me so far?'

'Not much. Dead, but no visible or obvious cause. She's been dead for less than twelve hours; rigor is partial. It's early days for this one.' She turned back to the body. 'Daisy's witness will have more to say for himself than mine at present. Now get out of here before we both suffocate and let me do my job.' She sounded a little more brusque than usual.

Callum rubbed a knuckle against his eyelid. Perhaps she was also suffering from sleep deprivation.

'Hmm.' He shuffled a step to the left and peered around her. The corpse was female, young but fully mature, with thick black curls much longer than his shoulder-length hair, and wearing some form of long pink nightdress, similar to what his grandmother wore. Her bare feet protruded below the hem, and he noted that both toe and fingernails were painted pillar-box red.

'Out, MacLean.' Martha flapped a gloved hand at him, her focus on her task, and he obliged.

He stepped out of the tent, eased the cricks out of his neck and stood to his full height. As a lanky youth, being tall had embarrassed him, but he had grown into his frame and was happy. The crisp autumn air chilled his chest from the inside out, and the hammering of a woodpecker made him homesick for Scotland.

Inside the cordon, near the closed gate of the cottage, was a boarded-out white van, the back doors open. A man sat on the rear sill; head sunk into his hands. He wore work boots, denims and a checked shirt with the sleeves rolled up to the elbow.

Callum pegged him as a probable local but didn't recognise him. He did recognise the blonde ponytail of Daisy standing next to the man. He was in capable hands.

He fastened the buttons on his jacket. Sunlight glinted on the earring in his left lobe; his single act of rebellion at university, kept because Grace had liked it. His mother called it his worry bead.

There were a few bystanders outside the tape, most of whom he recognised after three months down south.

'Inspector MacLean?' An elderly woman, in a tweed skirt and wellingtons, stepped away from an ancient estate car and approached the tape. She tipped back her head to make eye contact with Callum, who was a generous foot taller than her. The retired headmistress was not one to waste his time or her own.

'Mrs Smart. Good morning, how can I help?'

'Good morning, Inspector. I was first on the scene apart from Paul.' She nodded to the man sitting in the van. 'I called the police for him and have already given my account to the officer.' She looked across to the constable with the clipboard. 'He told me to wait but I was wondering if I might take my boys for their morning walk now. I'd rather they didn't have an accident in the back of my car.'

The heads of her two black Labradors watched her through the windows.

'I'll be back home in half an hour. I promise not to do a flit.' She chuckled, her features softening from stern to approachable.

He liked both her intelligence and her directness. She was a plain speaker who did not dance around an issue. The downside of this was she tended to ask direct personal questions, which made him uncomfortable.

The constable joined them. 'Madam,' he said, 'I told you to wait in your car. Now stop bothering the inspector.' He looked up at Callum and shook his head, his expression expecting support.

Callum turned his back on the officer. As she had already spoken to the first responders, he saw no reason to make her wait. 'Perfectly fine, Mrs Smart. Sergeant Donaldson and I will call on you later this morning.'

She lived a stone's throw from his own rented house, so he would have no trouble finding her. And he disapproved of people who, when entrusted with power, used it overzealously to prove they were in control.

'Thank you, Inspector.'

She got into her car, started the engine, and revved up for take-off. If she continued driving like that, she was going to need a new clutch before her next MOT.

Ignoring the dissatisfied grumblings of the officer, Callum walked across the gravel towards Daisy, mulling over the information he had so far. It was unusual to have no probable cause of death. Bullet holes, knife wounds and blunt force trauma were all easy to spot and enabled his team to hit the ground running in the right direction. Until Martha gave them something more substantive, there was little they could do. A magpie flew across his path, its harsh *ka-ka-ka* amplified beneath the evergreen foliage. The sound reverberated in his head. He hoped it was not an omen.

'Morning, sir.' Daisy turned at the spit of stones beneath his boots. She glanced down at his new footwear and the corner of her mouth twitched before she focused on his face.

He valued her attention to detail and her observation, but less so when it was directed at him.

'This is Paul Barnes. He lives here in Forest Cottage.' She pointed to the dwelling behind the closed five-bar gate. 'He found the body this morning.'

The man raised his head. He was in his mid-fifties, clean-shaven with a thick crop of untidy hair that drooped over his brow. It looked like he had cut it himself, giving him a boyish innocence. Paul's eyes were watery, and his lower lip trembled. Discovering a body could have that effect, but it was surely an overreaction. There was no visible blood, no suggestion of injury or violence. Callum was about to comment when he caught Daisy's warning look in Paul's direction. The reason was unclear, but he trusted her judgement. She was more sensitive than him and quicker to pick up on people's needs. Or, perhaps, he was just more inured by the depravities of humanity.

In the back of the van, behind Paul, gardening tools were secured to the sides with disciplined precision. Two terriers sitting on a pile of folded sacks bounced forward to greet Callum, tails wagging. They seemed friendly enough, so Callum gingerly reached out a hand to fuss the dogs. He was not overly comfortable with animals; the larger they were, the less comfortable he became, and he usually left any close contact to Daisy.

'What are their names, Paul?' he asked.

'This is Frodo' – he brushed his broad hand over a tan-and-white head that had a hairless grey scar along its snout – 'and this one is Bilbo.' He had a strong local accent, and a voice much lighter in texture than his body weight suggested. 'The mum and them bubbies was left in a box at my gate, a long time ago. I saved them, but the mum's died now. She was old. I buried her in the orchard where all the dead dogs are.' His glance flickered beyond his cottage, then returned to the detective. 'Bilbo's got a black patch on his head. *B* for black and *B* for Bilbo. See?'

Daisy remained silent. It was unusual for her to have nothing to say.

'I do see,' said Callum. 'Do you like *The Hobbit*, Paul?'

A bright smile chased away the furrows of concern from Paul's brow. 'It's my favourite ever book I've got. They live in burrows, underground, and keep them very tidy.'

Callum reassessed the situation as Daisy took her notebook from her pocket.

'We need to ask you a couple of questions about earlier this morning, Paul, if that's okay with you.' Callum kept his voice low.

The older man glanced across to the tent. He plucked at the front of his shirt with soil-grained fingers, and his frown returned.

'Would you prefer it if we went into your house?' Daisy asked.

Paul nodded, stood up and the dogs jumped out of the van and trotted towards the cottage. Lifting the police tape for Paul to dip beneath it and open his gate, Callum exchanged a glance with Daisy and caught her half-smile. She liked going into people's houses and seeing how they lived. She said it gave her a more complete picture of them. Callum thought it drew attention to the things people wanted to keep hidden.

Chapter Two

They followed Paul and his dogs inside the open door of the cottage. Callum dipped his head to avoid the lintel that was so low it could explain Paul's liking of hobbits. He was grateful that the house he was having built had doors of a realistic height.

Bonfire smoke drifted in and floated towards two checked shirts draped over a string stretched between beams. The ceiling, once white, was bruised by years of woodsmoke curling up the chimney breast from the open grate. The smell of dogs, with an undernote of cooking fat, filtered through the bonfire smokiness. Paul's eyes flicked to a congealing plate of eggs and bacon on the draining board. Callum supposed that if your day was interrupted by a dead body, then your appetite might suffer. He could not imagine eating that much fat at any time of the day.

'Let's sit down,' Daisy suggested.

It was not the worst kitchen he had been in, but Paul was not influenced by any hobbit habit of tidiness. On the dresser opposite the door, blue willow-pattern plates backed shelves busy with pens in chipped mugs; string in a jar; and a faded sketch of bluebells propped up by an old mobile phone. Light glinted on the prong of a mousetrap, and the brass caps of spent cartridges. It seemed that Paul deposited everything in the nearest vacant space, and there it stayed until it was greyed with dust.

Callum pulled out a chair and read the shopping list written on a board nailed to the wall: beef, bacon, sardines, pizza, melon, cosas – a product Callum did not recognise – and washing powder. The writing was neat and uniform, the spelling accurate, and it was all in the same handwriting. The man ate well, had a methodical approach to housekeeping, if not housework, and appeared to live alone.

Paul sat at the table and elbowed the breadboard aside, scattering crumbs, and Bilbo and Frodo licked them from the floor. He rested his bare forearms on the table, thick ropes of muscle that bulged when he clenched his fists.

Daisy dragged a chair away from the table, the beech legs squealing on the quarry tiles.

Paul's hands were broad, with calloused pads, paint on the knuckles and jagged skin edging grainy nails. Working hands, shaped by physical toil. Callum's own fingers had short, clean nails; more used to painting pictures than walls.

'Can you tell us what happened this morning?' Callum's burred voice was soft.

Paul stared up at the ceiling through his fringe. He looked like a small boy searching for lines he must remember for his teacher.

'The boys barked, I didn't hear anything, but we went out for a look-see.' He spoke slowly as if the words were echoes of those already rehearsed in his head.

Was this his standard response to figures of authority? Or unusual situations? Callum had to acknowledge that, for most people, it was unusual to discover a dead body outside your house.

'Were you expecting someone?' Callum asked.

Paul nodded. 'Dave Green. I always services his mower before he puts it away for the winter.' He looked at Callum. 'Lawnmower,' he added, perhaps doubting that Callum knew what he meant.

Dave Green was the local man who was building Callum's new house. 'And was it him?'

Paul scrubbed at his eyebrows. 'There weren't no one there. Just 'er.' He paused and slid a sideways glance at Callum. 'But a van was driving away.' He looked down and picked at the skin edging his thumb.

'Tell me about the van.'

'It was white, and it was a Peugeot Partner like mine. They're very good vans. Reliable. Don't rust.'

'Did you recognise it or get the registration number?' Callum held his breath as he waited for an answer.

'It was just a van. Me and the boys runned over to help her.' He looked from Callum to Daisy. 'I tried to make her breathe again. Then Mrs Smart came in her car.'

Callum imagined Paul kneeling beside the body where Martha now knelt, his heavy hands pummelling the ribcage.

'It doesn't always work though, Paul,' Daisy said.

'You did the right thing,' Callum said. 'Do you recognise the girl, Paul?'

Paul shook his head. He reached down to pat his dogs, one corner of his mouth lifting as his shoulders relaxed. 'We've done the right thing, boys.'

'Did you see anyone?' Callum asked.

'Mrs Smart. She patted my shoulder, like when I was at school.' He was silent for a moment. 'I like Mrs Smart. She's nice to me. She called the police.'

Daisy flipped closed her notebook. 'Will it be all right if we take your fingerprints, Paul? And we'll need to take a look in your van.'

Paul paused for a second, then nodded and stretched his hands out towards Daisy.

'Not just this second,' Callum said, 'but we'll get that sorted so we can eliminate you from our inquiries.'

* * *

After the hovering dust of the cottage, the outside air felt cool and clean. Callum breathed in an infusion of pine, laced with damp vegetation and bonfire smoke as he leaned against the wing of Daisy's silver Navara, and waited for her to join him.

'Get Bird onto a house-to-house, concentrate on the white van.' His eyes flicked to Paul who had come outside and stood in his garden watching them, elbows resting on the top bar of the gate.

'If we're lucky, it might have been caught on a doorbell camera.' He couldn't remember seeing many, but it was worth checking. In his first case here, he had been unprepared for the lack of CCTV coverage. It blanketed most towns but was largely absent from this rural setting. 'Or a dashcam,' he added. 'And tell Cookie to get a list of local white-van owners, smaller than Sprinters, but don't restrict it to Peugeots. Then check with Missing Persons, see if they can shed any light on the girl's identity.'

Daisy finished writing notes and slid the book into her pocket. 'I'm onto it.' She took out her phone and surfed for a number.

'What did you make of him?' Callum asked while she searched.

'He talks so slowly. I wanted to wind him up.' She rotated her head in a circle without taking her eyes off her phone. 'Harmless enough. Do you think he's a sardine short of a shoal?'

She had read the shopping list.

He shrugged. 'You saw that list, meticulous, perfect spelling, good uniform handwriting, and he reads books. I get the impression that he's long practised at thinking before he speaks. I wonder why that would be.'

'Perhaps he's just not used to company, other than Bilbo and Frodo. Nice little dogs, aren't they?'

Callum grunted. She rarely passed up an opportunity to tease him about his wariness of animals. She was renowned for knowing all the local pets by name. That was another two she could add to her tally. In the last three months, he had learned a lot from her about animals and was more comfortable with them now than when he first arrived. However, her recent suggestion that he try riding one of her horses, to see how much fun it could be, had fallen on deaf ears. She would have a long wait before that happened.

'Perhaps he doesn't meet too many people in his day-to-day,' he said, ignoring her question, 'or he's acting the way people expect him to.'

'Do you think so?' She tipped her head to one side and looked at him, squinting against the bright sun.

On their first case together, he realised that Daisy was nosy and angled her head when gathering information. Curiosity made her a good copper, but he was working on ways to deflect her attention from him. She was tenacious and it was proving difficult.

'Get Bird to find out what he can about Paul. I'm just going to check with Martha and then I'll meet you at Daphne Smart's.'

He heard her car door snick closed. Her tyres chewed into the turf behind him and hummed along the tarmac. A freshening breeze ruffled the trees, and the gentle creak of lifting branches was overtaken by the solid tread of his boots crossing the gravel to return to the tent.

'You again, MacLean.' Martha sounded a little flustered and had pinpoints of colour on her cheeks.

'I'm just off, Martha. Anything to add?'

She swivelled to face him, sat back on her heels, and blew out a long breath behind her mask. 'Sorry, MacLean. She has got a couple of broken ribs, but I think our heavy-handed helper might be responsible for that. No punctures, no wounds, no signs of percussive impact, no fractures to the laryngeal cartilages, the hyoid is intact, and no petechial haemorrhaging, so probably wasn't strangled. And incidentally, no ID – which is what you might expect for someone wearing a nightie.'

Callum took a last critical look at the body: late teens or early twenties, wavy black hair, large facial bones, and a wide forehead that made her look intelligent. The only jewellery he could see was a silver cross and chain around her neck. Her hands and feet were now bagged for forensic examination, and it gave the body a doll-like appearance.

'Any other jewellery?'

'Just the cross that you've already noticed, and gold stud earrings.' She lifted the tangled hair away from her ear, and he saw the small, round gold ball in the lobe. 'One only, the other's missing.'

'Hmm. Okay, thanks.'

The pink nightdress was old-fashioned, not what he would have expected a young woman to be seen dead in unless that style was back in fashion. Since Grace's death, he had avoided lingerie – finding it impossible to dissociate it from the memories of his wife. Late wife.

'What do you think of her nightdress?' he asked.

Martha was amused. 'I think it's several sizes too small for me, and way too dated for my taste. It's the sort of thing my granny used to wear along with check slippers and hair curlers.' She shifted her weight, and above her mask, the lines on either side of her eyes bunched together. 'Now myself I prefer…'

Callum held up a hand to stop her. 'Never spoil a man's dreams, Martha.' He enjoyed the harmless banter they shared. It helped them both cope with the grim situations they encountered.

'Your loss, MacLean. Seen sufficient?' Her grey eyes studied his face, giving him the impression that she was trying to see inside his head.

'For now. Let me have your report as soon as, please, Martha.'

She drilled him with a steely look following his superfluous comment, and he smiled a quick apology before backing out of the tent.

He slid onto the driver's seat of his Kia Sportage and pressed the button on the dashboard. The display lit up like a space station before settling down and asking him to confirm English as his chosen language. He fastened his seat belt and closed the door with a dull clunk, like the toll of a cracked bell. He missed Grace. And he would have to read his own manual.

Chapter Three

The thorny stands of ever-grey gorse on Hale Purlieu were sprinkled with yellow-flowered confetti, the scent falling between coconut and cat's pee. He caught a whiff through his open window. The sun filtered through the ochre foliage of silver birch trees, burnished the scorched bracken, and strobed into his eyes. Endless undulations of heath rolled away to his right, crests bright, troughs shadowed with the promise of autumn. The dark hollows were the same peaty brown as the girl's eyes.

He slowed as he came up behind a herd of wild ponies trotting single file along the edge of the heath, tails swaying, manes lifting away from their necks with every stride. This year's foals were leggy. Their short, curly tails marking them out from the mares. Daisy, being a horse owner, was always keen to supply him with equine information, even if unrequested.

When the open forest gave way to dwellings, he turned left at the crossroads, towards the village green. The large teardrop of close-cropped turf was surrounded by a narrow loop of tarmac. The green was common ground, used by ponies and people alike, apart from a reserved rectangle of lush turf near the middle, the cricket wicket which was protected by rusted railings. Thatched cottages were sprinkled along one side and across the bottom of Hatchet Green, each squatting smugly behind a hedge or picket fence, their gates secured against the roaming ponies.

He passed the village school on his left, an oversized cottage marked out by the bell canopy on the roof. Pupils were forming two lines in front of a teacher. His cottage was two along from the school, and he shot an anxious glance at the gate. It was closed. He had already mistakenly left it unfastened a couple of times and returned to find his garden full of ponies. It would not have been a problem if they just cropped the lawn, but they were indiscriminate grazers and ate trees, flowers, shrubs and vegetables with equal relish and surprising speed.

The first time they had got into his garden, they had proved difficult to evict, in part because he was wary of them. He had been rescued by a schoolboy. The lad had chased behind the small herd, flapping his arms as if attempting take-off. Steady progress towards the open gate was accompanied by calls of 'Git on, you buggers. Shift yer arses.' Callum had wondered if the lad was older than he looked. The wonky smile of milk teeth he had flashed at Callum when rewarded for his efforts with a few coins, had disproved the suspicion. The following week, when Callum arrived home, he once more found his gate open and ponies grazing on the lawn. His helper, who was 'just passing, mister' was on hand to assist with their removal but was disappointed when Callum decided not to part with any more coins. Much as he applauded enterprise, he was not seeking a long-term business partnership with the young entrepreneur. His own boyhood experiences in Glasgow were a long way from Hale village.

Daisy was already parked beside the picket fence of Snowdrop Cottage. The whitewashed walls were shaded beneath the overhanging thatch of the roof that looked like an oversized hat. She was leaning against the wing of her vehicle, arms folded, head tilted to catch the warmth from the sun. When Callum parked behind her, she levered herself upright and opened the wicket gate to Daphne Smart's cottage.

He followed her in, and she pointedly clicked the gate closed and rattled it against the catch. She had heard about his exploits with the ponies. It must take extreme measures to keep anything secret in a place like Hale.

The blue door swung inwards. Callum dipped his head under the lintel and was instantly struck by the difference between this kitchen and Paul's. Daphne's was bright and clean, scoured to operating theatre standards with not a whiff of dog. Paddy and Rufus rushed to greet Daisy, claws clicking on the quarry tiles, and she smoothed the broad black heads. Their tails wagged so enthusiastically that both dogs swayed from side to side.

The retired headmistress looked sternly at her. 'Daisy Donaldson, I am trying to foster the impression that they are guard dogs. You are not helping.'

'Sorry, Mrs Smart.' Daisy flicked a look at Callum.

He hoped she had managed to appear more contrite as a pupil than she did now.

'What can you tell us about this morning, Mrs Smart?' Callum said.

'Do sit down, Inspector.' Daphne gestured to her kitchen chairs; seats covered with quilted floral cushions secured by tape ties.

'I take the boys for a long run every morning, and this morning I drove along Hale Purlieu towards Woodgreen just after seven o'clock – the news had just finished on the car radio. When I drove round Densome Corner…'

'Where's that?' Callum still struggled with local versions of place names.

'The right angle in the road where Hale becomes Woodgreen.' She paused until he gave a confirming nod. 'I saw Paul Barnes outside his cottage down at the far end of the lane. It is quite a distance, but he seemed to be carrying something. When I got nearer, I saw that I was mistaken and he was actually kneeling next to that poor girl, pounding at her chest with those ham fists of his. He was concentrating so hard that he didn't seem to hear me arrive.'

'Doing CPR?' Callum clarified.

'His version of it,' she confirmed. 'His dogs were in the back of his van with the doors open and when I stopped, they flew out and started barking at me. The little black-and-white terrier was quite feisty.' She paused and looked across to her dogs sprawled on their beds. 'You could take a lesson from him, Paddy.' She returned her attention to the detectives. 'Paddy's far too friendly and he tries to lick people to death. Now, the girl was dead, but Paul didn't realise. He was pumping her chest, so I put a hand on his shoulder and said, "I think you can stop now." He seemed a little distressed. Then I phoned you.'

She pulled her elbows tight to her sides as if she was holding herself together. However professionally qualified Daphne Smart was as a teacher, Callum doubted that her training encompassed what to do when finding a dead body.

'How did you know she was dead?' His question was more interest than interrogation.

'Her colour, or lack of it. Her eyes were open but glassy, cloudy, and when I placed my fingers against her neck, she was cold with no pulse.' She touched a hand to her own throat.

'Did you recognise her?'

'No, Inspector. She was not a pupil at my school.'

'Did you see anyone else, any other vehicles?'

'None. Your constables were the next on the scene and then of course the screaming hordes turned up. I imagine a body is always good for a bit of gossip.' Her tone was disapproving.

'You didn't see a vehicle leaving the scene?'

'No. That doesn't mean there wasn't one. It might just mean I was a second or two too slow getting there. We don't all drive like Stirling Moss.'

When Daisy frowned at the mention of the racing driver from a past era, Callum knew she would write it down and look it up at the station.

'Now I don't condone gossip, Inspector, but Daisy's too young to remember and you're an incomer.' She settled herself more comfortably in her chair, her hands loosely clasped together on the snow-white tablecloth. 'There's something you should know about Paul.'

Callum maintained his neutral expression. What people thought he should know, and what he needed to know, were not often the same thing.

'I'll keep this as succinct as possible as I have a history society meeting later this morning. We have a man coming to give us a talk about the observation bases built for the LDV in this area.' In response to Daisy's expression, she added, 'The Local Defence Volunteers, who later became the Home Guard. Dad's Army.' She glanced at the wall clock.

Callum was about to ask her to focus on the matter at hand, but she returned to the subject without his prompting.

'Paul, and his sister Mary, came to the village when he was six, and she four. Their mother, Susan, brought them to visit their grandparents, Jim and Esther Barnes who lived in Forest Cottage where Paul still lives. Then, Susan – following some form of altercation, I suspect – left without the children, and didn't return. She never did get along with her father. He was too autocratic, not an easy man.' She sniffed a breath in through her nose. 'Esther enrolled them in my school. Jim was not particularly sociable and never used two words if one would do. People used to say they could carry on a whole conversation with Jim without him uttering a single word.'

Callum smiled. She had just described his grandfather, a man happy with his own company but prepared to tolerate the overtures of others.

'Now, in the summer, children have always gone down to the River Avon for a swim. Sadly, his sister Mary drowned. Paul was about ten and he was found kneeling over Mary. He was pummelling her chest and howling. It was thought that the child had got tangled in the weeds and pulled under.' She sighed and the dogs both lifted their head to look at her. 'This morning, Inspector, when I saw Paul kneeling over the girl's body, the incident came flooding back. Probably the same for Paul, which might explain why he was overly upset when I reached him.'

Callum realised that when they had spoken to Paul, the only animation he had shown was when he addressed his dogs.

'He's a quiet man?' He made the statement sound like a question.

'He didn't use to be. He was a chatterbox, quite the life and soul of my classroom before Mary died. After that, he retreated into himself. Spent too much time with that grandfather of his and not enough with other children. As a young teacher, I found Jim a little scary, if I'm honest.' She lifted her head to glance out of the window. 'That cottage has a beautiful setting. It's a blaze of bluebells and celandines in the springtime but it was too isolated for a grieving ten-year-old. Poor little chap. Esther blamed him for Mary's death.'

'Why was that?' Callum asked.

Daphne dipped her chin and eyed him over the rim of her glasses. 'We can only surmise the reason, but I'm afraid to say Esther abandoned him too. Jim said she went to stay with her sister in Hereford and died there.'

'I don't remember her,' Daisy said. 'I only remember there being Paul and old Mr Barnes.'

'Paul would have been about fourteen then. It was just him and Jim after that.'

'He lives alone now?' Callum said.

'He does. I had hopes that he would meet some nice young woman who would bring him out of his shell but, you know, time passes. He's an exceedingly kind young man and would do anything to help people.'

'Does he work?' Callum thought her description of him as a young man was an age-related observation.

'Yes. He delivers logs in the winter, and in the summer, he does people's gardens. And he's very good with his hands. If you have machinery that needs repairing, he's the man to take it to. He could have had a career in engineering with the right encouragement.'

'Does that provide him with a living?' Callum asked.

Daphne looked at the clock and stood up. 'He's very well organised. He has that big orchard behind the cottage, and he gives me apples and fruit every year. I bake him cakes and supply him with jars of jam and chutney. He does the same for many of us oldies. We couldn't manage without him now we're getting on a bit.' She pushed her chair tidily under the table and Callum and Daisy did the same.

'It is how they did things in communities after the war,' Daphne continued. 'The mend and make-do culture. Works very well in villages, Inspector. He's a bit of a throwback from those times, but he has a good heart and genuinely likes to help people out.'

Callum moved to the door and heard Daisy close her notebook and cap her pen. 'Thank you for your time, Mrs Smart.'

'Pleasure. Sorry to be so brusque, but I am rather busy today. This afternoon our art group are gathering for a session of plein-air painting on Hale Purlieu. We're hoping to catch the colours of autumn while we still have the weather for it. We meet every week throughout the year. I hear you are a dab hand yourself with a paintbrush, you should join us, Inspector.'

'Maybe one day, Mrs Smart, but not today.' He softened his refusal with a smile.

When he had first arrived in the New Forest, he had been pitched straight into a murder investigation before he had time to find a place to live. Daisy had given him temporary accommodation and had been impressed with the daily sketches he added to his pictorial diary. When that investigation was over, he had moved into a rented cottage whilst his own was under construction. He had not expected Daisy to share that information with the rest of the world.

Now Daisy turned away from him to pat farewell to both dogs and he recognised avoidance tactics when he saw them.

Chapter Four

Callum secured the gate catch and heard Daisy stifle a laugh. A chestnut pony was sawing backwards and forwards, enthusiastically scratching its rump against his door mirror. Returning to his car in Glasgow, he'd often found the doors keyed or the bonnet splattered with vomit. There was a first time for everything. Did the manufacturer's warranty cover that sort of damage?

Daisy shooed the mare away. The sun glinted on her copper coat and his breath snagged in his throat. His emotions were too close to the surface today, and triggers were stirring his memories. He needed to get a decent night's sleep.

The mare ambled onto Hatchet Green, lowering its head to nibble the short turf.

'No damage done.' Daisy released a few hairs caught around the edge of the mirror, then looked up and smiled as a green pickup stopped beside them.

The driver's window was down, and a tanned forearm rested along the frame of the logoed door, "J EASTWOOD – AGISTER". Callum realised how easily 'agister' had slipped into his vocabulary having never heard of one before he came to the New Forest. Now he understood that Jimmy's job was to keep all things Forest on an even keel in the fifth of the area that was his responsibility.

'Morning, boys and girls. How are you both?' Jimmy asked, and a piebald collie on the passenger seat stood up and wagged her tail.

'Hello, Panda. Good thanks, Jimmy. How are Sue and the tribe?' Daisy smiled at the boyishly open face.

Jimmy grinned at Callum, mimed tucking imaginary curls behind his ears, and raised his voice to a squeaky pitch.

'When's Auntie Daisy going to look after us again? We have such fun with her.' He spoke directly to Callum, his voice sliding back to baritone, his tone confidential. 'That's the same Auntie Daisy who doesn't have to do the washing when she brings them back from the pond soaking wet.'

Callum laughed.

'Unfair,' Daisy said. 'They ran me ragged, and James junior didn't fall in, he jumped into the water. I was knackered. I have no idea how Sue copes with four of them. She must be a superwoman.'

'She is.' There was a light of seriousness in Jimmy's eyes that pierced Callum with a stab of envy. 'Now, business, I'm afraid. A motorist rang me to report an injured pony by the roadside along Roger Penny Way.'

'Where exactly?' Callum asked.

'Deadman's Hill, just before you get to Telegraph Cottage. And it was a big dog, not a small pony.'

'Aww. Whose dog?' Daisy asked.

'That's just it. I don't know. Never seen it before. It was a bit of a mess but didn't look as if it had been hit by a car. I took it along to "Corgi" Pembroke.' He paused when Callum frowned. 'That's the vet at Fordingbridge, Colin Pembroke; you've met him, ginger hair, long nose and short legs?'

'I remember. What did he have to say?' Callum asked.

'That it was young and would recover with the proper treatment. It had previous injuries that were unprofessionally patched up using staples and superglue–'

'Ugh. Poor dog,' Daisy interjected.

'Not microchipped, ketamine in the blood and he's never seen it before.' Jimmy's mouth settled into a straight line.

'What breed?' Callum asked, suspecting where the conversation was heading.

'Pit bull type.' Jimmy's tone was serious, and Callum nodded.

Daisy's head snapped up and she looked from one man to the other. 'Pit bull? That's a banned breed...' Her voice faded away as she slotted all the information into place. 'Someone's been dogfighting. Who?'

'Your guess,' Jimmy said. 'New one on me.'

'And this is supposed to be a nation of animal lovers. Poor dogs,' Daisy muttered.

Both men looked down on her bowed head and held a moment of silence between them.

'Have you seen any activity that might be relevant?' Callum asked.

'No, but I'm going to ride Pirate over that way, get off the beaten track a bit, see if anyone has been about. The dog was on the verge of the road. It could have been tossed by a truck driving through. It might not have come to grief in our area. Not that it makes it okay to hold a dogfight,' he added swiftly, catching sight of Daisy's expression.

'Right. Better get on. See you later.' Jimmy glanced across to the grazing chestnut mare, probably assessing her in his official capacity, before leaving the road to drive down the narrow track that led to his smallholding in the sheltered dip behind the village hall.

Callum's phone pinged a text and Daisy scuffed the turf with the toe of her boot and waited. Fine, blonde hair had escaped from her ponytail, forming a halo around her head. She was not much over five feet tall, had a slim boyish figure, and did not look like a force to be reckoned with, but Callum had seen her in action. She was an officer you were pleased to have by your side.

'Back to the shop then,' he said.

* * *

Callum slowed as he neared the brick-built police station on the outskirts of Fordingbridge and in his mirror, saw Daisy pull into the car park behind him. Upstairs, the only occupants of the CID room were DC Thomas Cooke and a uniformed constable, both of whom looked up when Callum and Daisy came through the door. DC Almadia Levens, Legs, was on annual leave and someone had tucked her chair under her desk. Cookie jumped to his feet, lithe, snappily dressed apart from a ridiculous orange kipper tie, his thick black curls in need of a trim.

'Guv, nothing from Missing Persons for the dead girl so far. Dr Jones is doing the post-mortem this afternoon.' He shifted his weight from one foot to the other. 'I requested the info on white vans, and it should be through any minute.'

Cookie was a glass-half-full person, and it showed. 'I also had a look to see if we had any local criminals who had a record for doing anything that might tie into a dumped body.'

'Good. What did you find?'

'Nothing relevant yet. There are a few people with a list of summary and minor offences, magistrates' court stuff – shoplifting, criminal damage. I did find a small-time crim – burglary, receiving stolen goods and possession of class A. His last sentence was fourteen months but he's out on licence now.'

Every prisoner released on licence had to register an address with a responsible adult, although from experience, Callum knew that the definition of 'responsible' had a fluid interpretation. The more crowded the prisons, the more flexible it became.

'What's their name and address?'

'Frank "Ferret" Fenman, guv, and the approved address is his wife in Woodgreen.'

Not a name Callum had come across. 'Woodgreen will be covered by the house-to-house.' It was also the direction of the departing white van. 'Check where Fenman was this morning and let me know, Cookie.'

'Hunky-doodley, guv. And DCI Bellman wants an update on the body.'

Before the final word was uttered, he had turned back to his computer, curls bouncing as his fingers flashed over the keyboard. He nodded in time to music only he could hear and kept the beat by tapping a toe on the floor. Cookie existed in a bubble, untouched by the presence of others and, on occasion, was a source of great irritation to the rest of the team. But he was also gifted and intuitive with technology and computers, capable of producing information that had been invisible to the rest of the team. Callum grinned to himself. Cookie could be as annoying to work with as an overenthusiastic puppy. But he had a soft spot for the lad and keeping his team on their toes was never a bad idea.

Callum went into his office, a glassed-off portion at one end of the larger room that, to his mind, resembled a fishbowl. He reached across his desk for his phone, and it rang just before he touched it.

'MacLean.'

'That was quick,' Martha said. 'Anyone might think you were just going to ask me for an update.'

'I wouldn't dream of it,' he lied, 'but as you're on the phone...'

He heard her long exhalation hiss against his ear.

'That's the second PM you've stood me up on, MacLean. You're not squeamish, are you, or allergic to the sight of blood?'

He noted gleeful anticipation in her voice and marvelled that she could display such respect and consideration for the dead but delight in taunting the sensibilities of the living.

'Sorry to disappoint you, Martha. I have no problem with the sight of blood, or for the record, guts either. The only problem I have is being in two places at the same time. Any thoughts on a solution are more than welcome.'

'If I had the answer to that one... never mind. Business. Bit of a puzzle, this one, until I cut her up. Female, late teens, generally in good health but a bit overweight. Muscles were flabby like poached pastry, not enough exercise. She has not been to a dentist in the last couple of years, her hair is natural, nails are manicured and polished, but a home-done job, not a salon. Her left hand is painted to perfection, the right is messy, so she's right-handed.'

Callum jotted down the points as she made them and sketched a figure in the margin. Sketching helped him think.

'Now, this is where it gets interesting, MacLean. Her cause of death. She wasn't stabbed, or shot, or strangled... An untreated triple A rupture did for her.'

'Which is?' Callum asked.

'An abdominal aortic aneurysm. Unusual in females, very unusual in young females, but she was a smoker, and when you find out who she was, you'll probably find there is a familial history of it. She bled out internally. Losing consciousness would have been very quick, probably less than an hour start to finish.'

'Then why did they move her? Why dump her on someone else's doorstep and why not call an ambulance if she was that ill?'

'Probably no time for the niceties, and it's your job to answer questions like that. And to help you on your way, here's a bit more info. She has old scars on the insides of her arms, upper and lower, that I opine are evidence of self-harm. They are well-healed and there is nothing new for a while, so she conquered her demons somewhere along the line.'

Had there been a change of circumstances? Or had she grown to like and respect herself, or perhaps someone else had come to like and respect her? Maybe she had gained some element of control over her life that had previously been missing. Something had increased her self-worth.

'She has three broken ribs, post-mortem, down to her rescuer, I should think. No other signs of percussion. No abrasions…'

'But she was dead before she was dumped on the gravel?' It was unconscionable that someone had thrown her out and she died where she was found.

'She was. She had been dead for several hours before she was moved. Lividity confirms that she was on her side when she died, foetal position, and stayed there for some time after death. Now I have taken samples from under her nails, and they have gone off for analysis along with some sort of dust we found in her hair.'

'How long before we get the results?'

'Be patient, MacLean. Now, she wasn't a virgin but does not appear to have had sex recently. I have sent off intimate swabs, but I shouldn't hold out much hope.

Stomach contents were over-the-counter painkillers and water – sparkling, bottled, raspberry flavour. Tox report pending. Have you identified her yet?'

'Nothing from Mispers so far.'

'How many dog owners in the area, MacLean?'

'Practically every household has a dog or two. Why?'

'She has flea bites on her right thigh. Dog hair on the sole of one foot. Black and white. Could be anything from a spaniel to a Great Dane. Good luck.' Her soft chuckle against his ear was replaced by the purr of the phone.

All his neighbours around Hatchet Green had a dog. He was the only house without one. Hundreds of dogs were exercised daily on the heaths and lawns of the New Forest.

Her comment was as much help as bagpipes with no chanter.

Chapter Five

Callum was seated behind his desk, back to the wall, when Cookie scooted into the open doorway.

'I've got that white van list here, guv.' He waved a couple of sheets of paper at Callum. 'There're quite a few people on it. Frank Fenman's on it, and there's one really interesting one.'

He paused as the outer door of the office was pushed open by DC Tony Hampton. The tall muscular man shrugged out of his waxed jacket and dropped it over the back of his chair.

'Hi, Bird,' Cookie said, then his attention swivelled back to Callum. 'It's Jericho Hatcher, the local scrap-metal dealer.'

'What's Jericho done now, Cookie?' Bird pushed his shirtsleeves up to his elbows, exposing his inked forearms, a legacy from his time in the military.

'Nothing.'

'That's a bleedin' change then. Him and his brothers, Malachi and Gideon, are a pain in the bloody arse.'

'They're on my white van list,' Cookie said. 'That's all.'

'I should put them at the top of any list if I were you. If something has been nicked, they're always a good place to start looking.' Bird grunted, dropping onto his chair.

This was the first time Callum had heard the family mentioned, and he consulted his computer. 'Not too much by way of convictions, Bird.'

'Crimes and convictions aren't the same thing, guv. The only reason they get caught at all is because Jericho is a triumph of brawn over brains.' Bird leaned back in his chair and laced his fingers behind his head. 'Who goes robbing lead off a porch, in the middle of the night, and parks his sign-written van under a street light? I ask you. His rap sheet should be much longer, but no one has the balls to give evidence because they know there'll be reprisals. Jericho's got a short fuse, and it gets shorter when he's been drinking.'

Daisy came through the outer office and placed a mug of coffee on Callum's desk. 'I feel sorry for Sheena, his wife,' she said. 'He's turning his boys into mini-Jerichos. Sue Eastwood said Gabriel's been in trouble at school for bullying, and the next one down, Solomon, for thieving from the other pupils. The thing is, he doesn't see it as wrong – finders keepers – even if he found it in another kid's pocket. I can't remember what the little one's called.'

'Joshua,' Bird said, 'but you will seldom meet a more unholy bunch than that lot.'

'Bird, as you've dealt with him before, you follow up on Jericho. Promote them to the top of the list.' Callum heard the soft confirming grunt and turned back to Cookie. 'Chase up Missing Persons, and don't assume that she's local. Cast the net wide.' Something about her facial geography reminded Callum of holidays in Spain.

'Okey-dokey, guv. Right onto that.' Cookie raced back to his desk, his fingers skimming the keys before his backside landed on his chair.

Callum watched him for a moment, and then his phone pinged a message alert. It was just a thumbs-up acknowledgement of his text to Bryony Osbourne cancelling their planned visit to the cinema this evening. Last-minute changes of plan due to work were the norm and they had only managed two coffees and one dinner since their first meeting three months ago. He slid the phone back into his pocket. Her pro bono work for a woman's charity made her hours as unpredictable as his own. Their closeness would never progress to intimacy; he still missed Grace too much, but friendship filled a void in both their lives.

Callum called Martha's number but she was not there, so he left her a message.

'Right, people. Let's knock this on the head for today. And Cookie, check if the white-van owners also have dogs.'

'Dogs?' Cookie said.

'Martha mentioned dog hairs, and flea bites on the girl's body.' He scratched the back of his hand.

* * *

The cottages around the village green were springing out of the gloaming as inhabitants returned from work and put on their lights. The colours outside Callum's cottage were greying as dusk sapped the brightness. He clicked open the gate, pressed his keypad to lock the car and the glow from the interior light faded and disappeared. Shrubs in the garden assumed unusual shapes, and the evening breeze transformed them into dancing escorts as he walked along the path.

A silent shadow kept pace with him, weaving in and out of the bushes. The cat was still here. She had been waiting for him yesterday evening, rubbing against his legs when he unlocked his door. He had told her to go home and closed the door when she had tried to come inside. She had headbutted the locked cat flap and later, when he checked to see if she had taken his advice, she was still there, sitting patiently on his doorstep. He had relented, put out milk and had been rewarded with a chainsaw purr.

Now, he flicked on the overhead lights, leaving the door ajar, his hands full of papers. The tabby sauntered in behind him, tail held aloft, and rubbed her head against his leg, making soft noises in her throat.

'I'm not feeding you. Go home.'

He didn't want a pet, least of all a cat. Cats scratched and bit and clawed you. He looked at the lithe, short-coated body. It resembled a small tiger, a killing machine on velvet paws. The cat squinted its lancet-pupilled eyes at him and purred.

He put his supper in the oven and watched the cat lap at the milk he had given it. What harm could one more feed do? The cat flicked pearl droplets onto her face and up the side of the cupboard. When the bowl was empty, she used a paw like a flannel and washed her face and whiskers. Satisfied with the results, she curled up on the mat and slept.

Sitting at the table, Callum opened his sketchbook. The cat could stay until it woke up, and then he would put her out. He was not going to unlock the cat flap, installed by some previous tenant, because the cat was not staying. He held the pencil loosely at the end of the shaft and swept the point across the page. An image of the cat began to emerge, curled like an ammonite on the mat. He was soon engaged by the rhythmic skirl of his pencil over the white paper as he waited for the kettle to boil.

His habit of keeping a pictorial diary had started when his grandfather had given him a sketch pad on his first solo visit to the Seil Island croft, off the west coast of Scotland. The old man never had much to say for himself, possibly because his grandma spoke enough for both of them. Callum had been fascinated that every night, before he went to bed, his grandpa committed the events of his day to a sketch. Sometimes it was a single picture, but more often it was a series of recollections that produced a memory of his day. He had introduced Callum to this habit, and it had stuck fast. To a small boy, drawing was much more inviting than forming letters and avoiding words he couldn't spell. Now it provided a bubble of calm where the stresses of the day were eased away by the soft caress of graphite on toothed paper.

The comfortable cheesy aroma of lasagne swirled into the room as he lifted the dish out of the oven and put it on a board. He ran a knife across the middle of the dish and put half of the food onto his plate. The other half would do for tomorrow's supper. He made coffee and the radio played the opening notes of Mendelssohn's *Hebrides*. A surge of homesickness enveloped him, not for the living but for the dead. Grace barged into his head, his wild-haired witch, making coffee in their Kelvinside flat, the aroma blending with her perfume. He sat heavily on a chair and closed his eyes. He wanted to look round the room, catch a glimpse of her, as he had tried to do so many times before. He always failed.

The tightness in his chest eased and he opened his eyes. It was his memory clutching at the world that was slipping away. She was not here. She would never be with him ever again. This panic happened less often than it had done in the months following her death, but the impact was powerful, both mentally and physically. He felt weak, the sting of moisture burned his eyes, so he closed them again and took a steadying breath.

There were always triggers, always would be as long as he had breath in his body. Now, an individual stimulus rarely evoked an emotional response, but the smell of coffee and notes from her favourite composer had seeped through his defences. He wondered if Grace would ever leave him. Part of him hoped that she would stay in his heart forever, that the wound she had left would never heal. He would gladly put up with the inconveniences of sleep-troubled nights and stabbing memories rather than lose her completely.

His grandfather had said, 'If you're always looking behind you, you can't see where you're going, Callum lad,' and he knew that was true. One day, perhaps, he would put the memories behind him, but for now, he was not ready to face a world without Grace.

He selected a clean page and sketched the basalt columns of the Isle of Staffa. The marks on the page strengthened as his hand steadied, developing the entrance to Fingal's Cave, and the orchestral phrases washed over him like waves over the granite shore. At the top of the finished sketch, he wrote "For Grace".

Chapter Six

'Morning, sir.' Daisy followed Callum into the fishbowl. 'Mispers have found her.' Daisy paused in the doorway, taking up half the space that Bird regularly occupied there.

Callum motioned her in. Daisy was the best in his team at delivering bad news to relatives, so he earmarked her for the task.

'Her name is Conchita Gimenez,' she continued. 'She comes from Spain.'

He would rethink that idea. 'Who filed the report? Where did she go missing from? And when?' He briefly considered the possibility that she may have been trafficked.

'Her sister, María. They were on holiday in Bournemouth three summers ago, sharing a flat. The parents run a hotel on the Costa-del-something so never get away during peak season. I've sent Cookie to get the file.'

'How old was she when she disappeared?'

'Sixteen. That makes her nineteen now. She was a bit of a rebel, and it was initially thought she went off with a boy to annoy her sister. No proof though, and it doesn't look as if they put too much effort into finding her.'

'Busy time of year, mid-summer in a south coast resort.' A memory niggled at the back of his mind. 'Wasn't there a political party conference down there that summer?'

'I'll check,' Daisy said.

'Plenty of young people having a good time,' Callum said, 'and the police stretched thin. That's a recipe for low follow-up rates.'

'Maybe,' Daisy said. 'Here's Cookie. Let's see what else is relevant.' Her plait bounced against the back of her shirt as she went out into the office to collect the file. She leafed through it on the return journey to the fishbowl, before sliding back onto the chair.

'We didn't know this,' she said, eyes on the file. 'It looks like it was a kill-or-cure holiday. María was older by three years, and they were always at loggerheads. The parents sent them off to Bournemouth for a bit of peace at home, and to force them to get along.'

'Why Bournemouth?' Callum asked.

'The flat belonged to a friend of the parents,' Daisy said. 'Mum and Dad thought it would be educational and hoped that with none of their friends around, the sisters would find some common ground. You know, a bit of an adventure for them and they would come home best buddies.'

Sometimes, Callum thought, people just didn't like their siblings or the things they stood for. Unless you harboured

35

the idea that you could bully or bribe them into changing, and some did, it was better to walk away. His own three bossy older sisters had adored and indulged him, but not everyone got to play happy families like he had.

'Hmm. And did that solve the problem?' he asked.

Daisy referenced another sheet of paper. 'Here we go. Conchita had run away twice before from her home in Spain when she had argued with her sister. Both times she came back herself, so her parents weren't particularly worried. Same pattern of behaviour. This time, the girls had a big row because María was spending time with boys instead of her. María told little sis to get over it. Conchita was a self-harmer and responded by cutting her arms.'

'That ties in with Martha's observations about the scars on her limbs. What happened then?' Callum asked.

'Aah. This makes more sense,' Daisy said, reading on. 'María had met a boy the night before and wanted to spend time with him to practise her English.' She snorted a breath through her nose. 'Practise something!'

'And?' Callum said.

'He had a boat moored along the coast at Poole, and they sailed off for a fortnight playing water gypsy. María was really angry at Conchita for being uncooperative and needy.'

'Did they check with this lad?' asked Callum.

Daisy flicked through a few sheets of paper. 'Yes. Julian Dove. He confirmed taking María out on his father's boat for two weeks straight. They sailed along the coast and moored every night on any empty buoy.'

'No sightings of Conchita after María left? No use of her credit card or mobile?'

'Not a dicky bird. Nada. Nothing. María returned a fortnight later, found the door unlocked, dried blood on the kitchen and bathroom floors, and the place trashed. It looked like a burglary gone wrong, but all of their belongings were still there except for Conchita's passport. The only traces were from the two girls and the blood was

Conchita's. María said her sister had probably had a hissy fit and trashed the place herself and done her usual runner. Forensics agreed.'

'Immature reaction if that was the case. Was she admitted to the hospital? Did they check to see if she had been abducted and stowed on the boat by María and Julian before being dropped in the Channel?' Callum asked.

'You've got a dark mind,' Daisy said, making a horrified face. 'They searched the boat, prints and DNA everywhere but none of it was Conchita's. And no trace of her attending any hospital for treatment.'

'Any CCTV in the town?'

'Oodles of it – you were right about it heaving with politicians and press, but no helpful coverage according to this.' She tapped the file. 'No substantiated witness sightings.'

'The more people around, the easier it is to be invisible,' Callum said.

'You think she didn't want to be found?' Daisy asked.

'She had plenty of time to come forward in the intervening years. Why didn't she?'

'Met someone and went with them? Was punishing her family? Trying to get María into trouble? Perhaps she was fed up with the arguing and wanted to get away and leave it all behind her. Fresh start. Who knows?'

'Conchita did, but we can't ask her,' Callum said. 'Contact the local police in Spain and get them to inform the parents. They will need to come over and ID her body. I hope we will have more to tell them when they arrive.'

Daisy went back to her desk.

It would be a relief to Conchita's parents to know that she had been found. In time, Callum thought, they would take her back to her hometown and bury her. They would raise a headstone, worship there on high days and holidays, and sanctify their daughter. All her tantrums and misdemeanours would be erased to be replaced by purified memories of their perfect, sainted offspring.

His face felt suddenly warm, and he closed his eyes as a memory played across the back of his lids. Grace's ashes, lifted by the breeze above Campsie Fells, swept into a whirling dance that lifted them high above his head. He had watched until they had almost disappeared. Then they had gently floated down, surrounding him, the sound of the keening wind mingling with his quiet sobs. He ached to hold her in his arms just one more time, to rest his cheek against her hair and feel her breath caress his throat.

He opened his eyes. Three years, three months and... and it was the first time that he could not remember the exact number of days. The thumb of his left hand absently massaged his naked ring finger.

Bird's muscled frame filled the doorway. The man's hair grew in grey patches over his bronzed scalp, shaved so close it resembled an archipelago of small islands at low tide. It didn't seem to be normal hair loss, but keeping it short minimised the impact. Callum rarely asked personal questions of colleagues and hoped that would dissuade them from probing into his history.

'Guv, you asked about Paul Barnes. He's a bleedin' saint.' Bird rasped the back of his thumbnail against his stubbled chin. 'Not even got a speeding. Drives that van like a little old lady. And Forensics say there was no trace of Conchita ever having been in or near the van.'

'Did they find anything of interest?'

Bird referred to the sheet of paper he held. 'About a ton of bleedin' dog hair from those Jack Russells of his. Plenty of sawdust. There were some traces of blood, but it was his own and the only prints were his as well. Soil from the tools, grass clippings, and a drop or two of oil. Couple of petrol receipts, a note from a customer asking him to cut the hedge and an invoice from a lawnmower spare firm in Christchurch. That's near Bournemouth, guv. Everything they found was consistent with his being a gardener. We've got nothing on him.'

'The invisible man, Bird. What about the con on licence – Fenman, wasn't it?'

'Frank Fenman's tagged, and I thought we'd got him because he broke his curfew and was out all night. He didn't get back until about 0830 hours yesterday morning, which was after we found the body. My cuffs were getting itchy. Then Wonder Boy there' – he nodded across the office to the back of Cookie's head – 'had a moment of inspiration and we found out where he was all night.'

'Where?'

'Hospital. His missus drove him to Salisbury A&E at about 2230 hours and he was there all night. They had a nasty RTC come in just before midnight, that lorry–car collision on the A36?'

Callum nodded. He had heard it had been fatal.

'That pushed all the minors to the back of the queue. Eventually, they stitched and bandaged him, and the wife collected him about 0800 hours and took him home. It's all documented.'

'Why did he need stitches, Bird? Was he involved in a fight?' Brawling would be against the conditions of his licence.

Bird grinned. 'Yeah, but not the sort of fight you're meaning. This fight was with his dog and, with the number of stitches he's got, I reckon the dog won the show.'

'Good work. Daisy and I will go and check him out, see if he had the opportunity to slip out and dispose of a body.'

'Right. She'll probably want to give the dog a medal for biting him.' Chortling at his comment, Bird went back to his desk.

* * *

Haystick House was much more salubrious than Callum had expected. A neat post and rail fence enclosed the kempt front garden of the brick-walled property. The pitch of the tiled roof suggested it might have once been thatched, and the original fenestration had been replaced with double-glazed units. But the updating had been done thoughtfully and looked in keeping. Someone had thrown some cash at the place to make it to their taste. Callum knocked on the heavy oak door and heard a deep bark from the bowels of the property.

'Playmate for you, Daisy,' he said as they waited. He was confident that if the hound was let out, it would make a beeline for Daisy like everything else on four legs.

'My lucky day.' She grinned at Callum. 'This is a bit smart, isn't it, sir? Not your usual crim pad.' She nodded towards three vehicles parked near the house – the white van they were concerned with, a recent-plate silver Mercedes SUV and a shiny red sports car. 'Not short of a penny, then. I–'

Callum interrupted her by placing a finger on her arm. Without moving his head, he lifted his eyes to a spot above the door where a bug-eyed camera kept watch.

She understood his warning that they might be heard as well as seen.

The house was not what he had expected, and neither was the woman who opened the door. She had highlights in her hair, wore a dove-grey skirt suit, and dangerously high heels that showed off her shapely legs.

Daisy fidgeted beside Callum in her functional walking boots.

The woman tipped her head back to accommodate his height and slowly ran an assessing eye down his body and back up to his face. She glanced at Daisy.

Callum's interest was piqued. Why did Frank Fenman think it necessary to have his solicitor to hand? What was he going to protest that he hadn't done?

'As I don't know you, I assume you are after my husband,' the woman said, in an educated voice. She fixed her enquiring eyes on Callum's face without removing the arm braced across the door opening.

He hoped his preconceptions didn't show. 'We are looking for Mr Frank Fenman. And you are?' He tossed the question into the air, and she fielded it deftly.

'His wife, Madelaine Fenman.' She examined their credentials and then returned them. 'Come in, Inspector MacLean. First door on the left.'

The front door clicked closed behind them and their feet sank silently into the plush ochre carpet.

'Frank,' she called into the back of the house before following them into a sitting room. 'Do sit down, officers. He won't be a moment.'

This polite exchange differed from the welcome he sometimes received from the wives of suspects, but welcomes weren't always what they seemed. Callum speed-read the room – a quality three-piece suite, curved wide-screen television, antique furniture, oak flooring and an inglenook fireplace complete with bread oven and a log burner.

Madelaine followed his movements. 'All paid for by me and I have the receipts to prove it.' She nodded to a davenport against the far wall.

Callum wondered who kept the paperwork for the purchase of their entire house contents unless they were obsessively organised and loved paperwork, or had something to prove.

'There you are, Frank. These officers are here to see you.'

Frank Fenman had made no sound as he came through the house and now stood in the open doorway with two small hairy dogs behind him. He was shorter than his wife, even before she donned the killer heels. Slightly built with a narrow face, his sandy hair swept back from a low brow above small eyes, making it easy to see where his nickname had come from. His right arm was swathed in bandages and supported by a narrow black sling stretching from wrist to neck and back again. The dogs transferred their allegiance to Daisy and squirmed at her feet.

'Good morning, officers.' His eyes moved to Daisy. 'Apologies for my attire, my dear.'

Golden chest hair sprouted above the low-cut navy vest – presumably, all he could ease over the bandages. His fawn slacks were pressed with a knife-edged crease down the leg and the empty sleeve of his toning cardigan hung limply at his side.

'I was bitten by my dog, as I expect you know.' He looked at his wife and then at his dogs.

'You were teasing the silly little thing. What did you expect?' Madelaine smiled back at him before addressing Callum. 'Sorry to run out on you, but I have meetings this afternoon. No peace for the wicked. I just popped back at lunchtime to check that Frank was all right. I'll leave you in his capable hands. Hand,' she amended and dropped a kiss on her husband's forehead.

The action would not have been out of place at the school gates when a pupil needed reassurance from a mother. Callum felt uneasy.

Frank waited until the outer door clicked closed. 'Do sit.' He indicated the sofa with his good hand and dropped into an armchair.

'That looks painful,' Daisy said, sitting forward, elbows on her knees. 'How did it happen?'

Frank settled the cushions to his liking and carefully positioned his bandaged limb along the armrest. 'Mitzi heard something outside and I let them both out into the garden. Her hackles were up, and she was growling. It might have been someone snooping but it was probably the fox. She always knows when he's out there.' He crossed his legs and used his good hand to adjust the crease in his trousers. 'I had a quick look but couldn't see anything, so I called them back inside and threw her ball down the hall for her to chase. She was still a bit wound up and when I tried to pick it up to throw it again, she got hold of me.'

Frank winced and so did Daisy. 'What's the other one called?' she asked.

'Dodo. They're named after my aunts. Anyway, Maddie made her let go of me and I needed a few stitches. It hurts rather a lot now the anaesthetic is wearing off.' A bead of perspiration appeared on his brow when he attempted to find a more comfortable sitting position.

Callum had expected a greasy little grunt with a chip on his shoulder and an unhelpful attitude but was confronted by a well-dressed, well-spoken man who would not have been out of place at a civic reception. Were it not for the tag on his ankle, just visible above the leather loafer, he might have questioned if he was addressing the correct man.

'Just a routine question, but where was your van the night you ended up in hospital?'

'Here. Maddie drove me to the hospital in her car.'

'And the keys to your van?' Callum asked.

Frank made to stand up then changed his mind. 'If you go in the kitchen, they're on the hook by the door. Peugeot, blue key fob.'

Daisy went into the hall and after a moment, Callum heard keys jangling against each other.

'They're here, sir,' she said, then added, 'Hello, my lovely girl.'

'Don't touch her.' Frank lurched forward in the armchair and took a sharp breath.

Callum felt the hairs on the back of his neck move and looked out into the hallway.

'I forgot. She's in the utility room behind a stair gate.' Frank's eyes were fixed on the doorway. 'She can't get out.' The statement sounded more hope than fact.

Callum listened. Daisy was uncharacteristically quiet. All he could hear was his own breath in his throat. Ten seconds and he would go out and see what she was doing. He heard the clack of the dog's claws on a hard floor accompanied by a soft whine.

'I know,' Daisy said gently, 'you're such a beautiful girlie. We'll play ball next time.' She came back into the room and both men eased back in their chairs. 'She's a lovely girl, really friendly, isn't she?' said Daisy.

'She can be.'

'What breed is she?' Daisy caught Callum's eye, and he hoped she wasn't finding problems where none existed.

'Better ask Maddie. Ruby's hers, my dear.'

Daisy turned to Callum. 'She is beautiful but has big strong jaws. Lucky you weren't bitten by her. That would really have hurt, Mr Fenman.' She smiled sympathetically at the dapper man in the armchair.

'Being bitten wasn't pleasant.' He looked at her thoughtfully.

'Van keys were there on the hook,' Daisy said.

Callum nodded. 'Does anyone else have a set, or use your van?'

'No,' Frank said. 'It's only insured for me to drive.'

That was easy to check. A law-abiding criminal was a mass of contradictions and Callum and Daisy shared a moment of stunned silence.

'Look. I've seen the error of my ways, Inspector. I'm reformed. No more capers for me. I've got too much to lose.' He ran his eye around the room, sighed and looked back at Callum.

'I'm delighted to hear it, Mr Fenman. Then you won't have a problem with my team taking a quick look in the back of your van?'

'Be my guest. I've got nothing to hide.'

Callum nodded at Frank's bandage. 'I assume you will be here for the next hour or so?'

'It would be illegal to drive a manual in this state, I expect, so I will be here until my wife comes home from work.' He grimaced. 'To be honest, I don't think I could drive at the moment.'

'Do you have painkillers?' Daisy asked.

'The hospital gave me some.' Frank leaned back into the chair and closed his eyes for a moment.

'Good.' Callum stood, making the room seem suddenly small. 'What does your wife do for work?'

'Estate agent, and she's exceptionally good at her business.'

And extremely well remunerated, Callum thought, giving a final look around the well-dressed room.

* * *

'Thoughts?' Callum asked as Daisy slid onto the passenger seat.

'He wasn't what I expected, and neither was she, come to that. He doesn't look like a crim, looks more like a businessman.'

'Crime is a business these days. Organised gangs steal to order, and expendable foot soldiers are paid a pittance. The boss doesn't get their hands dirty, just sits back and counts the money. It's a full-time occupation for some.'

'Do you think that's what Fenman's involved with? I didn't think we had too much of that on our patch… yet.'

'There's too much of it on every patch. Until we get more officers, more resources, the problem will keep growing.' He changed up a gear with unnecessary force. 'There's more of them than there are of us. It reduces their level of risk and increases their incentive. The law is only for the law-abiding, Daisy.'

He was stating what every policeman was muttering into his sleeve. It was a constant irritation that they were forced to prioritise and make choices, with some crimes going un-investigated. He heard his grandfather's burred voice in his head saying, 'Only worry about what you can change, *ogha*. The rest is someone else's worry.' Callum sighed, that was easier said than done.

'What was so interesting about your new playmate, Daisy?'

'She's really rather nice,' she said. 'Beautiful dog, but big and I mean big. Must have been about eighty centimetres tall at the withers and probably weighed about eighty or ninety kilos.'

Callum did a thumbnail conversion in his head. That was about two and a half feet tall and fourteen stone if her assessment was correct. About twice as heavy as Daisy.

'What breed is she?' He was allowing her to show her knowledge rather than being particularly interested in the answer.

'Not sure, but he's lucky he just got bitten by that little fluffy thing. If she had bitten him, I reckon she could have done him some real harm. Do you believe that he's going straight, Callum?'

A neat row of thatched cottages flashed past. Were the inhabitants as forthright and law-abiding as they would like him to believe? He was certain Frank was not.

'Not for one minute. Let's search his van, see if there's any trace of Conchita.'

He caught a glimpse of a red burglar alarm box like a pimple in the hairline of the last thatched house. Did they all have window locks, alarm systems and security cameras? He thought not. Families had been in the village for generations and thought they knew and could trust their neighbours. And if they couldn't trust them, they kept an eye on them. There were probably a great number of eyes trained on the likes of Frank 'Ferret' Fenman and the Hatcher clan.

* * *

Something was nagging at Callum. Later, he drove alone to the spot where Daphne Smart had first noticed Paul with the girl's body and stopped his car. To his left, Godshill Wood Inclosure ran the length of the wide verge that was poached and rutted by the hooves of animals.

The tarmac road sloped gently downhill, and at the far end, Paul's van was still parked outside the five-bar gate.

Callum slumped down in his seat, banging his knee against the underside of the dashboard as he assumed the height of the retired headmistress. The verge on either side of Paul's drive was raised in a bund and the gravel itself was below his sightline. The van was visible from the top of the wheel arches upwards, and he could only see the top three bars of the gate. Nothing below that was visible from this proximity.

He sat up and rubbed his knee. Daphne could not have seen a girl lying on the gravel as she turned the corner into the lane, but she had seen Paul. He wondered how good her distance vision was. When Daphne got to his cottage, Paul was attempting resuscitation, so had he scooped up the girl only to change his mind and set her back down? Had he panicked? It wasn't every day that you found a body outside your gate.

Callum drove down the road at a Daphne-Smart speed and stopped where he had parked when the body was found. All that remained of the police presence was a short length of tape fluttering from Paul's closed gate.

A short distance further on, the lane disappeared around a curve and plunged into a dark tunnel of overhanging oak trees. That was the reported direction of Paul's white van. It would only take seconds to travel to that bend in the road. The white van would have disappeared long before Daphne arrived. And dumping a body was likely to make you heavy on the throttle. But why leave her outside a cottage when about seventy thousand acres of heath and woodland were available with less chance of being seen? He opened his door and got out.

The back doors of Paul's van were now closed. Dropping to his knees where the body had been found, he looked back up the lane to Densome Corner. He could not see the road from his lowered position, but he heard an engine growl and abruptly stood up. The post van was swinging round the corner, light glinting on the windscreen. Standing, Callum had a clear view of it speeding towards him. The red vehicle zipped past, and Callum followed the scarlet streak for a few seconds before it vanished into the leafy tunnel.

The wind changed direction, and smoke from the garden bonfire drifted towards him, bringing with it the rhythmic sound of a fork biting into soil. Callum watched Paul dig with practised ease. Season after season the same earth was turned, sown and harvested before the ground was restored and readied for future planting.

Sporadic drops of moisture scattered by a passing cloud lowered the temperature and warned Callum that worse would follow. The metronome precision from the garden was muted when he closed his car door, replaced by the steady sweep of his windscreen wipers as rain splattered against the tinted glass. The sudden squall bowed the pine branches and greyed the sky. Callum pulled out onto the glistening tarmac and in his peripheral vision, he saw Paul straighten up to watch him depart.

* * *

In summer, Detective Chief Inspector Bertram Bellman's office was dreary and grey. Now the lowering cloud base of autumn restricted the light still further and the room felt like a dark prison cell. Callum felt as if the walls were leaning in to suffocate him and experienced the urge to throw open the window. He would have loosened his tie; had he been wearing one.

'Good afternoon, sir.'

The man sitting behind the desk was slight, but his competence was well-respected at the station. Personally, Callum thought that Bellman should spend less time chasing budgets and more time chasing criminals. The eternal crisp white shirt and black-rimmed spectacles produced a monochrome effect with the man's face a mid-tone grey.

Bellman tidied some papers into a neat stack, guided them to one side of his desk and rested his folded hands in the space they had vacated.

'Inspector MacLean. Have you made any progress on your dead girl? I want a statement for the press.'

'Yes, sir. We've just identified her.' 'Just' was a flexible word that served well at reassuring senior officers that they were the first to be advised of new information. 'She's a Spanish national, Conchita Gimenez. Her parents are being informed by their local police.'

Bellman sat back in his enveloping leather chair and rested his elbows on the arms. 'Good. Do we know how she died?'

'Yes, sir. Natural causes.' Callum noticed the pinch of colour wash into Bellman's cheeks. He was probably relieved that he wouldn't need to defend the death to his overseas counterparts now there was no implication of murder.

'Natural causes,' Callum said. 'No signs of foul play.' If you discounted dumping a dead body in a public place, omitting to summon medical assistance, and failing to inform the relevant authorities of her death.

'Do we know who left her outside Barnes's house?'

'We are following up on the sighting of a white van in the vicinity. House-to-house is underway but nothing helpful yet.'

'Keep me informed.' Bellman removed his black-framed glasses, took a folded white handkerchief from his desk drawer and began to rhythmically polish the lenses. This was his signal that the business element of the meeting was finished.

'And how are you settling in, MacLean? Found somewhere to live?'

Callum quashed his annoyance. They had experienced a rocky start to their professional relationship due to the actions of the officer that Callum had replaced. It would take time to overcome the wariness they now had of each other, but at least Bellman was trying. As his contribution to maintaining the fragile *entente cordiale*, Callum briefly explained about building a new dwelling on the site of the derelict bungalow, then left.

* * *

Bird pushed back his chair when Callum entered the office.

'Martha phoned, guv, while you were with Bellman.'

'What did she want?'

'Just to tell you that, as per your question, there were no bruises on Conchita's back, significant or otherwise, and she will get back to you on the tox report.'

'Thanks, Bird.'

'What does that mean, about the bruising?'

'It means I have serious doubts that she was thrown from a white van. She was carefully placed on the gravel, not thrown. Her nightdress was thin but there were no scuffs or abrasive impact from the stones, and it is unlikely she would have landed flat on her back with her clothing pulled down to her ankles.'

Chapter Seven

The cat was waiting for Callum. She trotted, tail aloft, and rubbed against his legs as he turned the key in the lock.

'Still here then. I'm not feeding you today. Go home.'

The cat purred and sat by the cupboard where yesterday's milk had been placed.

'Are you really hungry, or do you get fed all around the village?'

He didn't like to think of it in need and he would probably not use all his milk before it was out of date. Feeding the cat was just recycling unused food.

The cat crouched down next to the dish and began lapping immediately.

Callum tentatively ran the back of his finger down its neck, and it stood up, pushing its head into his hand, milk droplets on its chin.

'You like that, do you?'

The cat purred a reply before returning to its drink. After watching for a second, Callum turned his attention to his supper.

A squeal of hinges followed the sharp click of his gate catch. Looking through the uncurtained window, he saw the silhouette of a man filling the gap in the fence. The security light marked his progress, and Callum recognised Dave Green. He opened the front door. Dave's navy overalls and stained baseball cap were replaced by pressed jeans, cowboy boots and a tooled leather jacket.

'Didn't recognise you for a minute there, Dave.' Callum filled the narrow doorway, throwing his visitor into shadow. 'Problems?' The cat slipped past his legs and went out.

'No, we're good. Didn't know you had a cat.'

Callum watched the animal morph into the shadows. 'I don't. It's attempting a takeover.'

Dave sniffed at the warm air seeping from the kitchen. 'Something smells good. I sent you a text earlier.'

'Sorry, I've been busy,' Callum said. In truth, he had forgotten about it.

'I've got a crib match at The Woodfalls Inn tonight and I'm cadging a lift with Sam Tanner. I saw you in your kitchen, so I thought I'd give you this instead of just pushing it through the letter box.' Dave reached into his jacket pocket and proffered a folded sheet of paper. 'It's just an idea about your lighting for downstairs. Here's a drawing for you. Have a look and let me know.'

Callum took it.

Dave gave him a hard look. 'I've outlined all your options. Now I need a decision. Then I can finish digging and move my machinery onto my next site. Please, Callum.'

'I know, I'll get onto that now. I was just thinking about it before you came.'

Looking past Callum's legs into the hallway, Dave said, 'And if you're looking for a cleaner, my oldest, Anna wants work. She wants to go to university.' He beamed a smile at Callum. 'First one from our family, and she needs to earn some money, pronto. She's putting leaflets through doors, so you'll probably get one later in the week.'

Callum smiled at the proud father. 'I'll have a think about that too, thanks. I might have a job for her. All the spiders in the village seem to have moved in with me this week.'

Dave laughed. 'It's getting cold outside, mate. You wouldn't want to sleep in the garden. Talking of which, if you're looking for a gardener, you could do worse than Paul Barnes. Now I've got to go, or Sam will leave without me, and I don't fancy walking far in these boots.' He waved a hand in farewell and clicked the gate closed behind him.

Callum had, in his naivety, thought he could put off the decision about lighting the basement until the bones of the dwelling were in place. But every change had a knock-on effect, and Dave had pointed out that changes cost both time and money.

Unfolding the sheet of paper, he smoothed it flat next to his plate. There were two pencil diagrams, one above the other. The first showed a bird's-eye view of the footprint of his new house with a grid protruding from both sides and had been executed with the broad strokes of a blunt pencil. The second showed an elevation of tall glass doors in a brick wall opening onto a small, tiled terrace. The perspective was off, but Callum interpreted it as his subterranean bedroom opening directly onto a tiled area of terrace through double glass doors. He imagined standing inside his bedroom by the tall windows and looking at a cerulean sky. His heart hopped a beat then excitedly raced to catch up. He hated being enclosed and this felt like someone throwing him a bottle of water when he was thirsty. He cut his food with the side of his fork.

When he had decided to make his move to Hampshire permanent, the only available property had been a bungalow that the agent described it as being 'in need of total refurbishment', and that was a conservative assessment.

Dave Green had accompanied him to a viewing.

'It's a knocker-downer, mate. And this will appeal to you, Inspector, being a Scotsman.' He had smiled to take the sting out of the remark. 'You don't get the VAT back on renovations, but you do on a new build, so you'll get a fifth of the build cost back when you've finished.'

Callum had walked around the orchard to the rear of the bungalow, avoiding the squelchy fallen fruit concealed in the tall grass. The perimeter hedges dividing the garden from the surrounding fields were topped by razor loops of brambles that stretched out to snare him. It felt like a fairy-tale hedge protecting a castle. His castle. And he loved the peace and seclusion.

Dave had joined him. 'The position doesn't put you off? Up here at the top of Tethering Drove, with no neighbours?'

Callum looked across the road at the endless quilt of open heath. Heather blurred from sepia to umber until it receded to an indigo smudge on the distant horizon. Low-growing gorse clumps dotted with yellow flowers clustered at the feet of trembling silver birch trees. The view was an inspiration, and he could have admired it for hours. His mind was already busy assessing the palette he would use to paint the scene.

'No, the location doesn't put me off.' Buying it had been an easy decision.

Callum pushed away his empty plate and studied Dave's drawing again. He liked this new idea. The thought of living with no natural light downstairs had been daunting, a dungeon in the bowels of the earth, plunged into perpetual darkness with no moving air, no sprinkle of stars in the night sky, no patter of rain against the glass. He wondered if he was a closet claustrophobic. When Callum read "Don't forget about sunpipes if you don't like this idea" pencilled along the bottom of the page, he had already decided that he would go with the basement-floor terrace.

* * *

The next morning, Callum pushed up through the closed doors of sleep. The transition was swift, a diver surging upwards to breach the invisible surface of wakefulness. He gasped a breath, reaching out a hand to silence the helicopter hum of his mobile. It was six fifteen.

'MacLean.'

Hurried footfalls echoed in his ear as he sat up in bed.

'Callum, missing eight-year-old girl. Last seen last night.'

He heard Daisy slam her back door and startle the early morning bird chorus in her garden into disharmony. She gave him the address.

'On my way.'

Questions queued for answers that he couldn't provide; why had she not been seen since yesterday? He pulled on his jeans. Where was she last seen? And, more importantly in his mind, why had no one reported her missing until this morning? He thrust his arms into the sleeves of his jacket and rested his feet, one at a time, on the seat of a kitchen chair to tie his bootlaces. Flicking off the kitchen lights, the hard planes of his face were shadowed in the early bright and he snapped the back door closed behind him. Jeanie Cowie had also been eight when she disappeared in Glasgow last summer. Cases of missing eight-year-old girls seldom had a happy outcome.

The predawn grey was melting away, replaced by a drifting lace mist that played hide and seek with familiar landmarks and made ghosts of the wild ponies. He pulled into Tethering Drove behind Daisy's Navara. Her tail lights went out, her door opened, and she dropped down into the lane. The avian choristers warbled high notes through the mist above the eerie whinny of a pony and a shiver slid down his spine. Dawn stumbled over the horizon, but it would take more than the lightening sky to brighten his mood.

'Tell me, Donaldson.'

'Morning, sir. Kim Tanner was last seen by her older sister Kelly last night. They went together to do night feeds for their ponies at about six in the evening and then came back here. The field is that way.' She pointed towards the open purlieu. 'SOCO are on their way there now.'

'Carry on.' He locked his car.

'Kelly came back earlier than her sister, leaving Kim to follow on.'

Daisy opened the wicket gate into the garden. The lawns were neatly trimmed, and the flower beds were weed-free. A clump of violet-and-yellow Michaelmas daisies raised drooping heads to the light.

'Parents?'

'Sam and Louise Tanner. They were at work together last night. They did a late shift at that nursing home in Downton.'

Light spilt onto the concrete path through the uncurtained windows of the brick-built semi as if something inside was trying to escape. Potted shrubs guarded the back door like miniature green sentries. Their compost was dotted with cigarette butts, and it was clear that the smoker in the house was expected to stand out in the cold in the interests of family health. Inside, a dog barked.

Before they had a chance to knock, the door was yanked open making the cat flap clatter. Filling the gap was a woman dressed in black trousers and sensible shoes, her logoed yellow tabard a splash of cheerfulness, despite red stains down the front of it. Her dark hair showed the first few streaks of grey, and wiry strands had escaped from her untidy ponytail, to hang like rats' tails on either side of her face.

Callum made his introductions, and they followed her inside.

The kitchen was cramped. A slightly built man with a deeply lined face leaned against the sink and agitated the coins in his trouser pocket. He seemed unaware of the constant jingling. His black shoes were scuffed and creased by wear; the toes turned up like pig snouts poking out below the hems of his trousers. He stretched out a hand.

'Sam Tanner. Thanks for coming.'

Callum felt the tremor in the sepia-tipped fingers and registered the smells of sweat and nicotine mingled with bleach. These odours attested to the man's night of hard work, but bleach could also be an effective crime scene cleanser. He pushed the thought to the back of his mind for now.

Slumped on a kitchen chair, elbows on the table, was a teenager with attitude. Ripped jeans, kohled eyes and a surly mouth, she was a study in kvetching discontentment. Callum's gaze rested on her for a second or two, during which time she turned her head to look up at him, rolled her eyes then glanced at her father. Callum caught a flash of colour from her hair clip of dangling rainbow feathers, like a Native American. Behind her on the wall was a list of chores divided vertically, one side for Kim and the other for Kelly – the ticks for completion were all sprinkled down Kim's side. Kelly flicked through her phone and seemed oblivious to the tension in the room.

Sam stared at her, his face stiff and tight.

'Kelly, make us a cuppa, please. We'll be in the other room.'

When she made no effort to move other than glance up from her phone, an intense look passed between father and daughter. Then the chair screeched backwards, skidded across the floor, and banged into the wall. Sam sighed and took his cigarettes from his pocket. He flipped the lid with his thumb, but when Louise, standing in the doorway, cleared her throat, he tossed the packet onto the draining board.

In the sitting room, a brindle hound jumped from the couch and wagged her way over to greet Daisy. The bookshelf displayed framed photographs of both girls with their ponies. Another – a family gathering that included grandparents – demonstrated the inheritance of family genes. Kelly took after Louise. She was taller than average, with generously fleshed bones and a confident smile, her long dark hair tousled, her eyes flirty. The other girl had the same delicate bone structure as Sam, but with cautious eyes, and a tentative smile as if she was expecting someone to play a trick on her. She looked like a victim. Callum's heart slid down a rib or two.

'Do you have a current photo of Kim that we might borrow?' he asked Louise.

Louise took a framed photo from the bookcase and handed it to Callum. 'This is her last school photo.'

Callum studied it. Kim wore a blue-and-white gingham dress, golden hair scraped back from her face, eyes dark and watchful.

'Thanks. We'll take good care of it.'

Sam and Louise sat side by side on the couch, weight forward, players in a game of musical chairs, in limbo, waiting for the activity to begin.

'Tell me about yesterday,' Callum prompted.

'Normal day, except we both worked last night,' Sam said. 'We left here at about five thirty and the girls were in the house. Kim was upstairs in her bedroom, she's doing a project on our native New Forest ponies, and Kelly was in here on her phone. That's usual – they never seem to be in the same room at the same time for more than five minutes. Lou had done their suppers and left them in the fridge for later.'

'So, you don't usually both work nights, Sam?'

'No. One of us is normally here with the girls, but with that bug going round, it lays people out cold for a couple of days and lots of staff are off sick, so we agreed to both do a night shift. Kelly's seventeen, but it's the first time we've ever left them all night.'

Louise pressed a tissue to her eyes. 'And it'll be the last. I worried all night while we were at work that something would go wrong. Sod the money, Sam.'

Her husband reached across and squeezed her hand.

'How did Kim seem?' Daisy asked. 'Was she worried about anything? Any unusual behaviour?'

'No. She was as smiley and cheerful as usual.' Sam wrapped his arms around his torso. 'When we were leaving for work, she showed me a drawing she had done of Drummer and gave me a hug goodbye.'

'You spoil her, Sam.' There was no accusation in Louise's voice. 'I thought she was a bit pale and wondered if she might be coming down with this bug. But she said she felt fine.' She pointed to a glass vase of yellow freesias on the mantlepiece. 'It was my birthday yesterday and she gave me those. She's always kind and thoughtful and I would have known if something was troubling her.' She gnawed at her bottom lip. 'She's very open and talks to me about everything. Too much information sometimes, quite the opposite of Kelly. Isn't she, Sam?' It was more a statement than a question.

He sighed. 'I told the girls to do the horses together before it got dark and then come back here for the rest of the evening and stay indoors. I think Kim would sleep in that stable with Drummer if we let her. She loves her pony.'

Callum's heart descended still further. In his experience, eight-year-old girls in love with their ponies were unlikely to spend the night with a boyfriend and creep home the next morning. He did not like this turn of events but concentrated on keeping his face devoid of concern. At seventeen, Kelly was old enough to be responsible for her younger sister; at that age, she could already have kids of her own or be serving in the armed forces. But age was no guarantee of maturity.

Kelly pushed the door open with her bottom, reversed into the room, and placed a tray of mugs on the coffee table. She stabbed a look at Sam and then turned to leave, retrieving her phone from the front of her shirt where it nestled against her breast inside her bra. She paused, waiting to see if her father would comment, but it was Callum who spoke.

'Tell me about last evening, Kelly.'

Her mouth drooped at the corners. 'I had to squid-sit the squirt while she drooled over Drummer and then come back and make sure she ate her tea and had the right yoghurt for afters.'

'She's lactose intolerant,' Louise interjected.

'Yeah, right. She just gets fancy food.'

'Kelly!' Sam looked startled at the volume of his own response. He was struggling to retain control.

The muscles of his neck were tight, like ropes holding him on an even keel and Callum wondered what happened when he lost that control. There was no right or wrong way to react if your child was missing. Just as everyone's characters are different then so, Callum had discovered, were their responses.

Sam sighed. 'Just… tell us what happened.' He finished in a quieter voice.

Kelly's eyes flashed defiance at her father before she half-lowered her lids and peered at Callum through mascara-heavy lashes. She seemed to have decided to make him the target for her answers.

'We went down to fill the hay nets. She was dribbling all over Drummer and wouldn't get a move on. I used the last two lots of hay to fill my net and hung it up for Topaz, and she was still wasting time. I told her if she didn't get a shift on, I was going home. She ignored me and kept talking to her stupid pony, so I went home.'

Sam sprang to his feet. 'You left her to carry a new bale across the field all on her own?'

'She should pull her weight; she's not made of glass. And you left me in charge. She should have hurried up like I told her.' She ignored Sam's lowering stare.

Louise was quick to lay a calming hand on Sam's arm and guide him back down into his seat before addressing her daughter. 'That wasn't very sensible, Kelly.'

The girl shrugged and looked down at her phone.

There was a battle of wills, a struggle for control going on between the pack leader and new blood. Youth often thought that experience could be overridden by enthusiasm and force of will.

Callum kept his focus on Kelly. 'Then you left the field and came back to the house?'

She nodded.

'And how long was it before you heard Kim come back?' Callum asked.

She shrugged. The silence stretched and Callum could hear the snuffling breaths of the dog that was sitting next to Daisy's feet. 'You did hear her come back?'

'Probably. I think so.'

Sam's sharp intake of breath slapped the air. 'You think so? You think so? Fuck's sake, Kelly.' Tears gleamed in his eyes, and he clenched and unclenched his hands.

'She ate her supper, Sam,' Louise said. 'Her empty plate is in the sink. She must have got back okay.'

'Kelly.' Callum's voice was firm. 'Do you know for certain that she came home last night? Yes or No.'

'No.' Her voice dropped to a whisper. 'When I came home, I took my supper up to my room and played music.'

'And you were there all evening?'

She looked across to Sam when she spoke. 'I stayed there all night.'

Kelly might be answering the questions he was asking but were the answers the truth, or were they what she wanted Sam to hear? Callum was less susceptible to Kelly's wiles. Seventeen-year-old girls lied when they opened their mouths in his experience. They trotted out the information that their parents expected to hear to confirm they were living the life their parents wanted them to live. There was often more truth in the things they did not say.

'Did you pass anyone on the way back here from the field? A dog walker or car?' asked Callum.

Daisy had told him it was only a short distance away and would not have taken Kelly much time, but it was still a possibility.

Kelly looked at Callum. 'A white van drove past me when I was nearly home...' She hesitated.

'For God's sake, tell them what you saw, Kelly. I can't believe you let her come back on her own,' Sam shouted.

'Did you recognise it?' Callum asked, ignoring Sam's outburst.

She seemed about to answer but paused, before giving one sharp shake of her head.

Callum looked at her bowed head for a long moment. 'Are you sure, Kelly?'

He sensed that she was about to add something but instead she said, 'Yes. I'm sure.'

Callum wondered why she was lying.

The prescribed procedure had to be followed. A missing child would capture the fears and imagination of every parent, and the investigation had to be carried out by the book. The eyes of the public would be on them, and Callum did not want to make an error. No detective wants an abductor, or worse, a killer, to wriggle out of a conviction and go unpunished because investigators had failed to walk the correct path.

And that path began with a search of the house which revealed nothing relevant. The walls of Kim's room were covered in posters of ponies, and more photos of her and Drummer lined the windowsill. An old computer sat on a small workstation, and piled to one side were pages of handwritten notes in loopy script. Louise was quick to permit Daisy to remove the computer and the diary she located on the bookshelf. The wardrobe was so full of clothes that Kim would have struggled to get inside it to hide if that was her intention, and she was not under the bed.

There were no hiding places in the house that went unexplored. Callum could sense the growing impatience of the stressed and tired parents. He knew that they thought he should be out running around looking for Kim, and he could feel their eyes on his back as he pulled down the loft ladder and peered into the void. It would not have helped them to know that he had once located the body of a missing boy hanging from the roof trusses in his own home, so he didn't tell them.

Chapter Eight

Hale, like many New Forest villages, had evolved over a long period. Some dwellings existed even before William the Conqueror had decreed it his hunting ground in the eleventh century. Cottages had crept out of the earth like scattered mushrooms, most with a small accompanying field for pasturing a house cow, a working pony, or a pig for bacon. It had been a necessity of a way of life that no longer existed.

'The Tanners rent a small paddock for the girls' ponies. It's opposite the houses at the top of the drove,' Daisy said.

They covered the short distance to the field, Callum with long ground-eating strides and Daisy trotting to stay with him.

'What did you make of Kelly?' he asked.

'Either unconcerned about her sister being missing, or she's heading for a career on the stage. And I don't think it's the stage.'

'Granted. She might know where Kim is and is covering for her,' Callum proffered.

'Doubt that. There doesn't seem to be any love lost between the girls and Sam is piggy in the middle.'

'Louise seems to be the peacekeeper,' he said.

She jogged a couple of strides. 'Callum, it's often a family member who's responsible. Do you think Sam knows something about Kim's disappearance?'

'Often the case, but I don't think he's involved. But he is a man close to the end of his tether.'

'Perhaps she was ill and has just collapsed somewhere and is being found as we speak.'

She was off on a flight of fantasy, running off on tangents, testing possibilities. He had got used to her doing this when there was no clear path to pursue.

'It's possible.' His reply lacked conviction.

When young Jeanie Cowie went missing, she had been fit and well, full of life, but he had failed to save her. He pushed the memories back into the dark where he needed them to stay if he was to concentrate on finding Kim.

'Take a look at their phone records and finances. Cookie's checking that they were at work all night. Let's wait and see what he says before jumping to conclusions,' he said.

'If the Tanners were stinking rich, I might be able to persuade myself it was a kidnapping for ransom but I'm struggling with that idea.'

Callum thought back to the worn chairs, scuffed carpets, and double shifts at work. Teenage girls cost money. 'You and me both.'

They eased their way past the parked scenes-of-crime vans and along the muddy track that ended at the field where Kim was last seen. The thick hedge gave way to a closed five-bar gate. A dozing chestnut gelding tied to the gatepost, head down and resting a back leg, was uninterested in the invasion of its field. A uniformed officer stood inside the gate, chafing his hands together in the early chill.

'Morning, sir.' He opened the gate to let them through. 'We've got to keep the gate shut because we can't catch the other pony.' He pointed to a smaller, bay gelding with four white socks, who watched the unfamiliar activity with his head held high and the whites of his eyes showing. 'They want to check its headcollar for evidence, but it thinks it's Shergar.'

Callum recognised Drummer from the photos at the Tanners' house. 'See what you can do, Sergeant.' With horses of her own, she was the expert for this task.

Hands in pockets, Daisy strolled towards the pony, her quiet voice rising and falling, the words indistinct. The pony flicked his ears forward then sideways, listening to her. She stopped a few paces from Drummer and extended her hand, palm upwards and flat. He swivelled to face her, planted his hooves, and stretched his neck forward to lip at her palm. It was an inelegant pose. Daisy made no attempt to take hold of his headcollar but reached back into her pocket and again extended her palm, this time lower than before. The gelding walked up to her for whatever treat she was offering, and Daisy's free hand gently grasped the knot of rope that dangled at his chin. She rubbed the flat of her hand down his face and gave him another treat before leading him towards Callum.

'Well done.' Callum caught the whiff of peppermint on the gelding's breath as she handed the animal over to the gatekeeper.

The field shelter was open-fronted, of timber construction and large enough for both ponies to take refuge from winter weather or summer flies. He followed Daisy along the shiny walkway of stepping plates. The interior smelled of meadow hay and horse dung. Two metal rings, one in each rear corner, allowed for hay nets to be tied for the ponies to feed during the night. Both nets were now slack and empty, and a fine drift of hay had settled on the earth floor beneath them. A strengthening timber at waist height ran around the inside of the building and doubled as a narrow shelf. An older-model pink mobile phone was perched on it.

'Get that processed as a priority.' It had to be Kim's as Kelly had been glued to her mobile. The technician nodded his hooded head.

'Anything so far?' Callum asked him.

'Nothing yet, sir. There is a riding crop on the shelf next to the phone, over there.' He pointed with a gloved finger. 'We'll bag it for Forensics. The floor is hard-packed earth, and the ponies have been trampling on it all night. It's unlikely we're going to get any footprints, but we'll do our best.'

All Callum could detect were hoofprints from the metal shoes, nothing else stood out.

'That's not right.' Daisy pointed to one of the empty hay nets. He followed her finger and frowned.

'What's not right, Daisy?'

'The knot. You always use a slip knot so you can undo it in a hurry.' She stepped along the line of plates until she was close to the net. 'What you should do is pass the drawstring through the metal hoop, pull the net up as high as you can, and then slip-knot the end of the rope to a strand of the net and pass the end through the loop. Then the horse can't accidentally undo it or pull it down and get his feet caught in it.' She pointed to the empty net at the other end of the shelter. 'Like that one.'

Callum looked at the other hay net and saw the difference. Who would have thought that feeding a pony some dead grass could be so complicated? 'I see. And Kim would have known how to tie it up correctly?'

'Of course she would.'

'Kelly would have tied it correctly if she had done it but, by her admission, she had already gone home. Someone else tied the net and used the wrong knot.'

A thought occurred, and Callum stepped along the raised plates and out into the field. Daisy's boots tapped lightly behind him, like a muffled woodpecker. Tacked onto the rear of the field shelter was a small shed. Opening the door revealed a rough wooden shelf two feet above the ground with a bale of hay on it, a couple of pats missing from one end. The herby scent was pleasant, tickling his nostrils and better than the ammonia reek of dung and horse urine coming from an adjacent wheelbarrow. A short-bladed knife, a repurposed bone-handled one, rested on the timber cross member. It was probably used to cut the pink twine holding the hay sections together because discarded strings hung from a nail driven into the back of the door.

'What does a bale weigh, Daisy? Fifty, sixty pounds?'

'About that, depends on how densely it's packed.' She loosened a section of hay from the end of the bale. 'And that's pretty dense. Nearer sixty, I should say.'

'Not easy for a child to lift onto the shelf.'

'Impossible without help. She would have left it on the ground. It would take both girls to heave it up there,' Daisy said.

Callum closed the door and pointed to the other side of the field where a pole barn was stacked with small bales, partitioned from the field by a post and wire fence.

'And both girls to carry it here,' she added, 'but Kelly had already gone home.'

They crossed the field to the barn and stepped inside onto the springy hay floor. The only sounds were the cawing of rooks in the oak trees backing the field and the call of a startled pheasant, alarmed by their appearance.

There were no traffic sounds coming from the adjacent local lane.

Callum walked around the structure, but there was no corpse tucked behind a bale or hanging from the rafters. He tested the weight of a bale by grasping the pink strings and lifting it. The polypropylene pressed into the soft pads of his fingers. Kim, on her own, would have no chance of carrying it to the hay shed. He let go of the strings and the bale rustled back into the seed-strewn floor releasing a puff of herby scent.

'She wasn't on her own,' Daisy said. 'Somebody helped carry the hay and filled Drummer's net. Why?'

'She was ill or injured? She might have been physically restrained?' Callum left the thought 'or already dead' unvoiced. That was unlikely. Anybody who had killed a child and risked discovery was not going to stop to feed her pony.

He instructed the team to include the hay shed and the barn in their search. There was always the possibility that Kim's helper had dropped something with a fingerprint on it or snagged their hand and dripped blood. Leaving a passport at the scene would have been handy, but investigations were never that easy.

They walked back down Tethering Drove to their parked vehicles, and Callum rotated his silver earring, a quarter-turn for every stride. Some things didn't add up. He opened his car door, paused, and turned to Daisy.

'Why did she leave her phone behind? I could see that happening following a struggle but there's no sign of that, and it wasn't discarded, it was placed on the rail. Why didn't she take it with her if she left willingly?'

'Could be a school friend who helped her. Perhaps she went home with them and just forgot about it,' she said.

'Someone was there, but her parents have phoned all her friends and none of them have seen her.'

Daisy folded her arms and leaned back against the wing of her Navara. 'I prop my phone up like that when I'm mucking out Moses's box to listen to music. Perhaps she was doing the same.'

'Then ask Kelly if Kim was listening to music.'

'You're sure that Kelly isn't covering for her? Perhaps she expected her back before the parents came home and this is just a load of fuss for nothing.'

'They don't get along well enough for Kelly to cover for Kim,' Callum said. 'And, if she knows where she is, Kelly would be delighted to tell and get Kim into trouble.'

'I agree. What about the white van? She might have heard that we're looking for one in the Conchita case. Perhaps she's an attention-seeker. She was trying to flirt with you – did you notice?'

'That may be so, but she is lying about something. We just have to work out what.'

Chapter Nine

Daisy pulled away ahead of him. Parked cars were tucked under the hedge opposite the string of houses, their owners still in bed or eating breakfast before they faced the day. Callum drove slowly. Passing a paling fence, a dog barked his way along his side, before putting his front feet on the top of the gate and giving one last warning to the intruder on his territory.

Glancing into his building site at the top of the drive, Callum saw that the fencing was padlocked, hardly surprising as it was still early. He recalled the deep foundations where Dave was constructing a basement level to allow him two floors and still comply with the planning conditions. Were there other sites like this where Kim might be hiding? Or where someone had hidden her body? How many properties had cellars or outhouses where a child could be concealed?

He snapped his eyes back to the road at the sharp blast of a car horn. Swerving to the left, he braked hard and stopped, bonnet to bonnet with Dave's pickup. Dave eased over onto the verge to pull level with Callum and lowered his window. He leaned out and Callum smelt toothpaste on his breath.

'So, it's true? Young Kim's missing?' Dave's usual bantering tone had gone. The grapevine was working overtime. 'Louise rang to know if we'd seen her. I can't believe it. Not here. Are you sure there's no mistake?'

'We are keeping all lines of inquiry open at present.'

Callum knew that sounded impersonal, heartless even, when the tragedy struck at the very heart of a small community. The other thing he couldn't say was that from this point on, everyone was a suspect until proven otherwise. It changed the filter through which he viewed people, listened to their remarks, and observed their actions. It raised an invisible barrier isolating him from them.

'If she is missing, then it was after I left you,' Dave said.

'Why is that?' Callum watched Daisy's rear lights disappear ahead of him around the curve in the lane.

'I told you I was cadging a lift from Sam to the pub? When I got to his place, there was a bloke parked outside, and Kelly had her head in through the driver's window eating his tonsils. Sam wouldn't have been too pleased with her behaviour.'

'Do you know who it was?'

'Nah, sorry. Pop star looks, white T-shirt and ripped like a scaffolder but without the tats. Didn't look too upset about the treatment he was getting though. Kelly said she forgot to give me a message that Sam had to work and couldn't play crib, so I left them to it and hurried on up the lane to catch Jimmy Eastwood. He was on the team too, and I didn't fancy having to run in those boots.'

'Kelly didn't mention to you that Kim was missing?'

'Exactly, so she must have been there then, or she'd have been running round like a headless chicken looking for her instead of chewing on matey boy.'

'Can you remember anything about the car?'

'Nothing helpful like the reggo, if that's what you mean, but it was a Beamer, saloon. It was gone quarter past seven by then, and the light was going, but I think it was black or navy. Or maybe dark green.'

'Model?'

'Too early in the morning for twenty questions, mate.' He screwed his face in concentration. 'Old model. I thought it was a personal plate at first then I realised it was just an old motor. Pre-2000 and it had more spotlights across the front bumper than a football stadium.'

'And you only saw Kelly? Kim wasn't there too?'

'No, just Kelly.' Dave started to raise his window then lowered it again. 'Just remembered. I heard it pull away and his exhaust starting to blow. I hope you find her.' He raised his window and pulled across to the site fencing as Callum moved off.

The spikey gorse bushes on the open heath were still cloaked in a patchwork of spiderwebs, each strand beaded with the jewelled moisture of early morning dew. They stood in watchful groups, and behind them the heather rolled into the distance, glistening with iridescent pearls that would disappear with the heat of the day.

Callum, through his still open window, breathed in the moist chill air, laden with earthy peatiness. He pulled it deep into his lungs – sharing the smell with past generations who had used this road before him, had cast their eyes over the land, enjoyed her summers and endured her winters. Lived and then died here, their empty bodies nurturing the earth, perpetuating the landscape for their ancestors. He closed his window as he pulled out onto Forest Road. The harsh *skaaak* of a jay carried across the heather before the sound died away and he shivered at the thought of a wee girl, missing in this vast openness, fallen on the damp earth – hidden from people that could help her – or buried beneath it.

* * *

'Guv, possible sighting from the house-to-house.' Bird swatted the air with a sheet of paper as Callum came in from the corridor.

'What time? Where?'

'Tethering Drove. A girl spotted in a car with a bloke heading up towards Forest Road about 1930 hours yesterday.'

'Thanks, Bird. Daisy and I will get over there. See if anyone else's statement corroborates that and have a word with the Tanners' neighbours and friends, see what they say about the family dynamics. There's tension between Kelly and Sam.'

'Wilco, guv. And two people said they saw Jericho Hatcher's van in Tethering Drove earlier that afternoon.'

At the adjacent desk, Cookie was ending a phone call. His lamp-black curls riffled, his head bouncing to an inaudible beat.

Not submitting to his annoyance at the casual approach of the young officer was at times a struggle for Callum. 'Cookie, how's the alibi for the parents going?'

'I spoke to the nursing home. They were both at work when they said they were, and the outer door is controlled and has CCTV to stop the crinklies escaping.'

Callum frowned and wondered if Cookie would be using the same terminology when he was the relevant age.

'The staff go round in pairs when on duty, so they are fully accounted for by another person all the time,' Cookie added.

'And you've spoken to their respective work partners as well as management?'

'Well, no, guv. They'll be in bed asleep now if they work nights.'

'I don't care,' Callum bellowed. 'A girl is missing. Do it. Now, DC Cooke.'

Red-faced, Cookie's hand trembled as he reached for his phone.

Callum closed his eyes for a moment and added a mental note to discuss priorities with Cookie at a less pressing time.

'Daisy, with me.' He heard her footfalls behind him, and the sounds of normal service being resumed after the hiatus. 'Let's go visiting.'

* * *

They parked outside the paling gate where the dog had earlier chased Callum's car. Now the same tan beast bounced towards them stiff-legged, hackles raised, every stride punctuated by a deafening bark. It halted, head down, throat rumbling, and the flesh across its nose wrinkled as the lifted lips exposed large, white teeth. That dog had an attitude, or perhaps dogs could smell fear. Callum took a step back from the wicket gate.

The back door opened and a man wearing slippers and a tartan dressing gown stood on the path. He whistled once and the dog raced back from the gate and sat at his left side, body tight against his lower leg.

Callum introduced them both as Daisy opened the gate, swiftly dealing with the barred horse catch on the inside. He had thought them unnecessary until he had watched a mare press her chin against the thumb tab, lean on the gate and trot into his garden.

In the kitchen, the dog transferred its affections and leaned against Daisy's leg, earning her a surprised look from slipper man. The kettle bubbled, then with a click, turned itself off.

'Can you go over what you told the officer, please?' Callum asked.

The man righted two mugs that were draining by the sink. 'Okay. Like I told the other chap, last evening I left the newspaper in my car – I park it the other side of the lane – and I went out to get it a smidgeon after half seven.'

'You're sure of the time?' Callum asked.

'Can't stand *Corrie* and the missus loves it. I'm sure of the time.' He grinned at them, dropped a teabag into one mug, scalded it with boiling water and immediately fished it out and dropped it into the other mug. 'Missus likes weak tea.'

'Right. Tell me what you saw, please,' said Callum.

'A bloody great black BMW going too fast up the drove with his spotlights blinding me.'

'Who was in the car?' he asked.

'Well, I was on the driver's side, and he was a youngish bloke wearing sunglasses, at half past seven at night – I ask you.' He shook his head and slopped boiling water into the second mug on top of the already damp teabag. 'And there was a girl in the passenger seat – I couldn't see her clearly because it was getting dusk. But it was definitely a girl. Long hair, you see.' He took in Callum's long hair and gave a little shrug. 'Probably some holidaymaker. We get 'em all summer, lost, driving too fast. Drives the missus mad.'

'Good. Do you remember what colour her hair was?' Daisy said, and stroked the dog's head.

The man poked the submerged teabag with a spoon. 'Sorry. I can't be sure. Dark, I think. But the other officer said I needed to tell you anyway.' He stirred the brackish liquid once more, then lifted out the soggy teabag and plopped it in the sink.

'Exactly so. Thank you for that, and if you think of anything else, please let us know,' Callum said.

The dog walked quietly at Daisy's side and sat near her boots as she lifted the catches to open the gate.

Callum looked from the canine to Daisy and back again. Slipper man had a disbelieving look on his face that matched Callum's.

'Nothing to do with me, sir, he just came and sat on my foot.' She reached over the gate, closed the horse catch, and patted the dog's head before turning away.

Callum looked over the gate and stepped back with speed as the dog launched itself at the palings, rattling the ironmongery and snarling at him. Daisy chuckled as he zapped open his car.

'One day,' Callum murmured as he settled in the driver's seat, 'I may have to arrest you for hijacking people's dogs.'

Chapter Ten

'Do you want me to start looking for that vehicle to find out if that was Kim in it?' Daisy snatched at her seat belt and clicked it closed as Callum pressed the start button.

He shook his head. 'No. That was Kelly sneaking off for a bit of fun with her Romeo.' He registered the surprised look on Daisy's face then caught a movement in the rear-view mirror and killed the engine. 'Speak of the devil.'

Daisy shot him a glance, looked in the door mirror, and then released her seat belt.

Kelly was walking up behind them, her attention on her phone, and the brindle bitch sauntered in her wake at the end of a red lead.

'Perhaps she'll tell me what you're talking about.' Daisy's tone was caustic.

Kelly passed their car without noticing them and they got out and fell into step, one on each side of her. The dog wagged a welcome which was more enthusiastic than Kelly's greeting.

'What do you want? I already answered all your questions.' She slipped her phone into the front of her bra and kept walking. The feather hairslide swayed and rustled like a trapped bird trying to escape.

'You told us you stayed at home all night,' Callum said

'So?' Kelly stopped walking and faced him.

'So, I ask you once again, Kelly, where were you yesterday evening?'

'It's my business and it's private.' She lifted her chin defiantly. 'I know my rights.'

Callum sighed, everybody thought they knew their rights these days. 'If it has any connection to the disappearance of Kim, then it is my business.'

'It doesn't.' The dog pulled on the lead and whined, wanting to continue with its morning walk. 'Stop it, you stupid mutt-face.'

'I decide if it's relevant, not you. Tell me where you were.' Callum watched her shoulders droop forward, the defiant tilt of her head softening, as she tried a different approach.

'Look,' she wheedled. 'It was nothing important. And I don't want to tell you, cos you'll tell Dad and there will be a shit shower. Please.' When she got no response, she tipped her head to one side and smiled coyly at Callum. 'Pretty please?'

That ploy may work with her parents, but he wasn't her father.

'Tell me. Now,' he said.

She sighed. 'All right, but don't tell Dad. Jack came round and we went for a ride in his car. And then I came back home. We weren't long and the squirt was upstairs swotting – I think.'

'Your mum said she ate her supper, but you didn't check on her before you left?'

'I'm not her keeper.' Kelly tugged at the dog's lead. 'And if you must know, I threw her supper in the bin. I'm sick of them running round after her. She should get her own food.'

A muscle bounced in Callum's jaw, but his tone remained civil. 'What time did you eventually get home, Kelly?'

She hesitated, impaled by Callum's stare, then opted for her version of the truth. 'About ten.'

The bushes rustled in the breeze.

Callum added on another half an hour; she was probably being conservative with the truth. That left four hours when Kim was alone – if she had made it home. The more facts they uncovered, the greater his doubts. What kid would leave her phone behind?

The dog tugged again on the lead and whined so they recommenced walking.

'Did you see the white van when you walked back from the field?' Callum asked.

The surprised look on her face told him she had.

'Yes. Didn't I say so?' Her dog danced at the end of the lead and barked as they passed the paling gate with the zealous canine racing along the inside of the fence. 'Stop it, mutt-face.' Her dog ignored her until they had passed the property, and then it sneezed, expunging the scent of the rival.

'What's Jack's full name?' Daisy asked.

'Oh, God. You're not going to ask him, are you? How embarrassing is that.' She hurried her stride, and they kept pace.

'We need to know if there is any connection between him and Kim,' Daisy explained.

'She's just a snotty kid.' Kelly's laugh was fleer. 'What would anyone want with a kid like her?'

Callum knew that for all her worldly veneer, Kelly would have been very shocked to learn what some men would want from a child like Kim.

'His full name, Kelly.' Any hint that it was a question was quashed by his tone.

'Okay. Jackson Chambers and before you ask, he lives in Woodgreen and works in Verwood. Come on, dog.'

They were near the top of the drove where the ribbon of houses gave way to open heath, close to the site of his new house.

'God, I can't wait to get out of this place,' Kelly muttered under her breath as she turned away from them onto a narrow path that meandered through the heather, the rainbow feathers in her hair fluttering. They watched her, backs to Callum's building plot, until a stand of gorse eclipsed their view of her.

A lassie stood by the gap in the perimeter fence; cut-off jeans, a T-shirt too short to cover her flat, tanned midriff, hair strained back in a high ponytail. Her eyes followed the path Kelly had taken. Dave came to stand beside her.

Callum looked down at Daisy. 'Five minutes max.' It would not take long to tell Dave that he approved the basement lighting suggestion.

Daisy was watching the girl follow the direction of the departed Kelly. 'Are you friends with her, Anna?' she asked.

Anna nodded. 'She used to be in the top set with me.'

Callum caught Dave's grin out of the corner of his eye.

Anna moved aside to stand closer to Daisy, her back towards the men. The girls' heads were close together and their voices so quiet that Callum could not hear what was being discussed. He caught Daisy's eye, and she gave him an almost imperceptible shake of her head before turning her back on him. He took her warning to keep his distance and resumed his conversation with Dave.

'Let's go with your suggestion for the lighting,' Callum said. 'It seems to address all my concerns.'

'Paul made up the shortfall on the crib team last night and he had a couple of sensible ideas about lighting basements, but not as good as that one of Anna's. She made those drawings I showed you. She wants to be an architect,' Dave said. A motor started up behind him and he raised his hand in farewell to Callum and moved deeper onto the site.

The girls had moved along the verge and when Callum joined them, they both looked up at him.

'Here comes the boss.' Daisy's expression was thoughtful. 'Back to work for me. Keep in touch, Anna,' she added lightly.

'I will.' Anna's face and tone were serious as she walked back to join her father.

'What was that all about?' Callum asked.

'Anna says Kim was getting a bit of hassle at school, and she thinks she is being bullied.'

Callum clicked open his car door. 'By whom? Why does she think that?'

'She doesn't know who. Anna has just completed her Gold Duke of Edinburgh's Award and as part of that she was helping at Hale Primary. The school put on a production of *A Big Green Adventure*, mostly for the leavers, but Kim was in it as she sings in the school choir. Anna helped with the costumes and noticed bruises on Kim when she was getting changed.'

'What sort of bruises? And where?' He got into the vehicle; his interest piqued.

'They are all in places that aren't visible when she is fully clothed.' Daisy opened the door and slid onto the passenger seat. 'And it's not big bruises like she's been punched or beaten. It's more like lines of little bruises.' She pinched a line in the air with her finger and thumb.

'Did Kim know Anna had seen the bruises?'

Daisy nodded. 'She asked her not to say anything. Said it was all right and she didn't want to get anyone into trouble.'

'Does Anna have any idea who might be doing it, or why?' He pressed the start button and pulled onto the road.

'She doesn't, but I asked her what she thought – she is intelligent and well-informed. She says Kim is a bit babyish compared to her classmates. She doesn't really hang out with the other girls unless they have ponies.'

Before he could comment, Daisy continued, 'And she's mad about Drummer, as we already know.'

'Is that enough to make her a victim?'

Daisy wrinkled her nose. 'Girls can be very cruel if they put their minds to it.'

Callum gave her a swift glance and wondered if she was speaking from personal experience.

'Chivvy up Cookie checking her phone messages and emails and tell him to keep that in mind. There could be some connection there,' he said.

And any connection, however slight, was more than they had at the moment.

Chapter Eleven

Cookie halted outside the office door; a blue folder clasped to his chest with one arm whilst the other appeared to be conducting an invisible orchestra. He was silently mouthing words.

'What are you doing, Cookie?' Daisy asked as she and Callum came up behind him.

'Hi, Deedee, sir.' He folded his conducting hand across the file and pushed his back against the office door to open it. 'Just counting the tiles on the corridor floor.'

Daisy strode ahead of Callum, her ponytail swinging with each stride. 'Why? Haven't you got enough to do? I can find you more work.' There was an accusatory edge to her voice.

Cookie did not immediately answer her.

'Cookie,' she snapped.

Callum restrained himself from intervening, not wanting to undermine her.

'Okay. Sorry. I was counting the tiles because I was working out what percentage of the floor we actually walk on. It was just a mental exercise. It wasn't wasting time because I was doing it while I was walking.' Cookie's eyes were on Daisy's face and his voice faltered. Callum would have liked to see her expression.

'It's like naming the US states in alphabetical order when I can't get to sleep.'

The corner of Callum's mouth lifted. He had come across people like Cookie before. When their body was dog-tired, their brains were still active and couldn't switch off. He had experienced the same thing for a while after Grace had died. He had watched the clock go round and in the morning was sure he hadn't slept at all. If Cookie's overactive brain consigned him to that fate regularly, he felt sorry for the lad.

Daisy's hiked eyebrows suggested she had never experienced that problem.

Cookie changed the subject. 'I found something odd on Kim's phone.' He dropped the files on his desk and picked up the pink phone. 'And Forensics said just her prints and Kelly's on it.'

'That was to be expected,' Callum said, joining Daisy beside Cookie's desk. 'What was odd?'

'A text message that doesn't make sense. She sent lots of texts, mostly to school friends and horsy girls with a gazillion photos of her pony, but this one was from Anna Green?' He looked up questioningly.

'We know Anna Green,' Callum confirmed. 'What did she have to say?'

'She says, "You should tell your parents. If you want me to come with you, I will." I don't know what she means.'

'We think Kim was bullied at school, so Anna is probably encouraging her to speak to her parents about it,' Daisy said.

'There's nothing else relating to bullying, no threatening texts or any emails on her laptop,' Cookie said doubtfully.

'Check her deleted files, Cookie. And go and see her friends and class teacher, but bear in mind that you might be speaking to the bully.'

'Hunky-doodley, guv.' He slipped into his seat; Daisy's admonishment seemed to be sloughed from his consciousness as easily as a snake's skin in spring.

'Bird.' Callum moved to the detective's desk. 'Anything else from the door-to-door?' Kim had only to walk past twelve gateways between her house and the lane that led to her field, so getting statements should not have taken long.

'Mrs Hammond, last but one, spends a lot of time looking out the window. She saw Jericho Hatcher, but it was earlier than 1800 hours. She saw "that Kelly girl" on her own just after six, but she didn't see Kim. When she was putting the cat out last thing, there was a car like Jackson Chambers's going down Tethering Drove, 2300 hours plus.'

'How does she know it was him at that time of night? It was dark,' Callum asked.

'"Lit up like a spaceship," she said.'

Kelly's story was holding up, even if her idea of time was a little fluid.

'Guv?' Cookie pushed back his chair. 'Sam and Louise were at work all night like they said. Sam's workmate was nearly driven mad by his worrying about Kim because it was the first time they had left Kelly in charge.'

Callum had had no serious doubts that their alibis would be confirmed, and it was another avenue closed.

'Good. Thanks. Daisy, I need you to go with Cookie to the school. You have a word with her friends and, Cookie, do the staff, including the lunchtime supervisors. If she was bullied, someone might know where she is.'

'No problem,' Daisy said. 'But I thought we were off to see Jericho Hatcher.'

'We were, but girls might be more prepared to talk to you. Bird can come with me. He could do with the exercise,' said Callum.

Bird grunted but was quick to scoop up his jacket and looked pleased with the prospect of getting out in the fresh air.

* * *

Jericho Hatcher's scrapyard was set back behind his house and accessed along a gravel track separated from the garden by a damaged paling fence. Callum parked on the verge outside the property, and they stepped across the cattle grid and walked along the track. The residential roof to their left was furred with moss disturbed by birds searching for insects, and the path below was speckled with green and brown debris. A television aerial clung drunkenly to the smoke-blackened chimney and overshadowed a shiny satellite dish that appeared to follow them along the track.

The yard comprised heaps of metal in various shades of rust, stacked in untidy umber pyramids. Along the back perimeter was a row of tall-sided skips and bins, some showing flaking brown poles protruding above their top lines. The only buildings were a dented red shipping container and a couple of wooden sheds. Backed by woodland, the ground was peppered with fallen leaves from the overhanging oak trees. Chattering jackdaws *chyak-chyaked* as they approached and flew away over the treetops as if they knew there was trouble brewing. When they entered the yard, the low sun behind them stretched their shadows into giants.

'Let's see if there's anyone about then, guv,' Bird said softly.

Callum heard the clanking of an unspooling chain and a muscular yellow dog with a record number of teeth charged out of the shadows and was jerked to a halt by his tether. Both men stood still, two strides away from the chain-testing canine whose raised hackles, glittering eyes and rumbling growl confirmed his bad attitude. Perhaps it was a mistake sending Daisy to the school with Cookie. She could have worked her magic on the beast.

They wore jackets against the crisp chill of early autumn but the man coming out of the shipping container wore a vest and jeans. He was accompanied by a skewbald terrier scurrying around his feet, yapping persistently. At first glance, the man looked fat, but closer inspection revealed his girth to be muscle; hard, well-used, ready-for-action muscle. Callum was pleased to feel the solidity of Bird's shoulder bump against his own.

'Jericho Hatcher?' Callum watched the thick fingers curl into fists.

'Might be. Who wants to know?' He hawked, spat phlegm into the dirt at Callum's feet and his eyes narrowed. 'Thought I could smell something. You're filth. Come to arrest me? What are you trying to stitch me up for now?'

'Just a couple of questions, Mr Hatcher, concerning a missing schoolgirl, Kim Tanner.' Callum pushed his hands into his jacket pockets and attempted to appear more relaxed than he felt. He watched as the fists gave in to gravity – one punch from them would have him in hospital for a week and he'd probably need a new passport photo.

Bird eased out a slow breath.

Jericho hooked his thumbs into his belt loops. 'Ask them then, then fuck off.'

The watchdog moved back into the shade, the chain chinked onto the earth and the terrier sped off across the yard in pursuit of a magpie that had lighted on a tower of tyres.

'Yesterday afternoon, your vehicle was seen in Tethering Drove, Hale. Were you driving it?'

'Yeah. So what?'

'Where were you going?'

'I had a bit of business. Why?'

'Where was this business?' Callum asked.

'None of yours, so keep your fucking nose out.' He had long eyelashes, too long for a man with a buckled nose and "HATE" inked across the bruised knuckles of his right hand.

Callum lifted his hand and pointed to the white van parked close to the house. The chain snapped taut at his sudden movement and a rumbling growl cautioned him not to move. Callum kept out of target range.

'Is that the vehicle you were driving?'

'Yeah. My Hummer's in the garage this week.'

Callum smiled.

Jericho snorted. 'Of course it's that bloody van. It's the only one I've got.'

'Where did you go?' Callum asked again and watched the fists re-form. 'Look. I am trying to eliminate you from our list of suspects. Help me here, man.'

'I don't talk to the filth.'

Callum snapped to attention and saw Bird's shadow do the same. 'Last chance, Jericho, or we're taking you in, and there's a long wait for the duty solicitor at the nick. You'll be with us for some time.'

'I've already got a solicitor,' Jericho snarled.

'I bet you have,' Bird said. 'But you'll still have to wait until we've got time to interview you. And we're very busy, aren't we, Inspector?'

'Surprisingly so,' Callum confirmed conversationally.

The taut ropes of Jericho's neck relaxed, and he flexed his shoulders. 'All right. I'll tell you where I was.' He looked towards the house where a dark-haired woman, pale face pressed against the smeared windowpane, was straining to catch their conversation. 'But don't tell Sheena.' Jericho moved closer to the detectives, putting his back to the property and shielding his face from her gaze.

'Fair enough' – Callum met the grey eyes in a steady stare – 'as long as it's legal.'

Jericho grinned, showing the gap from a missing incisor, a black hole amongst strong, even teeth, like the entrance to a dark cave in white rocks. 'Sort of. I was with a friend in Bournemouth.'

'Don't shit in your own backyard? Not normally your style, Jericho,' Bird said. 'Can you prove where you were all evening? Can anyone vouch for you?'

Jericho had a surprisingly joyous laugh that rose from his belly and boomed around the yard, bouncing from the rusted mounds, disturbing birds that lifted into the air like black rags and flew away. In another time and place, he might have been a more likeable individual but, with his anger simmering just below the surface, Callum thought that asking questions could be like throwing stones into a volcano.

Jericho was happy to share the joke. 'Try the cop shop down there. Me and Tracy had a few drinks at her flat before we went out on the town and then we had a few more and then some twat shopped us for fucking in an alleyway and we got arrested.'

'Name of the arresting officer?'

'How should I know? One of them make-believes playing at being filth. He'll be easy to spot though. I broke his bloody nose. Me and Tracy spent the night in separate cells, released this morning.'

Being released with a fine for laying hands on a police officer was a disquieting sign of the times.

Jericho leaned in towards Callum. 'Me and Trace have had a thing going for years and I told the missus I ended it, so I don't want her finding out,' he said.

'We'll need to check your van,' Callum said. Jericho had already told them where he was when Conchita was found, but it never hurt to check.

'I've told you I had nothing to do with any kid going missing. Don't you believe me?'

'Innocent until proven guilty in my book, Mr Hatcher,' Callum said calmly. 'If you've got nothing to hide then you surely won't object to a search.' He watched the conflicting emotions race across Jericho's face.

'We can always come back with a search warrant, Jericho. Bet the missus would love that,' Bird said, looking across to the indistinct figure behind the window.

'I got nothing to hide.' He was belligerent but flicked a look over his shoulder towards Sheena. 'You can search my bloody van. Give it a clean while you're at it.' Confidences over, his considerations returned to his image and his watching wife. He stepped back a stride and raised his voice. 'Now, fuck off, copper.' This time the gob of spit landed on the nose of the yellow dog.

They were nearly back at their vehicle when Callum caught a flash of gold streaking along the gravel behind them.

'Bloody hell. The bastard,' Bird said.

Callum pressed the key, yanked open the driver's door and hurled himself inside before the unfurling door mirrors and orange lights had finished their welcome. Bird slewed onto the passenger seat and his door slammed closed. Callum looked down at the crinkled nose, quivering flesh ridged above the threatening fangs. Back along the track, Jericho was laughing.

'He slipped his chain, MacLean,' Jericho shouted waving a two-finger salute.

'Like hell he did. Jericho did that on purpose, guv.'

'That he did, Bird.'

Callum pressed the start button and eased away from the verge. The yellow dog stood on the cattle grid, watched them in silence then turned to trot back to his master.

'Do you believe him about his alibi?' Bird fastened his seat belt, silencing the pinging sound, and looked at Callum.

'Oddly, I do. Get the CCTV checked and get Cookie to phone Bournemouth nick.'

'Wilco. The bloke who arrested him deserves a bleedin' medal for stupidity. I'd want to be mob-handed before I tried putting cuffs on our Jericho.'

'Good job we didn't have to take him in then.'

'It was. But I wasn't worried about it, guv. I was going to let you cuff him.'

Chapter Twelve

Interviews tend to fall into one of three categories, the 'no comment', the abusive, and the 'I want to tell you everything I know'. Callum and Daisy faced Jackson Chambers across the table and waited. Jackson placed his elbows on the grey surface and leaned forward. The bright flowers on his shirt nodded their heads towards the detectives with the same youthful innocence as the wearer.

'Do you have a problem with your eyes, Mr Chambers?' Daisy asked.

'Not now I've seen you.' Jackson's tanned face stretched into a smile showing his even, white teeth.

'Then please remove your sunglasses,' Daisy said.

He complied, dropping them onto the tabletop with a *click*. 'What's all this about?' he asked. 'You didn't need to bring me in for special treatment. I would have answered your questions at home. Saved you any trouble.' Jackson was an 'I want to tell you everything' interviewee.

The clock ticked as Callum identified the fragrances of ginger and citrus from the other side of the table. Deodorant and moisturiser? He felt old and out of touch and knew Grace would have laughed at his thought. He studied the boy-band face, smooth cheeks, arched brows, and soft skin. Jackson looked as if he might explode. That generation was so used to being bombarded with constant stimuli from phones and pads that they found silence uncomfortable and scary.

Callum relented. 'Tell me about last night.'

'Last night. Which bit?'

'All of it,' Daisy said, leaning forward, placing her elbows on the table, with cupped hands supporting her chin.

Callum sat back and let her take the lead as Jackson's eyes locked onto Daisy's face.

'I left work at the usual time and went home. I had a shower and a bite, played a game on my paddle against a mate and then left to drive to Kelly's.'

'Who can verify that?' Daisy said.

'Uhm, my manager. We had a new Merc in, and I asked him if I could have it for the night. He likes us to know how new cars drive so that when customers ask, it makes them think we know what we're talking about.' He grinned at Daisy.

She smiled at him. 'And did he let you borrow it?'

'Sometimes he says yes, but this time he said no because he wanted it for the evening. I can't think why. He's already got a missus. But he was standing by the Merc with the keys in his hand when I left.'

Daisy tilted her head to one side and her gaze played over his face.

Jackson sat back in his chair and folded his arms. 'Look, we have CCTV like any half-decent garage. Check it if you don't believe me.'

Callum looked down at his incoming text from Bird confirming what Jackson had just told them. So far so good.

'We believe you, Mr Chambers,' Callum said, by way of informing Daisy about his text. 'But we do have to check, or we wouldn't be doing our job properly.' Callum folded his arms and his eyes motioned Daisy to continue.

'Was your mother at home when you got there?' she asked.

'Sort of. She plays bingo, goes with our next-door neighbour and was just opening Mrs Bond's gate when I got home. She waved to me when I got out of my car.' He raised a hand and waved it at Daisy.

'And what time did you leave to go to Hale to meet Kelly?' Daisy made notes.

'Ten past or quarter past seven, maybe.'

'Can anyone verify that?'

Jackson's confident smile slid away, and the beginnings of a frown ridged his brow. 'No, I don't think so. I didn't see anyone, unless you count that dimwit Barnes creeping along in his van. He held me up all along Hale Purlieu driving in the middle of the road, until I managed to overtake him right at the end of the road and only then by driving on the verge. He probably doesn't use his mirrors, so he didn't know I was there.'

'What makes you say that?'

'Because I flashed him enough times and he didn't pull over.'

Callum thought that was no guarantee that Paul Barnes had not seen Jackson. It could just be confirmation that he didn't let the world hurry him.

'And then?' Daisy asked following a brief eye contact with Callum.

'And then I pulled up outside Kelly's. I normally park up the road a bit because her old man's a yawn, but Kel had texted me to say the olds were out. We had a bit of chat and then some chap in cowboy boots and a jacket with tassels had a go at Kel for not telling him her dad was working. When Crocodile Dundee–' Jackson paused and wielded an imaginary weapon '–that's not a knife, this is a knife.' He laughed and planted his elbows back onto the table. 'Love that film.'

'And?' Daisy prompted.

'Then the dude trotted off up the road and Kel got in my car.'

Callum studied the man, little more than a youth, with a certitude and assurance far beyond his years. When Jackson had arrived at the station, he had tossed his car keys to Callum so the team could examine his car. There had been no indications of ill ease, no nervousness or reticence.

'Good motor that, for now. Quality,' he had said, smoothing his hand across the bonnet, 'but I've got my eye on a Range Rover; black, tinted windows, real girlie-popper.'

He had winked conspiratorially at Callum who marvelled at the ability of the young to dream as if they would live forever and live as if they would die tomorrow. Had he been similarly assertive in his twenties? He thought back to university and concluded that he had been confident in his mental abilities but hadn't had the confidence that Jackson exuded. The lad was being open, almost enjoying the encounter, not because he thought himself superior to the law, but because he had nothing to hide. Callum began to suspect that the search would show no sign of Kim being in that car. Jackson was too honest, too forthright; helpful, but not overly eager to help. That would have made Callum suspicious, and currently his suspicions were ebbing with every subsequent answer.

Callum leaned forward. 'Did you see Kim?'

'No. I've never seen Kim. Kelly told me she's gone missing. Stupid squid… kid,' he corrected himself.

Callum heard Kelly's inflexion in his comment.

'Why do you say that?' Daisy asked.

'Because she's clingy, always needs looking after or things done for her. Ask Kelly. She'll tell you.'

Callum didn't doubt that.

'Where did you drive to and what did you do when you got there?'

Jackson turned wide eyes to Daisy. 'A gentleman never tells, Sergeant.'

'This one had better tell or he could find himself locked up.'

He was quick to reply. 'Okay. The exception proves the rule, so my gran says. I took her up to Turf Hill car park and we sat in the car and chatted.'

Callum didn't challenge the information. They were both over the age of consent.

'Did you see anybody?'

'There was a camper van there. They had a map and were trying to find the Rufus Stone.' He looked across at Callum. 'You know, where King William got shot by an arrow when they were hunting deer? I showed them on the map, and they left.'

'Continue,' Callum said.

'Like I said, we sat and chatted. And then we got back into the front of the car, and I gave her a driving lesson.'

Callum looked at the smiling youth. 'In the dark? Is your car insured for Kelly to drive?'

'It's not a public highway and it's easier to see if something's coming in the dark.'

'Ponies don't have headlights,' Daisy muttered. She looked at Callum, but he gave a shake of his head. He did not intend to pursue the issue. She turned her attention back to Jackson. 'What time did you get back to her house?'

'Half eleven.'

Daisy wrote it down. His reference to the time contradicted Kelly's version, which did not surprise either officer.

Chapter Thirteen

Callum wanted another look at the ponies' field. He parked in Tethering Drove in the last of the afternoon sunshine and, almost immediately, clouds appeared like stealth bombers and threw all they had at him. Cold rain slapped against his cheeks, beat on his scalp and trickled down the back of his neck. Shrugging deeper into his jacket, he lowered his head to keep the rain out of his eyes and watched the water bounce off the toes of his new boots onto the gravel.

An involuntary grin tugged at his mouth. His grandmother would say the deluge was his fault for buying new boots. 'You bought them, now God's making sure you get good use out of them.' She would duck her chin towards her chest and purse her lips. The unbidden image lifted his mood, and his shoulders relaxed for a moment.

The two ponies stood side by side, rumps pushed into the hedge to shield them from the rain. They seemed to get along better than the sisters. The gate was slippery, slicked with moisture, and the bottom rung dripped a wet line into the mud with a steady *plick*, *plick*, *plick*. Both animals swung their heads in his direction. He grasped the top rail, swung his leg over and splashed down onto the mired grass – hinges end, of course. He was learning. He cautiously glanced at the sheltering ponies and walked across the open field to the hay barn.

Flushed out by his approach, a cock pheasant whirred away in a flash of copper and soared over the hedge into a neighbouring pasture. Inside, the rain's tattoo on the galvanised roof eliminated all other sounds. It was like a regiment marching double time above his head. His boots disturbed strands of loose hay, releasing herby perfume into the air that lifted above that of sodden damp peat. He loved the fresh smell of earth after rain, but it was preferable when the storm was over, and he did not have cold water running down his chin and into the neck of his shirt.

He looked towards the road but couldn't see it. No one in a vehicle could have seen Kim under the shelter of the galvanised roof. He moved into the field and took the shortest route to the ponies' shelter. He had gone several yards before he had a clear sight of the tarmac and then lost it before he reached the shelter. He turned and walked back towards the barn.

Drummer ambled towards him, ears flicking forward then sideways when Callum spoke.

'Please don't,' he muttered, but the pony ignored him, catching up with him on his second traverse. Callum crouched down until he assessed himself to be Kim's height. Bent double, he came to a spot where he could see the lane. When Kim reached there, anyone passing could have seen her. Drummer stopped behind him, nudged Callum's shoulder with his muzzle, and then lipped at his long, wet hair.

'I hope you know that's not hay, fella.' Callum stood tall and reached out a flat hand to rub the brown face, as Daisy had done. Water slicked off the thick forelock but the hair beneath the fringe was dry.

'Pity you can't talk; you could tell me who took your mistress.'

Large conker-coloured eyes watched Callum with the enduring patience of generations of his predecessors.

The pony dogged his footsteps and followed him into the shelter out of the rain. Callum stroked the surprisingly soft muzzle with increasing confidence. He still had all his fingers.

'Someone driving along the road looked across at exactly the right moment, probably saw her struggling with the hay bale and came to help.' Drummer made a whiffling noise in his nostrils as if he agreed with Callum.

'I don't think he intended to hurt her, or he would have dragged her into the shelter unseen. And there's no evidence of a struggle.'

Drummer pushed at Callum's pocket with his nose.

'Sorry. I don't have a pocket full of Polos like Daisy.' He continued with his theory. 'He put the bale in the shed for her, so she was still standing because she must have told him where to put it.' He walked in the rain to the shed with Drummer at his heels. He opened the door and put a restraining hand on the pony's shoulder as it tried to snatch at the hay.

'No, you don't, beastie. Kim brings your empty hay net; he lifts the bale onto the shelf and cuts the strings with the knife. Second opportunity, but there's no blood on the knife, Drummer.'

The pony flicked his ears sideways and followed Callum back into the shelter.

'Then, Kim propped her phone on the ledge, presumably to tie up your hay net. That's when something happened, and someone else had to tie up your tea. What happened, I wonder?'

He looked around the shelter. The only prints on the phone had been Kim's and Kelly's, so it was fair to assume that she had placed the phone up on the shelf herself. Then what? The only prints on the riding crop had been the girls', and again this was nothing more than expected.

'One stride from the phone to your net, so something happened in that last metre.' They had not found any blood, or any sign of impact and she would need to hit the wood hard to incapacitate herself. He patted Drummer's wet neck and found himself coming back to the same conclusion. Kim's visitor had tied up the hay net – albeit not to Daisy's satisfaction. The pony followed Callum back to the field entrance.

'Well, Drummer, my conclusion is that his motive was to help, not to harm. That's where the logic takes me. Do you agree?' He patted the pony before climbing back over the gate.

The rain was easing off and the hedgerow leaves gleamed as if they had been polished. Tucking his wet hair behind his ears, he walked back into the lane. His boots slapped into the puddles with a steady rhythm as the sun reappeared and drew tendrils of peaty steam from the verge. The sinking sun slid down towards the horizon, tinting the sky cadmium red behind charcoal trees.

He went over his theory on the drive home and quelled the stab of alarm that Kim had been missing for nearly twenty-four hours.

He was nearly home when something nagged at him. If she knew the person who helped her, why didn't they take her home?

'Were you waiting for me?' The cat was sitting on the doorstep. She trotted into the dark kitchen ahead of him. He heard the scrape of wood on the flagstones and snapped on the lights. She was rubbing against the chair leg. She blinked up at him and stood on tiptoes to push her back up against Callum's leg.

'You're a persistent wee beastie, aren't you?'

He opened the fridge and took out the milk.

'And a lucky wee beastie too. Tinned salmon tonight, and you can have the skin.'

After supper, Callum set up a desk easel on the kitchen table, taped a sheet of paper to his drawing board and found a 2B pencil. He held it, not with his index finger on top and close to the point as he would to write, but loosely at the end of the shaft, thumb uppermost. He scythed the graphite across the page in sweeping strokes, varying the angle of his hand. On the paper, the outlines of a tall hedge, the field shelter and the hay barn appeared. He roughed in the shape of two ponies, bulbous-bellied with spindly legs, standing side by side. His phone rang and he put down his pencil.

'Freya. How are you? I should have called, sorry.' A weekly catch-up with his sisters or parents had become the new norm and it had been his turn to make contact. He knew his mother worried about him. Freya, the peacemaker, was stepping up to the plate.

'I know, Cal.'

He could hear the smile in her voice and imagined her sitting by her big picture window with the wind-bent tree outside and the moon-bright loch beyond.

'We're all grand here, up in the frozen north. And you, little brother?'

When he heard her accent, he felt a surge of homesickness that made the back of his throat burn.

'Aye. Grand too. Busy at work with a couple of new cases and an abducted wee lassie and having to make lots of decisions about the new house.' He did not need to mention that he was finding it difficult to make them without Grace. His sister always understood.

'Is it built yet? How long will it be before you move in?'

Callum's laugh was spontaneous and full-bodied. 'You're worse than she was. You've no patience. It will be a good while yet. I took some photos, to keep a record of what happens when you build a house. Should I put them in a file and send them up?'

'Do that. I'll take them over and show the olds. They miss you.'

'I know they do. And I miss you lot as well, hen.' And Grace. I miss Grace most of all, he thought. His chest hugged his heart a little tighter. 'I've posted a card and gift voucher for Shona's birthday, tell her.'

Freya chuckled. 'Have you got a social secretary working for you? You forgot Dolina's.'

'Life of Riley, down here, me. I'm sitting with a wee dram sketching as we speak.'

'Glad you're good. Keep in touch, wee man.' She ended the call.

Callum smiled to himself at the use of their pet name for him. His three sisters had always referred to him as 'the wee man' and he felt a warm surge of affection for the girls, women as they were now.

Filling a jug with water, he dragged a brushful across the top half of the paper. Then he swept a wash of cerulean blue into the damp section, watching the colour run down like a curtain and stop when it reached dry paper. He tilted the board to stop it bleeding into the dry section. With the paint still damp, he pressed a screwed-up tissue against it to lift out some of the pigment, leaving cloud-shaped patches.

Ochre and greens were washed across the lower half of the paper using the same method. He dropped a mixture of viridian green and ultramarine into the base of the hedge and tilted the board to confine the bleed of the dark colours to the shadowed foliage. Then he left it to dry. Tomorrow he would paint in the two ponies, standing with their rumps pressed into the hedge. He wondered if he would ever see the Tanner sisters standing that close to each other. He would have given a lot to know that it might once again be possible.

Chapter Fourteen

Callum slept badly. His mind was flooded with pictures of Kim captive in attics, cellars, and other confined spaces. Images chased through his sleep, like cinematic frames, morphing together, overlapping, dragging his memories with them. His legs thrust against the covers as he chased after Kim. Pain stabbed at his chest in his effort to catch the fleeing figure. He reached her, clutched her shoulder, felt her flesh solid beneath his fingers and turned her towards him. But it was Grace who smiled up at him.

For a moment, he could not get his breath, then he folded his arms around her and cradled her, his face dropping to her hair. As he tightened his embrace, her body disintegrated until she became dust in his arms. He screamed her name and was jolted awake by his voice. Tears prickled his cheeks, and the tang of salt burned his lips as his final shout died away. All the pulses in his body throbbed like hammer blows and his trembling limbs were sticky with sweat.

He lay still until his breathing returned to normal. It was still dark outside, but the dawn chorus was limbering up, less vociferously than in the spring. This late in the year they no longer needed to impress a mate. For him, the night was over. It was too full of ghosts and horrors for any chance of more sleep. He dressed for running and as the first streaks of morning crawled over the horizon, he tied his laces and slipped out of the gate.

Dew iced the grass, turning paths into streams of silver that flickered beneath his feet as he ran through the swards of bronze heather and copper bracken. He ran hard, pushing himself, punishing himself until his chest burned. The woman with the shaved head crossed his path before disappearing back into the murkiness. They raised a hand to one another as they had done on previous occasions.

She was very thin, and Callum assumed, with her bald head, that she was coping with some illness. But he had never spoken to her. Like him, she ran alone and early in the morning.

Half an hour later, he slowed to walk the last quarter of a mile down Tethering Drove, past his dormant building site, past the Tanners' dark house, onto Hatchet Green and home. He stood under the shower, hot water pouring onto his head and rolling down his muscled body. By the time he reached for a towel, his memories were safely back in their box. Night was banished to the shadows, and he was ready for a new day. What he still was not ready for was a life without Grace.

* * *

Despite his early start, the office was bustling when Callum arrived. Cookie was crouched over his keyboard, head bouncing to some internal beat, so business as usual there. Bird was scribbling on a sheet of paper, his thumb absently massaging his stubbled chin. Daisy sat at her desk and stared into space.

'Morning, people.'

Acknowledgements from the two men confirmed that they were listening to him. He was not so sure about Daisy. He shared his thoughts about Kim never having returned to the house after she fed her horse.

'Occurred to me too when she said she threw away Kim's supper,' Bird said. 'That Kelly is a piece of work. Every time she opens her mouth, she tells us a lie.'

'Or her selective version of the truth,' Callum said. 'So, let's suppose Kim didn't go home that evening. That makes the last confirmed sighting of her at six o'clock in the field. We need to find her.' He heard the urgency in his voice and knew he had spoken louder than usual, prompting startled looks and, he hoped, firing them with enthusiasm.

Daisy turned and faced him. 'Aren't you just guessing?' Her tone was accusatory.

'Maybe,' he said carefully. This was a side of her he had not seen before. 'But tell me why she left her phone in the stable?'

'In a hurry, forgot it, thought she had it with her… look, I don't know. People lose their phones all the time. It could have been accidental.'

'Fair comment. Would you tie up a hay net incorrectly?'

'Of course not, and neither would Kim.' Two spots of pink rode high on her cheeks.

'So it's a safe assumption that she would have retied it if she had been able.'

'Don't treat people like idiots just because they aren't frightened of horses.' Her eyes were shining, her breaths snatched.

Bird looked from one to the other and Cookie's head was suddenly still.

Callum studied her for a moment, jerked his head at the fishbowl and headed towards it. He did not look back and, after a couple of seconds, heard her follow him. Hand on the handle, he waited until she entered and then closed the door. Something was out of kilter with his sergeant, and he was going to find out what it was. Her sparkly, sunny disposition had been overtaken by a confrontational antagonist and he had no intention of working with her in that arena. He moved around his desk, sat in his chair, and indicated that she should sit. After a short pause, she perched on the edge of the chair, her back ramrod straight.

'What's the problem?'

'No problem. Sir.' She lifted her chin, jaw rigid, and avoided his eye.

'There is from where I'm sitting.'

'Nothing. I'm sorry I snapped at you.' She blinked once or twice before meeting his eye. 'It won't happen again.'

'Damn right, it won't, Daisy.' His voice was firm. 'If you have got a problem, I want to know about it before you bring it into work and impose it on the others. Understood? And if it is a problem with me, talk to me about it. Your attitude affects the whole team.'

She did not respond other than to swiftly dip her head. He thought she might be hiding tears behind the veil of blonde hair that fell across her face, and this concerned him. Tears had never touched her before, however dire the circumstances they had faced, except for the night that her dog had been killed.

She looked up at him. 'I'm sorry, I thought I was coping, Callum.'

Admitting to a problem was halfway to solving it. 'Still think that's the case?' he asked.

She shook her head.

'So, what's the problem, Daisy?' His voice was softer than before, the burr more pronounced.

'It's mostly Kim going missing.'

'Because?' he probed.

'I know her and will probably know the person who abducted her. It's not a comfortable feeling. Makes you look at people differently – even friends.'

He nodded. It was the village she had grown up in. Her safe place. The safe place for all the other girls who had ponies. And in a safe place, they should feel safe. He appreciated her concerns but sensed she was still holding something back.

'And?'

Her voice shrivelled to a dry whisper. 'Gran had a heart attack last night. She's in hospital having an op now.'

Callum had met Daisy's mother, Katherine Donaldson, the military attaché in Paris, and although a force to be reckoned with, he had liked her very much. This was the first time her grandparents had been mentioned.

'And your grandfather?'

'He died a long time back. She lives on her own.'

'Call the hospital and see how she's doing. If you need time off, then let me know.' A missing youngster was paramount and he felt he owed it to Conchita to find out where she had been imprisoned. He was gambling that Daisy would choose activity over sitting and worrying. And he had read her correctly.

'I'm planning to go and visit her tonight. I'll keep working.' She looked less strained.

'Fair enough. It is your decision.'

'Thanks.'

She left the fishbowl with a lighter step than the one that had carried her in. He watched her walk away and caught Bird looking her way too. Callum had not been alone in registering her change of mood. He hoped they would soon find Kim, safe and well, and change all their moods for the better.

After a few moments, Bird caught Callum's eye, dipped a questioning glance at the fishbowl and received a nod of assent.

'This is the report from yesterday's search of Jericho's van.' Bird stood in the doorway. 'And Jericho is not a happy chappie. And neither is PC Kent, come to that. Jericho's Jack Russell nipped his leg.' Bird gave a short guttural laugh. 'Bet that made the lazy bastard move a bit quicker than usual.'

'What did they find in the van?'

'Not what we wanted. There was no trace of Conchita or Kim. The back was rammed to the rafters with scrap metal and our lot had to unload it piece by piece, which amused the hell out of Jericho. Even asked them to sort it into the appropriate skips while they were at it. Which didn't happen, of course.'

Callum could visualise the scene.

'Then the boys got a bit excited when they found a bag of white powder, but Jericho had the last laugh there. It turned out to be washing powder and he was just taking the piss. Jericho stood and grinned throughout the search. That was until they examined the driver's seat. Then the smile was wiped off his face.'

Callum's interest sharpened. 'What did they find?'

'He had two knives stashed in a sort of scabbard attached to the underside of the seat and a lead priest for despatching fish, although I never saw him as a likely fisherman. Very well concealed. I think our Jericho does a spot of poaching on the side. He wasn't too pleased when we found them. And he was even less pleased when we found traces of dried blood on the knife blade.'

'How did he explain that?'

'Said he carries them for humane purposes.' Bird feigned surprise. 'I didn't think our Jericho knew what that meant, but he says it's so he can despatch roadkill.'

'Hmm. And the blood?'

'A pheasant he hit on his way back to his yard. Said it was very tasty. Sheena had put the feet and feathers in the bin, and they were fresh. We confiscated the knives anyway. He's a rum sort of cobey, that one.'

'A what?' Vernacular slang reminded Callum that he was an incomer.

Bird laughed. 'Sorry, guv. Cobey – rogue, rough sort of chap. In Jericho's case an all-round pain in the arse. And Bellman wants to see you. Soon as.'

'Understood.'

Callum left the office to update Bellman. All he had to share was that Kim had probably been missing for even longer than they had originally thought.

Chapter Fifteen

Bellman looked him over from head to toe and seemed discontented with what he saw.

Callum lifted his hand, intending to rotate his silver earring, but instead tucked his hair back behind his ear and waited for Bellman to speak.

'And you're quite sure that she has been missing since early evening and not the next morning as I was initially informed?'

'It looks that way, sir. Her sister only assumed Kim had come back from feeding her pony. We now know that she didn't see her.'

'This changes the whole complexion of the case, MacLean. Have there been any sightings? Have you conducted a house-to-house search, followed up any leads, checked her phone records, checked where the parents were?'

Callum studied the wall behind his superior's head. Was Bellman questioning his competence or being supportive? An assessing glance made him think it was the former.

'All under control. There was a possible sighting of her in a black BMW close to her home, but we now know this was her older sister, Kelly Tanner. I am working on a possible connection between her disappearance and our finding Conchita Gim–'

'Concentrate on finding the child, MacLean.'

Bellman fell silent and Callum thought that the interview might be over, but he was wrong.

'I am organising a press conference to come out on this evening's news.'

'Right. Good idea,' Callum lied. They would get reports of Kim from Devon to Dundee – most of them spurious, and they would waste hours they didn't have following them up.

'What time will you need me?' He was aware that his voice sounded flat, but he disliked the press almost as much as a senior officer interfering in his investigation.

'I don't, MacLean. This is a uniform job – instil a bit of confidence in the abilities of the force – and I'm sure you have plenty to be getting on with.'

Bellman did not directly say that he disapproved of jeans and long hair on an officer who resembled an extra from *Braveheart*, but Callum knew he didn't fit snugly into any mould. This might cause disquiet among the upper echelons, but not to him. It was results that he was after, not a best-dressed copper award. He felt the flutter of a muscle in his jaw and gritted his teeth.

Walking back to the fishbowl, he conceded that Bellman would doubtless make a better impression on the public with his polished buttons and emblazoned jacket. Callum's objective was to do the best for Kim, the Tanners and Conchita. And if he could achieve that by his senior officer parading around like a Christmas tree, then that suited him just fine.

* * *

'Got a treat for you, MacLean.' Martha loomed in the doorway of the fishbowl, her generous frame brushing both door linings.

Callum smiled a welcome, nodding towards the chair on her side of his desk.

'Don't mind if I do,' she said, dropping onto the seat that squeaked a protest.

Callum's ponytail had fallen forward onto his shoulder, and he flicked it back out of the way.

'I'm sad to say your hairstyle is growing on me. Still, none of us are perfect, are we?'

He was not sure if the implied imperfection related to his long hair or the fact that Martha was getting used to it.

'Right then, MacLean, remember the flea bites and dog hairs on your Spanish girl? Well, one of the techies has checked what sort of dog it was.' She paused and correctly interpreted his expression. 'Don't look so surprised. You can do that now, narrow it down to a breed. He's doing some sort of study on it, so it was right up his street. Unfortunately, they can't tie it to a particular dog – yet. But watch this space.'

'And?'

'And the hairs come from a Jack Russell terrier.' Martha laughed at his expression and left the office.

Callum could name at least ten owners of the terriers and Daisy would know many more. Paul Barnes, in his zealous attempt at resuscitation, had peppered the body with dog hair. Jericho Hatcher had a Jack Russell terrier, but the search of his van had already eliminated him. He sighed.

The way this investigation was going, every new piece of evidence just expanded the field of possibilities. He needed to narrow it down, and the sooner the better for everyone concerned. And especially for Kim Tanner.

Callum was disappointed to be right about the forensic search of Jackson's car. He perused the report that Bird had put on his desk. The inside of the BMW had not been cleaned in a while. In the boot, an entire ecosystem was surviving unchallenged by any suggestion of human intervention. They found traces of eight different females on the upholstery, Kelly included. Jackson was indeed living as if he would die tomorrow, and the search spoke volumes for his use of his recreational hours.

When he was that age and in his last year of study, Callum could not recall being presented with the same opportunities. He failed to convince himself that he would not have taken advantage had he been served with them. He smiled to himself when he remembered his grandfather telling him, 'Never lie to yourself. Lie to the rest of the world if you must, but never to yourself, lad.'

He knew the old man was right. Kelly lied. She was painting herself as a victim and his gut told him that was not the case. It was something more than the jealousy and conflict between the two girls; there were undertones he could not identify, but he would before the investigation was over. He needed to question Kelly again. She was holding something back. But for now, they had nothing to link Kim to Jackson, or his car.

'Guv?' Bird paused in the doorway of the fishbowl. 'Nothing from the house-to-house for Conchita. No white van driving like an idiot or otherwise, and no one saw Conchita's body being dumped outside Barnes's house. It's looking like a dead end, guv. And no trace of her in Frank Fenman's van either.'

'Keep digging. Too many things don't add up,' Callum said before reaching across his desk to answer his phone.

Martha's voice sounded in his ear. 'I've just got back to my office and the tox report for your señorita is here, MacLean. Interesting. Very interesting.'

She was waiting for him to ask what was so interesting, so he obliged her.

'Zilch showing. Just the over-the-counter analgesics we already knew about. Otherwise, clear as a bell.'

'Thanks, Martha.' He turned his attention back to Bird.

Chapter Sixteen

'Guv, one thing keeps cropping up.' Bird folded his arms across his chest.

'Which is?'

'A white van. Unidentified.'

A fleeting expression crossed Callum's face.

'I know,' continued Bird. 'I'm fed up with hearing about bleedin' white vans too. One old bird on Conchita's house-to-house said she didn't know anyone with a white van, but by the end of the visit had convinced herself it was the fish delivery man who dumped her body.'

'How many concrete sightings in Kim's case, Bird?'

'Five so far, and that includes Kelly's.'

Five sightings did not mean there was only one van. 'Get a timeline on each of them. Plot possible routes, then check any CCTV cameras. The last house in Tethering Drove has a camera. There could be others.'

'Wilco.' Bird hurried back to his desk. Callum watched the tightness in the detective's shoulders when he pulled out his chair. More than thirty-six hours since Kelly had left her sister in the field and despite house-to-house and outbuilding searches, there was no trace of Kim. The only clue was an unidentified white van.

'Cookie.' Callum waited for him to scoot across the office. 'Extend your perimeter for white vans. Check hire companies. Bump anyone on the PNC to the top of the list and give me a copy. Where were they on that evening? Check any reported stolen and bring any cross-references to the top of the list.'

Cookie nodded and made to leave.

'Wait. I haven't finished.'

'Sorry, guv.' He shifted his weight from foot to foot, his mouth an unusually tight line.

'This is not a situation any of us like, lad. Now, any vehicle without confirmed whereabouts, get it searched.'

'Do you think Kim's still alive?'

'Yes, I believe she is alive.'

He hoped he was right because hope was all he had to hang on to.

He sketched a white van in the top corner of his paper whilst his mind was filled with the memories of the body of an eleven-year-old girl in a Glasgow cellar. The rhythm of the short pencil strokes was interrupted by someone entering the fishbowl.

'Brick dust,' Daisy said from the other side of his desk.

Callum pulled his mind back from his speculations. 'What are you talking about? What brick dust?'

'The dust in Conchita's hair is brick dust. And it's not a modern brick but an old type, probably locally made. I thought bricks were bricks.'

Callum had thought much the same before he had become interested in building materials for his new house.

Before he had a chance to respond, Daisy continued.

'And when Cookie and I went to the school, no one had noticed any change in Kim's behaviour or had suspicions of bullying. If anything, her classmates were quite protective of her, and she was a popular pupil. Her friends are mostly pony-mad girls and could tell me chapter and verse about Drummer. Do you think Anna was right to think she was being bullied?'

'Noted.' He ignored her question. 'Let's concentrate on Conchita for a moment.' He sensed a connection between the two girls. 'Many small communities had local brickworks. If she was in an older property, it makes sense that the bricks were locally made.'

Many of the village properties were old and probably constructed from local materials. Some had cob walls, but there were plenty that were brick-built.

'It does tell us that she was in a specific area, in an old property made from bricks. And it's probably this area,' Callum said.

'That ties in with this.' Daisy referred to the report. 'There were a couple of tiny flakes of green gloss paint and whitewash in her hair as well. The paint is lead-based.'

'An old brick property with lead-painted doors.' Callum mused.

'Honestly?' Daisy said. 'That applies to about half the village.' Her tone was sceptical.

'Then we look at half the village.'

She pulled a face. 'Are you serious? Don't we need something else to go on? Shouldn't we be concentrating on finding Kim? And there was no DNA on Conchita, apart from her own and Paul's, which is exactly what we expected as he trampled all over the crime scene. And I know him, and he isn't the sort to keep someone captive.'

'Maybe not. You don't want it to be Barnes because you know him, but you need to stay objective. Look past your preconceptions, Daisy. I'll be having a word with Paul on my way home.'

Despite his friendly tone, she puckered her mouth as if she was sucking lemons. She seemed scratchier than usual, and he wondered how her grandmother was progressing but didn't think this was the best time to ask.

'So,' Callum continued, 'find out about local brickworks. See if you can source the make-up of their bricks.'

Her brow ruffled as she made notes.

'Compare the composition to our dust and that will narrow down a location for Conchita's captor. And as we can't dissociate Kim's disappearance from hers, it could move our second inquiry forward.'

'Where would you suggest I start?'

'Daphne Smart belongs to the local history society, she told us she had a meeting, remember? Try her for some local knowledge.'

Daisy nodded and made a note.

'And try a museum. There was a brickmaker at Sandleheath and one in Moot Lane in Downton. There will be others.' He caught her surprised expression but wasn't going to explain that, when driving around to familiarise himself with his new location, he had spotted the museum in Fordingbridge. He had checked it out online when he got home. Like him painting the background of a picture before placing the point of interest in the foreground, social history provided a backdrop for the inhabitants. Everything depended on, and grew out of, what went before.

He made a note to check how her grandmother was later in the day.

The more he discovered about the New Forest, the more he was struck by the dramatic differences between it and the familiar mining communities of his past. Equally striking were the similarities. Crime was universal and, in his experience, boiled down to motive and opportunity. Two words, seven syllables, numerous questions and, so far, no answers.

* * *

Rain mizzled down and the automatic wipers flicked it away as Callum neared home. He detoured to drive past Forest Cottage, but Paul's van was not there and there were no lights on in the property. He opened his window, leaned his head out into the gloom and heard the dogs yapping. His questions would wait until the morning.

The weather worsened as he drove alongside Hatchet Green and stopped outside his cottage. His eyes probed the wet shrubs that edged his path expecting the silent shadow to materialise and join him as he reached the door. His bubble of anticipation was punctured by a stab of disappointment.

He put his key in the door. Maybe the cat had gone home to her real owner and was, at this second, curled up in the dry. Perhaps his salmon had not been a satisfactory offering, although the cat had been quick enough to eat it. If he remembered tomorrow, he would ask Daisy if she knew who owned the animal. He turned the key in the lock and pushed open the door, pausing to wipe his boots on the doormat. As he turned to close the door, the cat streaked from the shelter of a shrub and skidded into the kitchen. She gave him a throaty greeting and shook the water from her paws, one by one.

'What kept you?'

Happy with the state of her feet, she did her tiptoe walk, brushed her wet coat against Callum's jeans and purred. Callum ran his hand along the arched back and up the flagpole tail.

'You're wet.' He wiped his hand on his jeans. 'Best I can offer is tuna,' he said, opening cupboard doors. 'Do you like tuna?'

The cat ate slowly and carefully, crouching beside the bowl and taking delicate bites of the pinkish meat.

'Okay. You like tuna.'

The cat responded by purring as it chewed.

'Did your mother not tell you it's rude to purr with your mouthful?'

Callum reached down, unlocked the cat flap and flicked the swinging door open before it closed again with a snick.

The cat lifted its head to watch him.

'It's just for tonight. I don't have time to stand here watching you eat; I have to go and watch a man make a speech. You can let yourself out.'

In the sitting room, with a clean page open in his sketchbook, Callum blocked in the positions of the rolling heath-clad hills, a fir plantation and a stream that meandered through the landscape and flowed out of the left foreground. He reached for a sharpener and paused to turn up the volume on his TV as Bellman appeared on the screen. The man looked the part, and his performance achieved a perfect balance between urgency and confidence. He was good. Callum sharpened his pencil. The phones would probably be ringing before Callum had swept the curled cedar shavings into the bin. Tomorrow, they would know if any of this new information would help him find Kim alive.

When he went into the kitchen for a whisky nightcap, the rain was heavier and, encouraged by the rising wind, it beat against the door. The cat was curled up on the mat, sleeping off supper, and would probably steal out when the weather improved.

'Just for tonight, understood?' Callum snapped off the kitchen light and tried not to think about that Glasgow basement.

Chapter Seventeen

The following morning when Callum zapped open his car, Daphne Smart was walking past on her return home with her dogs. The two black Labradors stood in front of Callum and wagged their tails.

'Morning, boys.' Callum smoothed the top of each head in turn, unable to determine which was Paddy and which was Rufus. Only Daisy and Daphne seemed able to tell them apart.

'Good morning, Inspector. You're about early.'

'As are you, Mrs Smart.'

'Not fair to sleep in when the boys need a walk. I'm not looking forward to these dark mornings we have coming though.'

'Looming on the horizon as we speak,' Callum said. 'I was wanting to ask you something,' he added quickly as she prepared to walk away.

'I gave young Daisy the information about brickworks. If it's not that, then ask away. If I can help, I will.' Her dogs lowered their haunches onto the damp grass of the village green and sat patiently at her side.

'You mentioned underground shelters from the last war. Built by the Home Guard?'

'Yes, it was an interesting piece of local history. The operational bases were constructed as auxiliary unit hideouts in the Second World War. Designed to be used by the LDV.'

He was transported back to his childhood schoolroom by the sharp attentive look in her eye behind the round glasses.

When he nodded, she continued. 'A selected group of locals formed a special unit and were given weapons and training. In the event of an invasion, they were to hide in the base until the advancing troops had passed, then sabotage them by employing guerrilla tactics. All very cloak and dagger.'

'And we had hideouts around here?'

'OBs – operational bases, not hideouts. And most likely we did. This area had a lot to defend. Did you know there was a secret bombing range out on the forest? Ashley Walk, near Pitts Wood Inclosure?'

Callum shook his head.

'Well, there was, and they tested Barnes Wallis's bouncing bomb there amongst other things. A few local girls worked there and used to photograph what happened when a charge exploded. They exploded a thousand-pounder once and the blast was so strong it broke the windows in the houses up at Mays Firs.' She chuckled to herself.

'Not that much of a secret bombing range then. And the bases?'

Daphne ignored his observation. 'And we were knee-deep in soldiers and airmen here – Canadians, Australians, Poles, many nationalities. There were small aerodromes, at Fritham and Ibsley, to name just two. You should come to one of our meetings, it's fascinating, Inspector.'

The dogs sighed.

'I'm sure it is.' He concealed his impatience behind his tactful response. 'Do you know if we had any bases in this village, or close to it?'

'I wasn't around then.' She paused and looked over her glasses at him as if challenging him to argue the point. 'And they were secret – that was the whole point. Invisible from the air or anyone walking. They weren't built by locals. Royal Engineers came in, built them using local materials then left again. Never told people where they were – need-to-know basis.' She tapped a forefinger against the side of her nose.

'What happened to them after the war? I assume they were never actually used.'

'Not in anger, just for training. After the war, the Royal Engineers came back to seal them up or destroy them.'

'So, none would still exist.'

'Probably not.' She looked thoughtful. 'Inspector, I'm having coffee with the major later. The bases are a pet interest of his. I'll ask him. It will get him off the subject of his geraniums for a change. Will that help?'

'It would. Ask him if he knows of any local ones surviving. Thank you.'

'Is it important to your job?' When he didn't answer, she narrowed her eyes and gave a shallow nod. 'Right. I'll let you know as soon as I can. Good morning, Inspector.'

The dogs sprang to their feet and trotted across the village green towards Snowdrop Cottage and breakfast. Callum watched the departing figures and thought how much easier his investigation would be if every person was as straightforward and intuitive as the retired headmistress.

* * *

'Nothing yet, guv,' Bird said in response to Callum's questioning look as he entered the office. 'I hate appeals to the public. Brings out every nutter and attention-seeker on the bleedin' planet.'

Callum smiled to himself. 'And the Tanners' finances?'

'Still checking,' Bird said.

'Keep me informed,' Callum said over his shoulder as he went into the fishbowl.

Daisy followed him in carrying two mugs. She placed a steaming black coffee on Callum's desk and then wrapped both of her hands around her drink. 'I went to see Gran last night in Southampton Hospital.'

'Thanks. How is she?' He studied her face over the rim of the mug and realised he had forgotten to ask her yesterday.

'Amazing. Had the op and sitting up in bed asking about food.'

Callum laughed. 'That's always a good sign.'

'They expect her to make a full recovery and are talking about sending her home soon. I want her to stay with me, but she said that I'm almost never home, so there's no point.'

'Will Mrs P help out?' Katherine Donaldson's retired housekeeper took over the day-to-day tasks for Daisy when she was time-challenged by her job, making sure there was always food in her fridge for an evening meal. Having stayed with Daisy when he first arrived in Hampshire, Callum knew that Daisy's priority was her animals and she always ensured that they were well-fed and cared for, but sometimes she forgot about her own well-being. Just at this moment, he could do with a Mrs P of his own.

'You've got it in one. Mum's still in Paris but she's organised for Mrs P to stay with Gran at her cottage for the first few days until she's back on her feet and, for once, Gran has agreed to being looked after.' Her eyebrows reinforced her surprise at her grandmother's ready acquiescence.

'Good news,' Callum said.

'Thanks. What I came to tell you was that I drove back from Southampton across the Forest last night and saw some sort of lights over near Pitts Wood. It might have just been the night sky; it was quite a pink sunset, but I thought I'd mention it.'

'Very observant, Sergeant. Have a chat with Jimmy Eastwood and see if he is in that direction today. If he can take a look, that's fine, but if not, we'll get someone out there.'

Daisy turned to leave the fishbowl as Callum's phone buzzed. He looked at the caller display and raised his finger to indicate to Daisy that she should wait as he put the call on speaker.

'Morning, Jimmy. I was just going to get Daisy to give you a ring.'

'Saved you the trouble then. What did you want?'

'Daisy came back along Forest Road late last night and thought there were lights near Pitts Wood. Are you out that way today as it is off the beaten track?'

They heard his intake of breath followed by a noisy exhalation. 'I was ringing to tell you that this morning a woman rode through Pitts Wood and the track's all churned up and there were some patches of blood. She wanted to know if it was something to do with me or Forestry England so she could complain.'

'But it isn't?'

'No. Sounds more like deer poachers. I'm going to Godshill later, so I'll look in on my way home.'

'Thanks, Jimmy.' Callum ended the call and returned his attention to his sergeant. 'Looks as if you didn't imagine it, Daisy. Get Cookie to see if there's anything logged for last night anywhere along Roger Penny Way.' In his peripheral vision, he glimpsed Bird moving towards the fishbowl. 'And I dropped in on Paul Barnes on my way home last night. His dogs were there but he was out. After I've had a word with Bird, you and I will go and see him.'

Daisy passed Bird in the doorway. Bird often loitered in doorways rather than entering a room and Callum thought it might be so he could keep an eye on both rooms simultaneously. But it could just be that he did not like the idea of being trapped in one place. He was a planner, thorough, considering all eventualities. Perhaps he subscribed to the theory that being prepared for every possibility minimised risk.

* * *

Callum and Daisy drove in amiable silence along beside Hale Purlieu. The low sun backlit the white daubs of cloud that floated across the faded cerulean sky. Shadows slithered over the pink bell heather, darkening the flowers to purple. Then the clouds were blown away, and the heath brightened once more.

Daisy looked out the passenger window and Callum saw her face reflected on the glass. She looked calm and relaxed, undoubtedly reassured by the positive prognosis for her grandmother. Gorse bushes edging his side of the lane sprinted past, their gnarled wind-bowed trunks bent like knees and elbows. The russet bracken was punctuated by the gleaming white exclamation marks of silver birch trunks.

Daisy turned towards him. 'Okay if I turn the radio up a bit, Callum? I like *Farewell to Stromness*.'

He flicked his thumb against the steering wheel and the simple piano melody joined them in the warm interior. The bleakness of the Orkneys suited his mood, and he let the notes wash over him. It was one of those melodies that invaded your brain, seeped into your soul, and he knew the haunting music would stay in his head for the rest of the day.

'Thanks.'

'Pleasure.' Sometimes the smallest of gestures kindled a warm satisfaction inside you that stemmed from helping someone else. The more you stoked it, the hotter it burned. He wondered if it ever became all-consuming, if the need for gratification grew faster than the flames.

He stopped outside Forest Cottage and Daisy immediately jumped out of the vehicle to answer her phone. They had missed Paul again and the place looked deserted. The soles of Callum's new boots crunched the gravel and, although the bonfire had gone out, he could still smell smoky notes in the cool air. He leaned in to reach for the gate catch and looked back to see Daisy end her call, pocket her phone, and catch up with him. The dogs barked as they had done yesterday.

'Looks as if we missed him again. His van's gone. Strange he didn't take Bilbo and Frodo with him though,' Daisy commented.

He held the gate open for her. 'Does nothing get past your radar, Sergeant?'

She grinned. 'Not much. That was Cookie on the phone. Last night, gone eleven, a woman from Cadnam drove home along Roger Penny Way after a meeting in Fordingbridge. She had just passed the cricket pitch at Godshill when a white van swerved out in front of her from one of the gravel tracks. She braked hard but the van clipped her offside front wing. The other driver stopped, apologised, and owned to it being her fault. They exchanged details and the van driver reassured her that any damage was covered by insurance. Then she drove away.'

'And?' Callum asked impatiently as the terriers continued to bark in the cottage.

'And when she got home, the car driver reported the collision to us, including the index number. The van driver was very keen to get away. She thought the woman had been drinking.'

'A white van. Why didn't she ring it in immediately? We could have had a unit there.' He took his phone out of his pocket, searched for a number and rang it.

Daisy fidgeted. 'No phone signal along that bit of road.'

'And the van belongs to?'

'Frank "Ferret" Fenman.'

'He's curfewed.'

'She described the driver as a "hoity-toity" woman with a sharp tongue and streaked blonde hair. It was Madelaine Fenman driving.'

The ring of a mobile phone came to them through Paul's closed door.

'Someone's ringing Paul,' Daisy said.

Callum cancelled his call, and the ringing stopped.

'Oh. It was you,' Daisy said. 'What's the point of having a mobile phone and leaving it at home when you go out?'

Callum was thinking much the same but acknowledged that the phone he had spotted on Paul's dresser didn't look as if it had ever been used.

'We'll come back later.' Callum closed the gate behind them. 'Where had Madelaine been in Frank's van at that time of night, I wonder?' He could visualise Madelaine doing many things, but poaching wasn't one of them.

'Better go and ask her as we can't find Paul.'

Callum looked down at an incoming text. He was silent for a moment. 'Shit, shit, shit.' He had always subscribed to the theory that swearing was just verbal confirmation of a poor vocabulary and a short temper. But sometimes no other words would do.

'What is it?'

'There's been a road traffic accident along Forest Road. Paul Barnes is dead.'

Chapter Eighteen

An ambulance, Bird's vehicle and Jimmy Eastwood's pickup were already on scene. Paul's van was nowhere to be seen.

Jimmy was standing next to his open passenger door. The black-and-white head of his collie dog strained round the door frame to see who was approaching. Jimmy stretched out a hand and fussed her ears.

'Here comes your friend, Panda.' The dog tried to get out to greet Daisy but Jimmy pressed his hand against her shoulder to stop her, and the dog gave a soft whine of frustration. 'Panda, stay.' She huffed air through her nostrils, circled once on the passenger seat and sat down.

'Morning, Callum. Deedee.'

'Morning, Jimmy. What happened here?' Callum asked.

'I spotted the tyre tracks on the road and then crossing the verge. I thought it was some damn-fool holidaymaker treating the place like a racetrack.' He pointed to the pair of dark parallel lines, where a vehicle had vaulted over the bank and gouged lines in the turf. 'There. I followed the tracks. Over that ridge and down the slope to a copse of trees. You can't see it from here.'

'What did you do then?'

Bird would already have asked Jimmy what he had done, but Callum was trying to assess how much he had contaminated the scene of the accident, if it was an accident.

'Paul's van is at the bottom of the slope, smashed head-on into a tree with Paul in it. I opened the driver's door and checked for a pulse, but he was cold. Then I went round the back of the vehicle and opened the side slider door–'

'Why did you do that?' Callum interrupted.

'To check that the dogs weren't in the back. He usually takes them everywhere with him, and I thought they might have been injured. But they weren't there. I climbed back up to the road to get a signal and called your lot. Bird's down there now with the medics.'

Callum and Daisy followed the tyre tracks. The van was visible at the bottom of the incline. Bird stood with his back to them, hands pushed into the pockets of his sleeveless wax jacket, watching the two medics at the driver's door.

'Morning, guv, Deedee.' Bird moved to the rear of the van and waited for them to join him.

'Definitely Paul Barnes?' Callum asked.

'Yeah. And definitely long dead. Bump on his forehead the size of an ant's egg, so I doubt that killed him, and no blood. Did you see the tyre marks on the tarmac, guv?'

'Looks as if he braked hard but still left the road,' Callum said.

'I'll call Martha.' Daisy reached for her phone.

'Done it, Deedee. She's on her way,' Bird said. 'Too late for the medics.'

On cue, the two green-clad figures joined them at the rear of the crashed vehicle, response bags hanging from their shoulders.

'Nothing we can do for this one. I understand' – the medic nodded at Bird – 'that Dr Jones has been called, so we just confirmed the death but haven't touched him.'

'Good call,' Callum said. 'Thanks for your assist.'

He watched the two figures ascend the slope, boot treads biting into the short turf. Their radios crackled into life as they climbed into a signal area and then they disappeared over the top.

Callum walked around the van and viewed it from all angles. The trunk of a birch tree had crumpled the front bumper and grill, raising an arch in the bonnet. There was no damage to the sides or rear of the vehicle. He examined the tyres and looked back up the slope. There was no deviation in the course, no turf forced into the treads from braking, no indication that Paul had made any attempt to change his gravity-dictated journey into the waiting trees.

'There's ample tread on the tyres. Why didn't he brake?' Callum asked them.

Daisy frowned. 'Perhaps he was shunted and didn't get the chance?'

'No damage to the back or sides,' Bird said.

Paul's face had greyed, his skin was waxy, and his head was bent forward, chin resting on his chest, blue lips edging his open mouth. He looked peaceful, held upright by his seat belt.

'I didn't move him,' Bird said. 'Like Jimmy, I just checked for a pulse. None found.'

'Anything else of note?'

'Not really. A bunch of flowers and a box of chocolates in the front passenger footwell probably flew off the seat on impact. The side slider was open but that was Jimmy checking for the dogs.'

Callum nodded. Jimmy and Daisy shared a similar regard for animals.

Daisy was looking through the open door into the back of the van. 'He's been shopping. He's an Asda man. There are groceries everywhere.'

He glanced over her shoulder. Half a dozen bags for life had been tipped over, the contents lodged between Paul's gardening tools. Callum touched a tub of ice cream and a packet of frozen fish fingers. They had both defrosted, the cardboard was soggy, and the ice cream was liquid, even though it had been a chilly night. He lifted a strip of paper caught in the teeth of a rake.

'Has he been here all night?' Daisy asked.

'This till receipt is timed at just after 8 p.m. yesterday evening. He's been here, sitting in his van since then.'

'Poor bugger. That's over twelve hours. What a way to go,' Bird muttered.

Kim had been missing for over forty-eight hours. He pushed the thought to the back of his mind, glanced at the scattered shopping as he slipped the receipt into his pocket, then looked round when he heard his name called.

'MacLean, I'm not into mountaineering.'

He strode up the slope, took Martha's case from her unresisting fingers and offered her a supporting arm. She grasped it just in time to stop her feet from sliding out from beneath her.

'I see the new boots are earning their keep,' she said with a glance at his footwear. 'What have you got for me this time?'

Callum brought her up to date with the salient facts as she glanced into the cab.

'Right, off you toddle. Go and chase some criminals; this one's past running. He's been dead a good half a day at first assessment.'

'I went to see him this morning,' Callum said. 'I have some questions that only he can answer.'

'Better get yourself a Ouija board, then.' Martha turned her back on him and snapped open the catches on her case.

'That's telling you then, guv.' Bird's laughter rumbled in his chest.

Gallows humour was Martha's way of lifting the mood, lightening the moment to keep it bearable. Losing his main suspect in a child kidnap case with the girl still missing was doing nothing to lighten Callum's mood. This had happened to him once before, and that child had died. He couldn't let that happen again.

* * *

From the shelter of his Sportage, Callum and Daisy watched the wind whip up a squall that shook the rain from the heavy clouds. It drummed a tattoo on the roof rivulets poured down his windscreen and the landscape became a blurred watercolour. Then just as suddenly the rain stopped. The sun pierced the clouds and glazed the beads of moisture until they shone like molten gold.

'Bird will get the van recovered when Martha has finished.' Callum started his engine. 'Get them to check it for any trace of Kim.'

Daisy looked across in the direction of the clump of stunted gorse bushes. 'Okay.'

They drove back along Forest Road towards the village.

'Let's go and see Madelaine Fenman. I'd like to know why she was on Roger Penny Way at that time of night.'

'Can you pull into Paul's cottage on the way past?' Daisy said.

'No problem.' He had been intending to stop at the cottage anyway. He wanted to make sure that nothing was out of place and to secure the property. 'I was going to call in, have a quick look around.'

'I want to check that Bilbo and Frodo have been collected.'

Paul's words came back to Callum from their first meeting – '*B* for black and *B* for Bilbo, see?' The careful words, the slow delivery that niggled at him for no good reason.

When they clicked open the gate, the only sound was a startled pigeon diving out of a fir tree, wings slapping the air. Callum watched it flap across the garden and swoop onto the edge of a raised bed of onions. No yapping terriers.

The door into the kitchen was unlocked and Daisy pushed it open. 'Good. They've gone. Poor little chaps.'

Callum ducked his head and followed her. The only differences from their previous visit were missing check shirts, no uneaten breakfast and different items on the shopping list. Everything else looked the same.

He ran his eye across the bricks of the fireplace; red, smoke-stained and old. The door frames had been painted white sometime earlier in the century but knocks on the architrave exposed dashes of dark green, as did the dust-coated skirting boards. It was too much of a coincidence that there had been traces of brick dust and flakes of green paint in Conchita's hair.

'Let's just have a quick look around as we're here. You do downstairs. I'll go up.'

'What's the point? There's no one here.'

'You don't know that.' Kim *is* somewhere, he thought. 'Now get looking.'

Daisy lifted her chin and met his eyes. He recognised the challenge in them. He placed his boot on the first tread of the narrow stairs. Daisy expelled a noisy breath.

The threadbare carpet had once borne a pattern of flowers, probably alizarin crimson, he thought, looking at the edges that still retained colour. His arms brushed the walls in the narrow space, and he found it easier to rotate his body and lead with one shoulder first. The house had not been built with his frame in mind.

There were three small bedrooms, and Paul's was the only one not quilted by a coating of grey dust and housing colonies of spiders. He started in the unused rooms. Through the bare floorboards, he could hear Daisy moving about downstairs. The wardrobe doors creaked when he eased them open. One housed clothes that might have belonged to Paul's grandfather – the legs were much too long for Paul – and another was full of women's garments. Moving the hangers along the rail, he found them all to be old-fashioned, at least half a century out of date, and the musty smell made him sneeze.

'All right, sir?' she called, after a moment of stillness below.

'Fine. Get on with it so we can get out of here.' He rubbed the back of his hand against the leg of his jeans to remove a sticky spider's web.

The smallest room was Paul's and was probably the one he used as a boy. It was dusted and tidied and the bed was made with a faded cotton patchwork bedspread tucked in tightly over sheets and blankets.

Callum could imagine Paul as a small boy being shown how to make the bed by his grandmother, and it seemed he still worked to her standards. There was no dust on the dressing table or bedside cupboard, but the air was stale, and the small-paned window had seldom, if ever, been opened. None of the drawers or cupboards upstairs held any garments that belonged to anyone other than Paul or his dead grandparents.

He took one last look around the room as he turned towards the door and banged his head on the low lintel. He groaned as he moved onto the landing and was sporting a red mark in his hairline when he joined Daisy in the kitchen.

She laughed as he massaged the bump that was rapidly forming. 'Hope Dave's making your doorways taller than these,' she said.

'What did you find?' He noted that her mood was back to normal, the threatened argument forgotten, for now.

'Nothing odd. No bodies lurking in cupboards. No belongings for any girl and nothing under the stairs. The bathroom is through that door in the kitchen, but the only toiletries are his. No nail varnish or hairbrush. You?'

'The same. One bed made up with sheets and blankets...'

She made a face. 'I didn't know they still made them.'

'...wardrobes filled with his grandparents' clothes in the spare rooms. His room has only his belongings, and clothes that would fit him.' He ran his eye around the kitchen one last time, but nothing piqued his interest.

'Where's the back door key?' Callum said.

'I don't think he ever locks his door. Some people don't around here.'

'Might explain the burglary figures.'

He ran his fingers through the dust along the top of the architrave above the door. He wanted to leave the building secure, even if there didn't seem to be anything inside it worth stealing. His fingers snagged on a key, grease-sticky and furred with dust. It fitted the keyhole and with persuasion and a squeak of protest, turned the lock. Once outside, nothing looked different from his previous visit, so he pocketed the key and headed for the gate.

Chapter Nineteen

The advance of autumn and last night's strong winds had stripped leaves from trees and widened the view. Callum noticed for the first time the cluster of buildings behind Haystick House. On his previous visit, they had been obscured by the overhanging tree canopy, but now he saw the buildings beyond the leafless twigs, like a child peering through their fingers. He supposed they looked agricultural, accessed from the gated track that ran along one side of the Fenmans' property.

He recalled a recent conversation with Bird. Financial returns had not kept pace with costs and the smallholders, the one-man bands, could not make a living from agriculture alone these days.

'It boils down to a choice, income versus tradition,' Bird had said.

Reluctant to part from tradition, they changed what they could without compromising their way of existence. Some worked a second, or third job. Some sold off the main house to incomers with money to burn but often retained the buildings for winter stock housing and hay storage. Callum thought this could be a case in point.

He waited for the click of Daisy's passenger door closing, then locked his vehicle. Upstairs, a curtain twitched before settling back into place. Before he could lift the brass knocker, a chorus of yapping started up inside the house and continued until the door was swung open by Frank Fenman.

This morning, he was dressed in red trousers, an open-necked mustard shirt, a paisley-patterned cravat at his throat and leather boat shoes. Noël Coward would have approved. He still sported the conspicuous bandage on his arm that rested in the black sling.

'Good morning, officers.' His smile was relaxed, his voice chirpy.

The pair of hairy canines dashed around his feet like animated wigs. It was difficult to establish which end was which until the barking ends snuffled around Daisy's feet. She stooped to stroke the squirming bodies and looked towards the open kitchen door. After Daisy's description of the large dog she had encountered on their previous visit, Callum was relieved it was absent.

'Good morning, Mr Fenman,' Callum said. 'Might we have a word?'

Frank inclined his head and beckoned them inside the house. The sitting room was the same as it had been on their last visit in all but one respect; an assortment of cushions formed a pyramid over one arm of a chair. Frank had been seated there before their visit and his crumpled morning paper was on the seat.

'How's your arm coming along, sir?' Daisy tilted her head to one side.

'Slowly. I had expected it to improve rather faster than it has.'

'Not able to drive yet?' Callum asked.

'God. No. Far too painful. And I'm having a bit of trouble moving my fingers.' He wiggled them experimentally to demonstrate and winced. They looked like pink tentacles protruding from the sling. Fingers that dabbled in how many pies?

'No Ruby today?' Daisy asked as she bent down to stop one of the snuffling wigs chewing her bootlaces.

'No.' Madelaine spoke from the doorway, and they all swivelled to face her.

Callum wondered how long she had been standing there.

'Unfortunately, she ran away this morning.' She moved into the room. 'I expect she'll come back when she is hungry.'

Callum exchanged a look with Daisy. The thought of the giant dog roaming unsupervised was more than a little scary.

Madelaine was dressed in a floor-length golden kimono-style robe, her hair concealed beneath a towel that was wrapped turban-style around her head. The robe was loosely belted at the waist. The dogs rushed to her, and she bent forward to fuss them, exposing a generous flash of cleavage and the lace edging of a white bra. When she straightened up, she did not attempt to retie the belt. She indicated that they should all sit.

Frank subsided into the chair with the heaped cushions and Madelaine took the other armchair.

'I was in the shower when you arrived. How can we help?' she said.

Callum sat on one end of the sofa, leaned back into the cushions, and crossed his legs at the knee. Daisy took the other end, but sat forward, her elbows resting on her thighs as the dogs chased around her feet.

'We have a report that you were involved in a road traffic collision last evening on Roger Penny Way. What were you doing along there at that time of night?' Callum's voice was soft, his tone conversational.

Madelaine's shoulders relaxed. 'I was on my way back from taking Ruby for a walk. Frank can't manage her with his arm bandaged like that. I had a late meeting at work, so I took her out for a run when I got back home.'

'In Frank's van?' Callum asked.

'I didn't want her muddy feet in the back of my Merc, Inspector.'

'Hale Purlieu and Hatchet Green are on your doorstep. Why did you go over to Godshill?' Callum's eyes were fixed on her face.

She ran a finger along her eyebrow. 'She can be a bit… strong with other dogs around. I took her up to Pitts Wood to let her off the chain.' She smiled at Callum, trying just a bit too hard.

He thought that her inclination was to tell him to mind his own business. Her body was speaking one language and her mouth another.

'A big dog like that needs a good bit of exercise,' Daisy said.

Madelaine frowned and switched her attention to Daisy. 'Have you seen her then?'

'The last time we called. She was in the kitchen. She's a beautiful girl.'

'You didn't tell me, Frank.' Madelaine's tone was sharp.

'Sorry, beloved.' He flushed. 'It slipped my mind. I was more worried about Mitzi nipping her after she bit me.' He lifted his bandaged arm and gave a forced laugh. 'She was probably still full-up from trying to eat me.'

'Silly man. You do make a fuss. It was only a little nip.'

Callum had spoken to the hospital. It had been more than a little nip. For such a small dog, Mitzi seemed to have a lot of teeth.

Madelaine rose and moved across the room to stand next to her husband's chair. Frank stood up with a surge of speed and an anxious face. A flash of her muscled thigh was exposed as she pressed Frank back down into the armchair with a firm hand on his shoulder, her thumb pressing on his collarbone. She perched on the uncluttered arm of his chair and pulled the edges of her robe together, one hand at her chest, the other at her thigh.

She confirmed her previous evening's brush with the third-party vehicle. Driving back from Pitts Wood, Ruby had barked in the back of the van and distracted her. She had pulled out from the gravel track and had swiftly taken evasive action, but not before clipping the approaching car.

'She was driving right on the crown of the road, but it was my fault entirely. I pulled out without looking properly. I hold my hands up for it.' Madelaine did so now, palms facing the detectives, silk sliding open, lace underwear on display.

Frank reached out with his good hand and pulled the fabric back over her thigh.

'Sorry about that,' she said, placing her hand over Frank's and giving it a quick squeeze.

'The other driver thought you might have been drinking,' Daisy said.

Madelaine laughed. 'Chance would be a fine thing, Sergeant. I value my licence far too much to be so selfish or stupid.'

She was saying all the right things, but Callum saw the surprised look that Frank gave her. She was showing Callum what she thought he wanted to see, telling him what she thought he wanted to hear, distracting him. He was more interested in the things she was not saying. The things she was hiding.

'I've already informed my insurance company this morning, Inspector.' She pushed at the turban with a painted fingernail as it threatened to slide down her forehead. 'It was entirely my fault. There won't be any problem with her claim, I can assure you.'

'Pleased to hear it.' Callum rose to his feet. 'We'll see ourselves out.'

* * *

Daisy silenced the pulsing beep from the car dashboard by buckling her seat belt and slid a sideways look at Callum. 'No prizes for guessing where she buys her underwear, Callum.'

'Can't say I noticed,' he said with feigned surprise, easing up through the gears.

She laughed. 'Wasted effort on her part then. You were meant to notice. That floor show wasn't for *my* benefit.'

He chuckled. 'Agreed. Frank seemed a little embarrassed by the performance. He was quick to cover her up when she pulled the hands-free stunt.'

'Perhaps he doesn't like sharing,' Daisy said.

'As smokescreens go, it was a pretty transparent attempt.'

'Not unlike her bra, then,' Daisy said drily. 'She didn't seem overly concerned about Ruby being missing, did she? I'd have been more worried if it were my dog.'

'And why lie about being in the shower?' Callum said.

'How do you know she was lying?' Daisy turned to face him.

'She had streaks of dry blood on the side of her neck. They would have washed off under a shower. The strands

131

of hair at the nape of her neck not caught in that turban affair were dry.'

'Okay,' Daisy said slowly.

Callum drove along Hale Purlieu and Daisy lapsed into silence. He thought she was replaying the conversation at the Fenmans', trying to ferret out something to explain those things she had not noticed. He could wait.

He slowed as two youngsters on ponies came towards him, riding side by side along the short turf of the purlieu. The girls wore jeans, short boots and jackets beneath the brightly coloured silks that covered their skull caps. Jockeys in the making. They both waved their thanks for his courtesy in slowing down. The hairy ponies plodded along completely unperturbed by his vehicle, so laid-back that Callum thought even blues and twos would not affect them.

'She was wearing underwear,' Daisy said suddenly. 'When I get out of the shower soaking wet, I towel off or I drip-dry for a bit before I put on underwear.'

'Too much information, Donaldson.' His memory flashed an image of Grace swathed in a white bath sheet like a film star, bare feet and rat-tails of hair dripping onto her shoulders. He blinked it away. He tried to forget the feel of the towelling sliding through his fingers.

'If she was dry enough to get into her underwear, it would have taken her no time at all to pull on jeans and a T-shirt. So why the robe? Have you thought that she might not have been getting dressed, Callum? I think she was getting undressed.'

He nodded. She had caught up with him. 'Agreed. So why didn't she put her clothes back on? That would have been as quick as finding a robe and twisting a towel around her head. And how did she get blood splashes on her?'

'Good question.' She looked at him, expecting more.

He gave her the benefit of some of his observations. 'Her hands were clean. There was no sign of her being injured… we had a good look at most of her body–'

'If you say so.' Her smile was impish.

'And Frank had no evident injuries, other than his still-bandaged arm. Where did the blood come from? Who was injured?'

'I'll pass on that one for the moment.' Her brow ridged with concentration.

Callum suspected Madelaine's clothes were bloodied, so she removed them rather than risk questions she did not want to answer. He would let Daisy mull that over for a little longer. He hoped the blood wasn't Kim's.

'In the meantime,' he said, 'get onto Cookie. I asked him to get me a list of properties built before the local brickworks closed. And get him to find out who owns those buildings behind the Fenmans' house.' He signalled and pulled into the station.

'Then update me on the Tanners,' he continued. 'Have they had any more thoughts on where Kim might have gone? Anything significant from her laptop or phone?' He pulled to a stop as she continued writing notes but did not kill the engine. 'Then see if Bird has anything new from the house-to-house.'

Daisy stood on the concrete and seemed to realise that he was not intending to come into the station with her. 'And where will you be, Callum?'

'Asda.'

She grinned. 'Never took you for an Asda man.' She closed the passenger door and headed for the building.

He had never taken Paul for an Asda shopper either, but there had to be a reason he didn't use the local supermarket. All he had to do was find out why.

Chapter Twenty

His visit to the superstore had filled him with hope. Adrenaline surged through his body on the drive back from Brook towards Hale. His eyes skimmed the land on both sides of the tarmac. A textured tapestry of russet bracken and burnt-umber heather; raw-sienna sand and lime-green moss; Winsor-green holly leaves with blood-red berries. Callum went over the information obtained at the store and tempered his growing sense of urgency.

The receipt from Paul's shopping trip had helped locate the till operator who had served him. Eileen was an older woman, a long-time employee who had an old-fashioned interest in her customers. Callum considered her just plain nosy. He followed her down a corridor and into a small, yellow-walled room with a wooden table, plastic chairs, and a food-splattered microwave on the cupboard by the sink.

Paul Barnes, she said, had been shopping there regularly for as long as she could remember, although she had not known his name. She just thought of him as Mr Check-Shirt.

'You can tell a lot about people by what they put in their trolley,' Eileen said. 'You get the ones who just buy ready-made meals for one – members of the "ping club" – and they always buy wine but never the cheap stuff. Then you get the ones who do the family shop and everything they buy is heading for the deep-fat fryer or is full of sugar. They never make anything from scratch. In my day–'

'And Mr Barnes?' Callum interrupted her quickly.

'He's a proper shopper. He comes a couple of times a month and doesn't buy ready meals.' Her nod was approving. 'He buys frozen meat and tinned goods, fresh fruit and dog food. He has dogs,' she added, unnecessarily.

Callum wondered, uncomfortably, what she would make of the contents of his trolley. He needed to buy food and made a mental note to do it on the way home this evening. And perhaps a tin of cat food.

'Maybe he grows his vegetables,' Callum said, remembering the raised beds at the cottage.

Her face brightened. 'I expect his wife uses those when she cooks.'

Callum felt an icy chill immobilise him for a heartbeat. 'His wife? Why do you think he has a wife?'

She smiled at his naivety. 'Toiletries and sanitary wear, silly. He wouldn't be buying things like that for himself, now would he.' It was a statement, not a question.

It explained Paul's decision not to shop in the village. The local gossip mill would have been onto that.

'I've never seen her come shopping with him, so I expect she's disabled or has a demanding job – although he doesn't look the sort to have an executive wife.' Her smile was smug.

Facts were clanging into place with the impact of the *1812 Overture*.

'Because?' he prompted.

She inclined her upper body towards him and whispered, 'He's a bit of a stranger to the iron, dear.'

Callum had sat back in his chair to assimilate the information. He felt a surge of satisfaction at being right. And sometimes, being right was the only thing that gave you hope. He passed her the receipt and asked her to name the items on the list. She looked at his face, decided he was serious, sighed, and took her glasses from her pocket.

Eileen paused after the seeded wholemeal loaf times two and looked up.

'Continue, please,' Callum said.

She returned her attention to the list. 'I don't remember him ever buying flowers before. Or a box of chocolates, come to that. He's more of a "value-for-money" man. Big slabs of dairy milk, it's cheaper per kilo.'

'And next?' Callum encouraged.

She sighed and began on the dairy section. 'Four pints of blue-top milk, that's full fat. Six lactose-free strawberry yoghurts–'

'Say again.' He leaned forward in his chair, and she repeated the details.

'Anything else lactose-free?' he asked.

She scanned the remainder of the list with an experienced eye. 'There's a lactose-free skimmed milk, a chocolate soya milk drink and of course the yoghurt.' She looked towards the door. 'We also do a lactose-free chocolate and orange mousse, new in. I wonder if he knows about that?' She refocused her attention on Callum when his chair legs skidded across the floor as he stood up.

'Thank you, Eileen. That was very helpful.' He plucked the receipt from her unresisting fingers and put it in his pocket as he yanked open the door, and almost at a run, threaded through the shoppers.

* * *

He drove back taking the same route that Daisy had travelled the previous evening. He was passing the turning to Fritham when his phone rang.

'I had a thought, MacLean.' Martha's voice was upbeat.

Callum detected something verging on excitement in her. 'Which was?'

'Well, first things first, the intimate swabs came back devoid of DNA, which is what we anticipated. That gets the factual stuff out of the way. Now. My thought. The girl is atypical.'

The same thought had occurred to Callum when he compared Kelly and Conchita. 'Go on,' he said, eager to hear her theory.

'No hair dye, and that's unusual in today's young. No cosmetics, and no residue of any; no mascara, nothing. And not much of a sun-worshipper, either.'

An image of Kelly popped into Callum's head, pink-streaked hair, heavily kohled eyes, and the rainbow feathers of her hair clip. What made these two so different? Kelly had a stable home life with two parents, her pony, clothes, an education, and a phone, yet she was kicking the traces and wanting more. Conchita was dressed in clothes that would have been better suited to his grandmother with no conscious diversions to make her fit into society. She was not trying to impress with her looks, so what was she trying to achieve? Who was she trying to please?

Martha's voice interrupted his thoughts. 'She's not been to a dentist in years; again, unusual. No trace of alcohol or drugs in her organs; again damned unusual – I'd go so far as to say unique – in this day and age.'

'So? What are you suggesting, Martha?' He felt a buzz of adrenaline, hoping her thoughts would confirm his own.

'Bit of a long shot, but your girlie doesn't seem to have been touched by society.'

Callum slowed his speed, a scenario firming up as Martha's observations melded with his. 'Thanks for that.'

'Pleasure, MacLean, but you don't seem too surprised by it. And good luck with finding young Kim Tanner.' She was gone before he had a chance to respond.

Could Conchita have been abducted from Bournemouth three years ago? It resonated with Eileen's conviction that Paul had a wife.

Martha's scenario did not explain why she had stopped self-harming.

He indicated right to turn from Roger Penny Way onto Forest Road. With her track record of running away when circumstances didn't suit her, even her family had not been concerned by her disappearance.

Now, as he neared the site of Paul's accident, he saw that the police presence had gone. He pressed his thumb against the steering wheel and found that he still had a signal. He was finding the unreliable phone connection a challenging aspect of such a rural beat – that and the lack of CCTV coverage. Bird answered on the second ring, his voice sounded weary. This week was taking a toll on all of his team. He hoped his good news would cheer them all.

'Yes, guv?'

'Bird. I'm on my way back, be with you shortly.' He heard Bird's grunt and the background noises from the office. 'And tell Cookie it's now urgent that I get the info about the old-brick houses. I expect it on my desk by the time I get there.'

Bird must have walked into the fishbowl while he was listening. 'It's already here. And Martha's done the prelim report on Paul Barnes and it's on your desk too.'

'Some good news, Bird,' Callum said. 'I'm ninety-nine per cent sure that Kim is still alive.'

Bird slowly released his breath. 'Good timing. Her sister, Kelly, has been attacked. She's in hospital.'

Chapter Twenty-One

Martha's pixie house was erected over the site of Kelly's attack. As Callum and Daisy walked towards it, he glanced across to a figure seated a few yards away on a log, his back towards them. A constable stood beside him.

Following a nod from Callum, Daisy changed direction and headed towards them.

Martha looked up when Callum stood in the opening of the tent. Tension made her fleshy face uncharacteristically taut, her mouth a straight line.

'MacLean. Second time today. We can't go on meeting like this. Now, I have a supper date arranged for this evening. Any chance you could allow me one meal today without interruption?'

'I'll do my best, Martha.' He met her eyes and recognised the sadness they shared that her attempt at humour could not override.

'What happened?'

'First indications are attempted manual strangulation. The caller said she was dead, which is why I'm here, but someone must have been watching over her.'

Callum held out his hands, thumbs together, encircling an imaginary neck. 'Front or back?' he asked.

'Front. She was facing her attacker.'

She didn't feel threatened by letting him get that close. 'So, she probably knew him,' Callum said.

'Him, or her. I'm all for equal opportunities. She broke a couple of nails so we'll see what we can dig out from underneath them, besides make-up and snot.'

He knew she was aiming for normality, not disrespect. 'Who found her?'

'Matey boy there.' She nodded to the figure sitting on the log.

Callum looked across and saw that Daisy was speaking to the uniformed officer. 'I sent him over there to wait for you. He threw up all over my crime scene. Cheese and pickle in white bread.'

Callum grinned at her censure. 'Not everyone has your stomach, Martha.'

She looked down at the bulge distorting the front of her crime suit. 'Bloody good job too, MacLean.'

Daisy was already crouched beside the seated figure whom he now recognised as Jackson Chambers. The lad was sobbing so hard that he began to retch. Callum needed information and fast but he wasn't going to get anything from him in this state. He stood behind him and placed his hands on the shuddering shoulders.

'Take a deep breath in through your nose… count to five… breathe out through your mouth.'

The shoulders lifted against his palms, then drooped again on the exhale. After an initial failed attempt, Jackson established a rhythm and regained control. Callum lifted his hands away and moved around to face him.

'Tell me what happened, Jackson.'

Jackson stood up. His eyes darted from side to side, skimmed over the tent and he shook his head.

'I can't.' He sobbed.

'Yes, you can. Take your time.'

Callum took a deep breath and Jackson did the same. After a couple of false starts, he found words.

'Kel texted me that she had a surprise.'

'For you?'

He nodded. 'But I couldn't find her.'

'Did you see anyone else?'

'Here?'

Callum nodded.

'Jericho Hatcher. He nearly ran me over.'

'You're sure it was him?' Daisy asked.

Jackson nodded.

Daisy took her phone from her pocket and moved away from them.

'Did you see anybody else, Jackson?' asked Callum.

He shook his head. 'I thought she was dead.' He retched and vomited the rest of his lunch onto the turf at Callum's feet.

'Sorry.' He wiped the back of his hand across his mouth. 'She just stared at the sky.' He heaved another breath and whispered, 'I touched her, but she didn't move.'

Callum did not think Jackson was in any way involved in the incident, other than finding her. That in itself would be sufficient to give the lad a few sleepless nights. Despite all his worldly aspirations, Jackson was an innocent.

Daisy returned, followed by a female officer, and assigned her to look after Jackson.

'Take a statement from him before he can overthink what he saw. Then make sure he gets home, and hand him over to his mother,' she said.

They went back to the tent. 'Martha, any sign of her mobile?' Callum asked. 'It might tell us who she was meeting.'

She shook her head and sat back on her heels. 'She might have it on her. Check with the hospital. You can't expect me to solve all your cases for you.'

Callum could tell that she was smiling behind her face mask.

On the walk back to his car, Daisy's phone was in constant use and Callum strode silently beside her along the now-closed track.

'That was Bird,' Daisy said. 'A few minutes after Jackson's triple nine, someone in Hale Lane reported a glancing collision between their stationary vehicle and Jericho's van. Jericho didn't stop.'

'Which direction was he heading?'

'Towards Woodgreen. He lives further along that road.'

'He's going to ground.' Callum made a phone call, and it was answered immediately.

'Inspector MacLean here. I want firearms officers and backup to Jericho Hatcher's address, and a welfare unit. Urgent.'

Daisy snapped on her seat belt when he started the engine.

'Check that the Tanners have been informed,' Callum said as he sped away. 'Let's go and flush out Jericho.'

He was aware of her quiet voice beside him, giving instructions and asking for information as he drove along the narrow lanes, praying a pony didn't choose that moment to walk out onto the road in front of him. The blood pounded around his veins, kicked on by the adrenaline boost that rushed through him at the prospect of action. Daisy was probably experiencing the same effect beneath her calm exterior. This was a situation where training, experience and control were tested.

Daisy ended her call. 'The FLO told the Tanners. Louise took it like a trooper, but Sam collapsed with a suspected heart attack and is being blue-lighted to hospital. They're keeping me updated.'

The banks and hedges flashed past in blurred streaks of green and brown.

Callum changed down a gear to slew around a corner. 'Keep me updated on Sam, too. And I want Jericho detained before he gets the chance to destroy any evidence of contact with Kelly. We've got firearms support en route. I don't want anyone getting injured.'

'What about his kids? They might be there.' She grabbed at the door as he surged round another corner.

'Priority is to detain the suspect. Welfare will be there for the wife and kids. We'll wait outside the property until everyone is in place, then go in together, hard and noisy. The best scenario is we surprise him and detain him in the yard. That's my Plan A.'

Daisy took her hand from the door and checked an incoming text. 'No trace of her phone at the hospital. What's Plan B?'

'I'm still working on that. Make sure you know her mobile number and have it available. We'll see if we can locate her phone at Jericho's.' He looked in his mirrors as the wail of a siren and a flash of blues appeared behind him. He barked into his phone. 'This is a silent approach; repeat, a silent approach. Kill the sirens and keep out of sight. Understood?'

'Sorry, sir. Understood.' The voice echoed out of his speakers and the offending vehicle fell in behind them and was still there when Callum slowed as he approached Jericho's yard.

'Firearms are already here, Callum.' Daisy nodded to a black vehicle parked under the lee of a hedge metres back from the property.

'Good. I have a feeling we are going to need them. Ready, Daisy?'

They went round to the tailgate and put on vests. Hers looked child-sized in comparison to his. He snapped his closed and checked that Daisy did the same. The firearms boys stood at the rear of their vehicle, kitted out, checking weapons and conversing quietly.

Callum led them to the track entrance where he and Bird had narrowly escaped the attention of the yellow dog. Bodies peeled off to the house to secure possible exits if Jericho was inside. It was a worry to Callum that if they cornered Jericho, he might react by taking his wife or a son hostage.

Moving out from behind the hedge, they stepped across the cattle grid and onto the track. Jericho came out of the shipping container in his yard and stopped when he saw them.

Callum shouted, 'Go. Go. Go.'

Boots pounded along the track, and shouts of 'Armed Police!' and 'Down on the ground!' startled a murder of crows into a black cloud that flew overhead, their raucous calls adding to the urgency. Jericho tossed something into a scrap bin and ran towards his van. The yellow dog dashed out into the yard to the full extent of the heavy chain, barked at the intruders, and then slunk back under the hedge.

Jericho ran, head down, arms pumping like an Olympic sprinter. The team raced forward, fanning out into an arc, shouting at their target, weapons raised and ready. Jericho ignored them all. Callum remembered the concealed weapons in his van.

Jericho covered half the distance to his vehicle and ignored all instructions to stop. A red laser dot appeared on his thigh as a Taser beam locked onto him.

'Taser! Taser!'

Before the warning shout was complete, an audible crackle of electricity burst into the air and Jericho stopped running. He plunged forward onto his face and made weak swimming motions with his arms and legs in the dirt. A circle of black-clad officers surrounded him, gun muzzles pointing downward as the prone figure was handcuffed with coordinated precision.

The thousands of volts that had snapped into his thigh had stunned Jericho's muscles into near inactivity. The same did not apply to his mouth. He swore without reservation as he was arrested. Callum had to raise his voice to make himself heard over Jericho's shouts and the barking of his dog. The phrasing that Callum had learned in Scotland when he first became a policeman was different from that used in England. It occurred to him, as he finished his speech, that Jericho had probably heard this version more times than he had himself.

Chapter Twenty-Two

They watched Jericho being assisted down the driveway towards the waiting police van as they released the fastenings on their protective vests. Having been tasered, Jericho would require medical clearance before he could be interviewed. The strength and aggression he displayed resisting his four-man escort convinced Callum that he would pass without any problem.

The arrest had gone as well as he could have expected. Not a punch had been thrown, and no one had been battered or stabbed. Callum was about to share his satisfaction with Daisy when a shout came from the house. One of the welfare team stood at the open front door and a pint-sized hellion hurled himself over the doorstep, swearing and swinging a baseball bat. Some nifty footwork secured a safe retreat, and the officer gave some pithy advice to the child. Sheena silently witnessed the proceedings from the threshold, arms folded across her chest, but made no attempt to intervene.

Daisy grinned. 'Like father, like son.'

Callum stowed his protective gear and thanked the support team members. Jericho was manhandled into the back of the van and the sides reverberated with a steady pounding rhythm that echoed like a bass drum.

'Enough, Jericho,' Callum shouted, raising his voice above the din. He then addressed the waiting officer in quieter tones. 'I think your prisoner is anxious to see the inside of a cell.'

'I'm always mindful of Joe Public's wishes, guv.' The driver grinned as he opened the front door and got into the cab.

'Get him booked in and let me know when he's been cleared by the doc, please.'

'Will do.' Muffled shouts came from the back of the van. 'Yeah, same to you with bells on, fella,' the officer muttered as he closed his door. 'Good luck with interviewing him,' he added as he pulled away.

Daisy followed Callum back along the track and into Jericho's yard. The breeze rustled sere leaves that clung like moths to gnarled twigs. A cloud of black corvids dropped one by one into the withering tree canopy and traded grating squawks as they furled their feathers. It seemed eerily still after the earlier burst of activity. The yellow dog rumbled a warning, but Daisy spoke softly to it as she passed and it thumped its tail on the earth, raising puffs of dust.

Callum kept one eye on it until he was sure it couldn't reach him.

'Have you still got Kelly's phone number?' he asked, and she nodded. 'Then ring it, Daisy.'

'What, now?'

'Yes, now.'

She pulled out her phone, made the call and waited for it to connect. Daisy raised her eyebrows in surprise as a jingling tune sounded in the yard. They headed through the heaps of twisted salvage towards a tall scrap bin. It was the one Jericho had tossed something into when he saw them enter the yard.

'Your arms are longer than mine,' Daisy said, pocketing her phone as she stopped beside the rusty, high-sided container.

Callum peered up at the bin. There was no way he could reach into it from the ground. Daisy was used to hopping up on horses. A stationary bin should be no problem despite her protestations.

'Not that long,' he said. 'In you go.'

'You've got to be joking.'

'Wrong.' He cupped his hands together to form a stirrup and waited for her to plant her boot on it before legging her up to sit on the rim. 'And don't drop the phone,' he added as she disappeared down onto the scrap.

He listened to her grumbles, the twang and scrape of metal against the sides, and then she reappeared, a purple phone enclosed in an evidence bag.

'How am I supposed to get down?' She perched on the rim, stray hairs floating around her head like a halo against the slate sky.

'Jump. I'll catch you.'

She made a face at him before carefully turning around and walking the toes of her boots down the side until she was dangling from her fingertips, still short of the ground. Callum reached up and grasped her around her thighs and stepped away from the metal drum as she released her grip. It took no effort to control her descent; she weighed almost nothing in his arms, and he let her slide through his grasp until her feet hit the floor. His heart raced a little from the exertion. He needed to get more exercise, more miles under his belt on his morning runs.

'I'm filthy.' Daisy held up her rust-streaked hands and then brushed at the knees of her jeans before heading for Callum's vehicle.

'You'll wash. Good work finding the phone. We'll get Jericho's prints from it without a doubt and, hopefully, the reason for their meeting. The whole world seems to text non-stop these days. Times like this, I'm pleased they don't speak to each other.'

'Whoever said that dinosaurs are extinct is wrong.' She grinned at him as she waited for him to unlock his car.

'Your observations have been noted, Sergeant.' It was, he conceded, difficult to argue with the truth.

* * *

The hubbub of the office paused for just a second when Callum and Daisy walked through the door before soaring to a new level of urgency. Cookie shot across the floor to wave a sheet of paper at Callum.

'The Fenmans own those buildings at the back of their cottage, guv.' He consulted his paper. 'They were purchased with the house, and the firm Mrs Fenman works for marketed the property. She works for an estate agent,' he added, unnecessarily.

Callum looked down on the tousled black curls. 'How long ago?'

'Five years, give or take. I found the sale particulars. When the farmer retired, he sold it all: house, outbuildings and the yard with it.'

'Thanks, Cookie. Get a warrant. I want to take a closer look at their house and those buildings.' Callum made to move into the fishbowl but stopped when Cookie continued speaking.

'Wait, guv. DCI Bellman wants to see you immediately.'

* * *

As soon as he entered Bellman's office, Callum was aware of the chill in the air.

'Inspector MacLean.'

'Yes, sir.'

'I have just come out of a meeting with my superiors about the Tanner case and this latest attack is a great disappointment.' The grey gaze was accusing.

Callum, eyes hard as obsidian, stared back at Bellman.

'I have already made an arrest, and we have irrefutable forensic evidence for prosecution. I will be interviewing him as soon as he's cleared by the doctor.'

'Doctor? I won't condone undue force, MacLean.'

'We had to taser him, sir.'

'And Kim Tanner? Are you any closer to finding the child?'

Bellman didn't add 'dead or alive' but that's what Callum heard. He felt as if someone had thrown a thick blanket over him, and it was interfering with his ability to breathe.

'There is very strong evidence to believe that she is still alive.' He did not add that the person he needed to question about finding her was now dead. He closed his eyes, and Jeanie Cowie was there behind his lids, trapped in the Glasgow cellar, her pleading eyes willing him not to walk away, challenging him to find Kim. Alive.

'Sir, I am close. The team have narrowed down the search area to a handful of properties and I am waiting for a warrant for one in particular.'

'Which one?'

'Haystick House, Frank and Madelaine Fenman. They are concealing something, and it could be Kim. In the meantime, we will be searching all the other possible locations.'

Bellman clasped his hands together and rested them on the desk. 'I hope, MacLean, that you find her. Safe and well,' he added. 'That's all. Keep me informed.'

'Yes, sir.'

The next twenty-four hours of Callum's life would be the most important ones he had ever lived. Not for him, but for Kim.

* * *

Cookie raced across the office towards him when he walked back through the door. 'You remember that list of old buildings you asked for? The Fenmans' place is on it.'

'Now, think back, all of you. Is there anything that connects Paul Barnes to the Fenmans? Or to their property? Does he rent those buildings from them? Might he be holding Kim there? Anything from the interviews?'

'Do you still think that Paul is involved?' Daisy said from her desk.

'The Fenmans are incomers,' Cookie said. 'She transferred from the London office to the local branch. Why them?'

'Because the forensics fit the bill for an old house like theirs,' Callum said. 'We've drawn a blank at Forest Cottage regarding a hiding place for Conchita, and I now think, Kim.'

Daisy rolled her eyes. 'Are you serious? Paul wasn't a killer, he was doing CPR, and Forensics said his van was clean.'

'But she was dumped there by a white van,' Cookie said.

'A white van that only Paul saw,' said Callum.

Bird scrubbed his hand over his tufted hair whilst he considered the facts. 'So, you think he invented it?'

'Effective lies stay as close to the truth as possible,' Callum said. 'Because of the fall of the land, Mrs Smart could not have seen Conchita on the ground by his cottage when she drove around the corner.' He gave them a moment to consider the information.

'Why didn't you tell us this before?' Daisy said.

'I'm telling you now.' He drew a breath to continue but was pre-empted by Bird.

'So, Paul was carrying her, he saw Mrs Smart's car and knew it would drive past, so he put Conchita on the ground and did CPR as if he had found the body. Is that right, guv?'

Daisy was still disbelieving. 'No way. That doesn't make any sense. And that would take quick thinking, and you've made it quite clear that you don't believe he's that bright.'

'That is not exactly what I said,' said Callum, 'but I think he was drawing on past experience – a lie that's close to the truth. Mrs Smart reminded us that when his sister drowned, Paul was found kneeling over her trying to resuscitate her.'

'That's a bit far-fetched.' Daisy folded her arms. 'He must have a good memory.'

'I disagree. I think the image of his dead sister would stay with him for his whole life,' Callum said. The image of Grace would stay with him forever. 'Martha said there were no abrasions or contusions on Conchita's body consistent with being thrown from a moving vehicle onto gravel, and the only DNA on her was Paul's. I have a hundred unanswered questions, but those are facts. I believe Paul was holding her captive when she died. Mrs Smart interrupted him when he was trying to dispose of her body.'

'I think you're wrong,' Daisy said, 'for the record.'

But Callum could tell that she was turning over the information in her mind. Testing it, to see how good a fit his theory was with the facts.

Daisy frowned. 'And because Conchita died, he took Kim, but you're saying she's not dead?' She exchanged a look with Cookie, who shrugged. 'It's not just that you want this girl to still be alive?' she asked.

Callum was motionless for a heartbeat. Cookie must have looked up the case of Jeanie Cowie. He blinked and saw the image of the small heart-shaped face, tear-stained cheeks, lifeless. They knew he had failed Jeanie. What they didn't know was that, devastated by his failure, he had taken leave and gone to stay with his grandparents. He had run away.

Now, he heard the old man's voice in his head. 'A mistake is only a mistake if you don't learn from it,' he'd said.

He focused on Daisy. 'Find me a connection between Paul and the Fenmans. That could mean that Kim is being concealed in those buildings at the back of their house. I believe she is alive. We found no trace of Conchita at Paul's cottage and we have to consider that he is keeping Kim where he kept Conchita. And it could be at Frank's.'

'It just doesn't add up. Sir.' She was distancing herself from his theory. 'And you're sure Kim isn't already dead?' she asked. 'There's been no contact from her, no demands from a kidnapper. What other reason does he have to keep her alive?' Daisy asked.

Callum could think of several reasons for keeping a young girl captive and alive, but none meshed with the current situation.

'Kim is alive.' It was almost a shout. 'You know what was in his shopping? Lactose-free products, we have his receipt. I spoke to the checkout operator, and that is not something he has bought before. Why else would Paul buy those products unless he wanted to give them to Kim?'

Daisy shot a sceptical look at Bird, who shrugged.

'The guv has got a point, Deedee.'

Callum glanced at them both. 'Paul knows where she is, and we know she is in good enough health to need feeding.'

'Knew where she is,' Bird corrected. 'He died before we could ask him.'

'Come on, people,' Callum said. 'We need to find this child.'

'Guv. Guv.' Cookie's voice was squeaky with excitement. 'I've found a connection.'

Chapter Twenty-Three

Cookie knew how to get an audience, and all heads swivelled to look at the bouncing curls.

'What is it?' Bird demanded.

'The Fenmans get Paul to come in and do the garden. The lady across the road has seen his van there. He cuts the grass too.'

'That doesn't mean he's responsible.' Daisy shook her head. 'That's circumstantial. And he does loads of people's gardens.'

They looked at Callum, waiting for him to comment.

'Kim is somewhere close by,' he said. 'Paul was nearly back home when he died. He only had to drive down Tethering Drove, past the Tanners' house, turn left along the Purlieu and he was home. Matter of urgency for that search warrant for the Fenman house and outbuildings, Cookie. Paul has been dead for sixteen hours. That's potentially sixteen hours for Kim without food, and more importantly, water.'

Cookie raced to his desk.

'Let's get a search of the other properties underway. Start closest to Forest Cottage and work outwards. And give the Fenmans a wide berth. I don't want them alerted before you've got that search warrant sorted. Clear? Now hurry it up.'

'Hunky-doodley, guv.' Cookie slid onto his chair, one hand reaching for his phone, the other for a pen.

'Jericho's been given the all-clear to be interviewed and his solicitor's here,' Bird said. 'Keen to earn himself another new Jag, I expect. He must love them Hatchers as clients. Nice little earner.'

'Right. Get me an update on Kelly. You're with me, Bird,' Callum said. 'Let's go and get this "no comment" interview over with.'

Bird chuckled. 'That is exactly what I expected too, guv. But the custody sergeant is complaining that Jericho is telling anyone who will listen that it was not his fault. Singing his head off, he is. Hope our entertainment licence is up to date.'

* * *

In the interview room, Jericho and his solicitor sat together on one side of the grey metal table. The solicitor finished scribbling a note on his pad before lifting his chin and looking down his long nose at the detectives. It was the sort of nose that invited you to hit it, hard, and Callum knew instantly that he was not going to get along with the man. He pulled out both chairs, sat, and felt Bird sit next to him. Callum placed his folder of papers on the table in front of him, palms resting on top of the blue cardboard.

'My client has prepared a statement, but other than that, he has nothing to say today.' The solicitor's voice was dismissive, bored, and oozed a sense of entitlement.

He was sure of himself and used to getting his own way. Callum felt a moment of sympathy for any girlfriend or boyfriend he might have trailing in his wake. He looked across the table at the agitated man beside the solicitor.

'Well, Jericho?'

'I didn't mean to do it, Mr MacLean.' The handsome face no longer looked boyish or carefree. Jericho's spade-of-a-hand shook as he rubbed it across his eyes.

'Tell me what happened.' Callum's voice was soft and persuasive.

The solicitor cleared his throat, and his immaculately tailored suit skimmed his torso as he leaned forward over the table. 'My client—'

'Shut the fuck up,' Jericho growled. 'She's been texting me, Mr MacLean. I've seen her about the village with that

153

wimpy-looking boyfriend and she said she wanted to meet me.'

The solicitor inhaled sharply, and his mouth bunched like a cat's bottom.

'Did she say why she wanted to meet with you?'

Jericho fidgeted on the hard chair. 'Not really. Well, yes. But no, not really.'

Bird grunted and Jericho raised his eyes, brow knitted, and stared at the detective constable. Bird stared back. 'Why did you meet her if you didn't know what she wanted? Bit stupid, wasn't it?'

Anger flashed in Jericho's eyes and his upper lip curled to show his teeth. Like yard dog, like master.

Callum touched a warning finger to Bird's forearm. They wanted information, not to pick a fight, and Jericho was an expert in that department. He felt the roll of Bird's muscles beneath his finger as he relaxed. Bird grinned at Jericho and then turned to his boss.

'Women always confuse the hell out of me, guv. They say one thing and mean something else. Then they do something completely different again. A fella has got to be a mind reader these days to figure out what's going on.' He looked back at Jericho.

Callum murmured approval for this revised approach. It had the desired effect and Jericho leaned forward, tattoos rippling over his forearms.

'That's it. I thought I knew why she had sent me them texts.'

'Why was that?' Bird asked. 'A bit of extracurricular?'

Confusion clouded Jericho's features.

'A bit on the side?' Bird rephrased.

The other man gave a sly smirk of confirmation. 'She said to meet her along the track.'

'Inspector, my client has nothing more to say.' The solicitor shuffled his papers together and directed a hard look at Jericho.

Callum detected an edge of frustration as the solicitor attempted to regain control. He was not used to being disregarded. Callum ignored him as if he had not heard the comment.

'And she was waiting for you as you expected?' Callum asked. 'What happened when you joined her?'

'Nothing. She was smiling and playing with that feather thing she wears in her hair.'

'Go on.'

'She came and stood right up close, and I could smell her perfume. She said she wanted money.' Jericho hesitated and lifted a hand to rub at the side of his head. 'She whispered it against my ear.' He gave a little shiver, as if suddenly cold.

'Why did she expect you to give her money?'

Jericho thought about his answer.

Callum watched his eyes shift around the room as if the information he was seeking might be on the ceiling or over by the door.

Jericho looked at Bird, then at Callum, and the tiny muscles at the corners of his mouth relaxed. He had decided on the truth.

'Inspector, I must insist—' the solicitor began.

Jericho's meaty fist crashed onto the table, and he swung round to stare at his solicitor. 'Shut the fuck up, you smarmy git,' he said, then turned back to Callum. 'She thought I had snatched her sister, that Kim kid that went missing. But I didn't. You know I didn't, Mr MacLean. But she said I did because she'd seen me driving past. She was going to tell you I took the kid unless I paid her.' Jericho's eyes glittered with indignation.

Callum suppressed a smile; being innocent of the crime he was being accused of was probably a new experience for the scrap dealer.

'So, you told her it wasn't you. Then what?'

'Too right I did. Then she called me a liar and slapped me.' He rubbed his palm across his cheek.

'So, what did you do then?' Bird asked. 'Hit her back?'

'Inspector–' the solicitor interjected, half-rising from his seat.

'I don't hit women,' Jericho protested, meeting Bird's eye and then looking swiftly away.

The solicitor sat back down.

Callum recalled the information on file. Perhaps a wife did not classify as a woman, in Jericho's eyes. He let it pass.

'When she swung her arm again, I caught hold of it to stop her hitting me. She just laughed and blew a kiss at me.'

Bird stole a quick look at Callum before saying casually, 'That sounds like an invitation, if ever I heard one, guv.'

'That's just what I thought,' Jericho jumped in before Callum could reply, 'but she was just a prick-tease. She took her phone out of her bra and started videoing me. When I tried to kiss her, she started screaming. I put my hands round her neck to shut her up. That's all I wanted to do. Shut her up.' He massaged the ball of his thumb against his forefinger as if he could erase the memory of her skin.

'You did that all right,' Bird muttered.

'I didn't mean to hurt her. She pulled at my hands and made noises, then just went limp.' He slumped back in his chair. 'Honest, Mr MacLean, I didn't mean to kill her. I was just defending myself. Like I said, she slapped me.'

The solicitor sighed and the legs of his chair grated against the floor as he leaned forward to add another note to his pad. He seemed to have accepted his role as a partial observer.

'Now, where's her phone?' Callum decided to keep the fact that Kelly was still alive to himself, for now.

'She said if I didn't pay up, she was going to tell you lot. I wasn't going to pay her for something I didn't do.' Jericho glanced at his solicitor before continuing. 'She dropped it when I tried to kiss her. I only had my hands round her neck for a second. Sheena fights and kicks but she just went limp on me. All of a sudden, like.'

Was Jericho telling the truth? Could it have happened as quickly as he was saying? And why didn't Kelly fight? She either had a low level of self-preservation or was supremely confident of her power over Jericho, convinced he would not hurt her. Callum looked at the heavyweight fists resting on the table. Or was she paralysed by shock at the unexpected turn of events? He remembered the ghostly face of Sheena peering through the cottage window. She had learned to read her husband and when to give him a wide berth, her decision fuelled by knowledge gained from years of living with him. Kelly had no such experience.

'And you picked up her phone because of the recording,' Bird said.

'And I ran back to my van and went home. I had barely got back when you lot arrived.'

'Where's the phone now?' Callum asked.

'I threw it away. You want it, you find it.' His confidence was returning. 'I've told you the truth, and it was an accident, so can I go home now?' He turned to his solicitor, his expression hopeful, and began to stand up.

Callum stood, towering over Jericho. 'Sit down. You're staying right here. Kelly is in a serious condition in hospital, and you'll be remanded in custody, Jericho.'

'You bastards. Why didn't you tell me she's okay?' Mr Nice-Guy had been replaced by a flush-faced thug who hammered his fist down onto the tabletop, making the pens bounce.

The solicitor sighed. 'Please, Mr Hatcher.'

Callum remained standing, hands holding the back of his chair, face impassive. 'After a serious assault,' he said, 'you can't expect us to let you out on bail. As well you know.' He looked at the solicitor whose features remained expressionless.

'I told you it was an accident. An accident. I want to see Tracy.' Jericho scowled at them and thumped the table again.

Bird did not seem surprised that his mistress was higher up the pecking order than Sheena and their kids. He scraped back his chair, stood next to Callum and grinned at Jericho.

'Disappointment is good for the soul.'

Jericho's impolite response was silenced by the closing door as the detectives went out into the corridor.

'Always supposing he's got a soul, that is.' Bird chuckled to himself.

Callum huffed a laugh that started in his throat and ended in his nose. 'We'll leave that one up to the jury to decide.'

Chapter Twenty-Four

Callum sat in the fishbowl and scrutinised the map Cookie had printed showing the locations of all the properties constructed from local brick. They were spread out across the parish with a handful sprinkled around the village green, his own rented cottage amongst them, and a few in each of the approach roads. There had been a good distance between those properties when they were built, but the gaps were now filled by more recent developments.

He leaned back in his chair and wondered how long it would be before Daphne would give him the information about observational bases that she was getting from the major. Until he had it, he wasn't sure what he was looking for. He remembered a conversation with his grandfather one summer, long ago. They had been moving a flock of sheep down the hillside in the late afternoon and the weather was threatening trouble. Callum had fretted that the dogs would miss some of them and they would get lost in the coming storm. The old man had briefly cupped Callum's skinny shoulder in his gnarled hand, the warmth seeping through his sweater.

'Work with what you've got, lad. No sense in inventing problems that don't exist. That's like looking for something you haven't yet lost.' He had ruffled the boy's long hair before whistling directions to his dogs. No sheep had escaped.

Now, Callum looked again at his map and went to the door of the fishbowl. Cookie was leaning over his keyboard, the supple fingers of his right hand racing across the keys, while the pen in his other hand beat a staccato rhythm on his desk.

'Anything back from the searches yet?'

Cookie swivelled in his chair to face Callum. 'Nothing yet, guv.' He waited for another question, but none came.

The skin of Callum's face felt tight, and a muscle crawled in his jaw. 'How far have they got?'

'They are just going to move onto the houses around the village green. Yours is on the list,' he added. He hesitated, then turned back to his screen when Callum didn't comment.

Callum was irritated with himself. If there had been anything to report, Cookie would have whooped and danced his way across the office and the whole world would have known about it. It was frustration that triggered his unnecessary question. Frustration that they hadn't yet found any sign of a hidden base; frustration that he lacked concrete evidence to support his theory; and his biggest frustration was that another little girl would die unless they found her.

Sometimes, when he closed his eyes, he still saw Jeanie. She had scraped at the door, until her nails had broken, and her fingers bled and dried tears streaked her pale cheeks. When Callum had crashed through the door, her body was still warm. The fact that she had died frightened and alone he found difficult to live with. It was the worm that writhed in his brain, that caused a sheen of moisture on his brow and a chill to slide down his spine. He paced the few strides from one side of his office to the other. He saw Bird turn his head at the repetitive movement, so he stopped abruptly. He needed to get out and do something.

Daisy was carrying a mug of tea towards her desk when Cookie waved a sheet of paper at Callum. 'Search warrant, guv.'

Callum scooped up his jacket and exited the fishbowl. 'No time for that, Daisy. Let's go, everybody.'

Chapter Twenty-Five

Callum parked on the verge near Haystick House. Through the rear window of the vehicle in front, he recognised Bird in the driver's seat. Cookie fidgeted next to him, and the passenger door swung open. Bird turned his head, and the door closed again without Cookie leaving his seat.

'Marked car is here now, behind us,' Daisy said, looking in the door mirror.

'Let's go and have a chat,' Callum said, 'I'm waiting for a dog handler.' He stood on the verge and motioned to the officers to join him.

Bird moved round to stand next to Callum under the shelter of a holly hedge that concealed their arrival from anyone at the Fenmans' house.

'Two cars and the van are at the property. I caught a glimpse of Frank through the window in the front room as I drove past,' Bird said. 'But I haven't seen Madelaine.'

'Perhaps she's out looking for her missing dog. I would be,' Daisy said.

Cookie had been cautiously parting the prickly holly hedge to peer into the garden. He hurried back to join them. 'A woman is hanging washing on the line at the back of the house, in the garden.'

'Unless they have a cleaner, that's the missus accounted for,' Bird said, then looked along the lane towards the muted sound of opening and closing car doors. 'Cavalry's here, guv.'

Callum strode towards the new arrivals and issued curt instructions. 'Keep the Fenmans in the front room and cuff them, if necessary.'

'Even with a bandaged arm?' Cookie asked.

'Yes. Give them no opportunity to dispose of anything. No dashing off to the toilet unaccompanied.' He turned to an officer who waited at his elbow.

'PC Andrews, sir. You requested a K-9 handler.'

'I did. We've seen three dogs on the premises but there could be more. My biggest concern is a dog called Ruby. The owner said she went missing earlier today but she could still be on the premises. She can be aggressive and fights with other dogs. The husband was attacked, they say by one of the little dogs, but I have doubts about that. If she's there, I need her contained.'

'Understood.' PC Andrews began sourcing equipment from his van.

Callum addressed the search team. 'We'll start in the house, then move onto the orchard and outbuildings. Remember, we are looking for any sign of a hidden shelter or underground base, anywhere that could conceal a child. Give an eye to paths that look well-used but don't seem to go to an end destination. Be thorough.'

Murmurs of agreement echoed through the officers.

'Ready?' Callum scanned them and received nods of assent. 'Then let's go, people. I don't want this child to die.'

* * *

Madelaine's protests, followed by threats of lawyers, fell on deaf ears and she and Frank sat, like bookends, on the pale-green sofa.

An officer stood in front of them, one hand resting on the cuffs attached to his belt. Frank leaned back against the cushions; his bandaged arm still suspended in the elegant sling. He crossed his legs at the knee, exposing a glimpse of a gold sock top and the tag against a pallid leg as the hem of his trousers rode up. Madelaine wore jeans and trainers. Perched on the edge of the seat, weight forward, she looked like a child waiting for the music to start so that she could spring up and run to another chair. The two 'wig' dogs dozed together in an armchair, not bothered by the unusual company or activity.

Officers worked methodically through the house, clearing one room at a time. Callum could hear their quiet conferring, the crackle of radios and the opening and closing of doors. They reported back to him with solemn shakes of their heads. No other persons or dogs were found in the house and no evidence of concealed entrances, but they did find a quantity of cannabis in the kitchen.

Callum stood at the kitchen window watching officers moving steadily through the orchard and a worm of doubt crept into his head. Why had he been so certain that this was the likely location? His gut instinct that the Fenmans were hiding something partly mollified his concerns. He looked across to the outbuildings and the scuffed grass that pushed up through the cracked concrete yard.

'Daisy, Bird, Cookie.' He inclined his head towards the outbuilding, and they followed him out into the yard, past the rotary washing line pegged with jeans and T-shirts, through a wicket gate and onto the hard standing.

'I can hear a dog in there,' Daisy said when they approached the breeze-block building.

There was only one door, and it was constructed from solid steel in mottled tones like a dapple-grey pony. It was a door designed to keep out the curious, and it looked good at its job.

'Get the dog handler over here. This is a bit belt and braces for an outbuilding.' His heart rate increased. 'And it's padlocked.' He hoped the team had bolt croppers in the van or they would have to wait a little longer to find out if Kim was inside.

Daisy rattled a bunch of keys at him and grinned. 'These were hanging on the board in the kitchen where I found the van keys on the last visit. I picked them up on the way out. I thought they might come in useful.'

'Well done.'

She found the correct key on the second try and eased the door towards her a fraction to look inside.

'Stop.' Callum jammed his foot against the base of the door to bar it from opening any further. The last thing he wanted was Ruby in attack mode hurling her heavy body against the inside of the door.

'Wait. Get the dog handler.'

'I'm here, sir.'

They stood to one side to give the expert access. A smell of animals, warm straw and disinfectant seeped through the opening along with the sound of more than one dog barking. Lights inside the building flicked on and a narrow rectangular mat of yellow light fell at their feet. They heard the booted footfalls of Andrews steadily moving deeper into the building, but no sound of voices.

'Clear,' Andrews called, and Callum opened the door fully.

He was looking along an inner corridor with the outer block wall on one side and a row of wire-fronted pens on the other. Andrews moved away from the entrance and went to the far end of the building where he stopped outside the last cage.

'I've found your dog,' he said, moving through the open door into the cage.

Daisy was soon beside him, her face bleached of colour. When Callum joined them, her fists were clenched into tight balls.

Andrews was crouching beside the barely recognisable red dog making a cursory examination. 'One ear partially torn, a wound on her right shoulder,' he said. 'Other sundry bites. No wonder she looks so miserable.'

'Will she recover with treatment?' Callum looked at the damaged creature resting on a pad of straw on the concrete floor. She raised her head to look at her visitors and Callum saw hope in her eyes.

'I should say so.' Andrews pointed to her wounds. 'I'll get her over to the vet, pronto. And sir, there's not enough blood for her to have been attacked here. This looks like the result of a dogfight, I'd say. Hundred per cent. Poor bitch.'

'Bastards,' Daisy said and moved briskly away.

Callum kept his eyes on her stiff back as she moved along the wire cages. She stopped and leaned against the side of one, her fingers curled around the mesh.

'Sir. Look.' Her voice was urgent.

Callum nodded to the dog handler and went to join Daisy. She was peering through the outer caged space to an inner section where a breeding bitch was nursing a litter of puppies.

'Same here,' she said, moving to the next pen. 'They look well cared for.'

Callum heard the scuff of boots behind him.

'You bet they're well looked after,' Andrews said. 'On the black market, each of those litters is worth more than the contents of my house.' He moved away and spoke into his phone.

'That explains why Madelaine had a near miss on Roger Penny Way that night,' Callum said to Daisy. 'She had been dogfighting with Ruby up in Pitts Wood. She couldn't afford to say it wasn't her fault in case the other woman called us, and we discovered an injured dog in the van.'

'And that's why Madelaine had blood on her when we turned up,' Daisy said. 'She'd just taken Ruby out of the van and put her in the pen.'

Andrews finished his phone call and returned. He glanced into the nearest cage. 'These are way better looked after than some I've come across. You can leave these to me. We will remove them later today. They're secure where they are for now.'

'Thanks for your help.' Callum turned away as Bird and Cookie approached from the rear of the building.

The earlier enthusiasm had seeped away from Cookie, and his steps were leaden. Callum watched the steady stride of the older officer and thought that even his military bearing did not satisfactorily disguise the despondent slope of his shoulders.

'Anything?' Callum asked.

'There's a medical room back there, like a vet's surgery. A drug room with plenty of supplies, all in date, including ketamine, and enough dog feed in the back room to keep my dogs fed for about ten years. And not cheap stuff either,' Bird said.

Callum sloughed off his irritation. 'No sign of any concealed access?'

'Nothing, guv. Sorry.'

Callum left the three officers standing together and went to look for himself. He glanced into each of the rooms and conceded that Bird's assessment was correct. Nothing seemed out of place. What had he been expecting? A sign on the wall saying "secret doorway"? He was annoyed with himself. He walked back to his three officers who stood, hands in pockets, their focus on the floor beneath their feet.

'Let's go,' he said.

Outside, they stood next to the damp jeans and tops flapping on the washing line. There was a flurry of activity as Frank and Madelaine were led out of the back door and along the side of the cottage to the recently arrived transport. They were both under arrest. Frank sauntered next to an accompanying officer. His arm was still supported by the sling and his cuffed hands were clasped together in front of his chest, like a man praying.

Madelaine was not so compliant. With hands cuffed behind her back, she still managed to make the short walk to the van difficult and noisy. She spotted Callum, and despite the distance between them, spat in his direction. Any semblance of the cordial and cultured estate agent had disappeared. An officer put pressure on the cuffs and Madelaine completed the remainder of the journey bent forward with one of the officer's hands pressed against the back of her head and the other grasping the handcuffs.

'Assault of a police officer,' Bird said. 'You letting that go, guv?'

'For now.' He turned back to look at the building they had just moved away from. He studied the roof line, then stepped to one side to view it from a different angle.

'Daisy, how far back did those pens extend?'

'Ten, maybe twelve feet, max.'

'And the feed store behind them, Bird?'

Bird tilted his head to one side and Callum wondered if he was envisaging his six-foot body lying along the floor as a guide.

'About another five or six feet.'

'So, what was behind the store?' Callum asked.

'Nothing. There was a solid breeze-block wall right across the back. Wasn't there, Cookie?'

Cookie nodded. 'The side wall of the feed store was the same, the medical room and drug store have cupboards along that side of the room.'

Callum ran over the layout in his head. 'Was there anything in the cupboards?'

Bird frowned. 'Of course. Most of them. Yeah.'

'One was empty, Bird,' Cookie said, looking up at the older man.

'Which one?' Callum asked impatiently.

'In the medical room, the room that stinks of lemony disinfectant.' Cookie wrinkled his nose as if he could smell the memory. He looked at Callum. 'On that back wall,' he said. 'Second cupboard.'

'What's the significance?' Daisy asked.

Callum pointed at the roof line. 'That building goes back further than six metres. See the roof? Each one of those sheets of galvanise is about a metre wide. That makes the building a good bit longer than our assessment of eighteen feet for the cages and rooms. They would only need six sheets of roofing.'

The team turned and looked at the corrugated roof where the narrow zebra stripes ran from ridge to gutter. At regular intervals, the fixings for each panel sprouted upwards, making parallel lines along the length. It was a study in perspective.

Cookie was muttering numbers under his breath and extending his fingers in sequence as he counted. 'I reckon there's about twenty roofing sheets.' Excitement made him sound breathless, and Bird dropped his hand onto the lad's shoulder for a second.

'Cookie,' Callum said. 'Walk round the outside of the building and see if there are any external doors or windows. Then come back here.'

Cookie was gone in the blink of an eye. A cloud of black corvids, disturbed by their activity, lifted off from the roof ridge and wheeled upwards before settling in the trees that bordered the yard. The mackerel sky eased slowly to the south-west. The breeze rustled the dying leaves in the treetops, and it sounded like sibilant whispering. Like gossip passing along a line of bystanders, mocking Callum's lack of success in finding Kim.

Cookie trotted around the far end of the building and rejoined them. 'Two windows have been blocked in, big windows, but not recently, and there are no doors. That's odd, isn't it? What do you think that means?' he asked.

'I hope it doesn't mean more dogs,' Daisy said.

'It won't,' Callum said. 'They felt no need to hide those, other than behind a padlocked door. But they are hiding something.' His heart bounced in his chest. He hoped they were hiding Kim, that they were not too late to find her alive, but as the thought surged through his mind, he knew that if she was there, in a building that size, she would not be alone. His mind spiralled to a dark place of sexual exploitation and captivity.

'Come on. Let's find a way in.'

Chapter Twenty-Six

Callum opened the empty cupboard. His fingers gently probed the inside surfaces until he located a metal nub near the door hinges. A little stub of a lever sited in a place you would never touch by accident.

'I've found it. Ready?'

Callum heard Cookie's noisy intake of breath then the sharp click of the mechanism and a complete section of the back wall, cupboards included, swung away and then to the left. The opening it exposed was covered by floor-to-ceiling strips of vertical plastic that overlapped and formed a seal. Callum pushed through the barrier and the heat and smell hit simultaneously. Cookie screwed up his face.

'Fuckin' hell,' Bird said. 'What a set-up. Not a whiff of that from outside.'

They followed Callum through onto the concrete-floored interior. The soft hum of a pump and the purr of fans filled the air. The glare and heat of the powerful overhead lights caused moisture to bead on Bird's brow.

Callum felt a chill slide down his spine. They were not going to find Kim in here.

What they had found was row after row of cannabis plants, neatly lined up in black tubs as precise as a fir plantation. The fronds swayed gently as the rotating fans moved the warm air over the leaves. A sea of green waved to and fro on an endless tide. The smell was pungent and musky. The plants nearest the door were in bud and the flowers gave off a strong skunky odour.

'Brilliant,' Cookie said, moving towards the green mass. 'Baby cannabis plants don't smell much for the first three weeks or so when they're in the vegetative state.' He walked deeper into the building, the lights throwing his shadow across the floor like a scurrying spider. 'Look. They've got giant scrubbers.' He pointed up to the foil-lined ceiling that was criss-crossed with silver hoses.

'What?' Bird asked.

'Scrubbers. Carbon filters.' Cookie raised his voice as he raced to the far end of the building. 'See the pumps? They're good ones. They pull the air through and sort of purify it. Takes the smell away. Then when the air gets outside, no one smells the cannabis.' He made his way back towards them. 'That next section is younger plants, so they have a constant supply coming along. It doesn't smell so bad at that end, Bird.'

Callum leaned towards Bird. 'Let's hope he gets questions on cannabis farms if he ever sits his sergeants' exam.'

'I'm going to bleedin' stink when I get out of here,' Bird grumbled, raising his arm, and sniffing at his jumper sleeve. 'Helen will probably make me undress in the yard before I'm allowed indoors.'

'This is brilliant.' Cookie was moving from one area to another. 'And this is where they dry it. This is all top-class stuff. It could be Malawi Gold, but I'm not sure.'

Callum glanced at the animated face below the unruly black curls. His constable seemed to know a lot about the illegal cultivation of drugs.

'See the irrigation pipes?' Cookie continued as he completed his tour of the premises and studied the ceiling. 'That insulation must be pretty brilliant too.'

Bird moved to the wall dividing the dog pens from this area. A section of it was covered with pigeonholes. He chuckled. 'Just what we need here, guv. Paperwork with names, addresses, and dates. A laptop. They must have been very sure we wouldn't find this place, or they wouldn't have kept any of this.'

'They were. I think it's been here for some time. There is nothing to give it away from the outside.'

'But you found it,' Daisy said, a thoughtful expression on her face. 'Shame we didn't find Kim though.'

Was she now considering his conviction that Kim was alive and captive? Callum noted the shift in her attitude but wasn't sure she was completely on side. Disappointment pressed down on him at not finding the child. His heart was shrinking inside his chest, and he wanted to curl his body around it protectively. Instead, he took a deep breath and pulled his shoulders back. Kim was somewhere close. She had to be. He had worked it through in his head and nothing else fit. He had failed Jeanie. He would not fail Kim.

'There was no way we could have suspected it was here. We only found the bleedin' set-up because we were looking for Kim,' Bird said.

'They thought we wouldn't look any further than those poor dogs,' Daisy said.

'Good job you clocked the roof, guv. Shall I give the team a tug to come back and let them sort it out?' Bird asked.

Callum nodded. 'And turn off the power.'

'It must be costing the Fenmans a fortune,' Cookie said, earning himself a sharp look from his boss.

'With the return from this little set-up, I reckon they can afford it,' Bird said as he clicked the door closed behind them.

* * *

Callum tossed his car keys to Daisy, and she slid behind the wheel of his vehicle. The vortex of birds spiralled above him, like black rags on the wind. A lone magpie, smart in his dinner jacket, cawed a raucous jibe as it strutted across the verge, green-tinged tail feathers swaying in its wake.

'I thought you were never going to let me drive it,' she said, moving the seat forward.

'I want to think. Don't hit anything.'

Daisy started the engine and eased the vehicle back onto the lane, the crunch of gravel sending the magpie up onto the gate where two more joined it.

'One for sorrow. Two for joy.' She nodded at the bird. 'Three for a girl.'

He sensed her look in his direction but didn't respond, just stared straight ahead.

He would not find Kim dead or alive on the whim of a bird. He dropped his chin onto his chest and went over the layout of Paul's cottage in his mind. None of the searches of other properties had been successful, and there were only two more to complete. They had found no hidden doors, no secret bases, no Kim. He must have missed something at Paul's property. Something important. His phone pinged a text message and he read it. The forensics were back and Kim had been in Paul's van.

'All right, sir?' Daisy asked.

Callum straightened up, as dense rhododendron bushes flashed past his window. The deep shadows beneath their foliage seemed dark and threatening. He read a second incoming text then cleared his throat.

'Let's go to Daphne Smart's,' he said.

'What now? I've got a mountain of paperwork waiting, Callum.'

'So have I.' He paused. 'Snowdrop Cottage. Now.' His voice was quiet and firm.

Daisy sighed, reversed into a driveway, and turned the car around.

* * *

'Head,' Daphne Smart shouted.

Callum ducked hastily and felt the tingle against his scalp as his hair brushed the low door lintel.

He sensed Daphne's scrutiny when they entered her neat, bright kitchen. His body was tense, shoulders held too high, limbs restless like a caged animal keen to escape. He knew that his usual affability was replaced by curtness that he was not proud of. He felt as if a bee was buzzing around in his head, ricocheting off the inside of his skull.

'Sorry for shouting, Inspector.' She poured two mugs of tea, unasked, and placed them on the table, one in front of each officer. 'I had an image of you knocking yourself out, crashing onto the kitchen floor and squashing my boys.'

Her dogs wagged their way across the kitchen to greet Daisy. The keyboard clicks of their toenails on the hard floor filled the silence when Callum did not comment.

'Dogs, bed.' Daphne pointed to the corner of the room. 'Now, Inspector, I have some information that might interest you.' Her eyes flicked to a neat pile of papers at the other end of the kitchen table. 'Courtesy of the major. I asked him about underground operational bases and fear I may have created a monster.'

Callum looked with interest at the sheaf of papers. 'What have you got?'

'The major belongs to an organisation up in, I think, Oxford, and they have archive information on these bases.' She shuffled the papers until she found a particular sheet.

'Here we are.' She handed it to Callum. 'These are construction plans for a base built during the Second World War – curved elephant iron roof, brick walls and railway sleepers or concrete floors.'

The plans were handwritten, the presentation of its time. Daisy leaned in to look at the drawings.

Daphne gave them a moment. 'There are two pieces of specific information that will interest you.'

Callum tilted the paper to one side to take advantage of the light from the kitchen window.

She looked at him over her spectacles. 'Now, Inspector, about six hundred secret bases were built, and methods were area-specific. In Scotland, for example, most were built into existing caves. In the north of England, they often utilised mine shafts; along the Cornish coast, they used tin mines where possible; and in this area' – her eyes met Callum's – 'they often built them in woodland.'

Daisy frowned. 'Are you saying they just dug a big hole, built a shelter in it and then covered it over and nobody knew it was there?'

'Yes, Daisy. I am. They were invisible. They left the contour of the land as they found it,' Daphne said patiently.

'You'd see the door though,' Daisy persisted.

Callum was looking through sheets of paper with a growing sense of excitement.

'No, you wouldn't.' He pushed a sheet of paper in her direction. 'Look at that. The entrance is a balanced trapdoor. It's hidden when closed. Trigger the mechanism and it lifts the trapdoor vertically upwards and then swings it out of the way to one side. See the pulley wires?' He pointed to the page.

'Like at Fenman's? I see, but I don't understand how it works.'

'Doesn't matter. You haven't got to build one. Just know that when the trapdoor is closed, you can't see it.'

'Okay.' Daisy's voice held doubt.

Daphne leaned back against her sink and sipped her tea. A happy teacher who had enthused her students.

Callum surfed through the papers and pointed at a drawing. 'You open the trapdoor and climb down a vertical ladder into the base. And at the other end of the chamber is an escape tunnel.'

Daisy leaned forward for a closer look. 'If the doors are concealed, I can't see how this is going to help us find Kim.'

Daphne opened a blue tin and cut two slices of cake, which she popped onto a plate and pushed across the table towards the detectives.

Callum pointed at another sketch. 'On the outside, it would just look like part of a bank, or a wall. No one would suspect that it was there. See that picture?' He reached for a piece of cake and took a bite.

'Okay. I get that.' Daisy took the other slice and used it to point at the papers before sinking her teeth into it. 'And men hid in them?' she asked through a mouthful of cake.

'Yes,' Daphne said. 'For guerrilla attacks on the enemy had invasion occurred. The major told me about the auxiliary group who used it. They were four local men: a farmer, Charles Harrison; a gamekeeper called Ben Hickman; a postman named Robert Deacon and James Barnes, Paul's grandfather. Sadly, it's a little too late to ask Paul for help.'

'Thank you for taking the time. It is appreciated.'

'My pleasure. It's quite fun trying to work it out – like doing *The Times* crossword but with exercise thrown in. Let me know if there's anything else I can help with. I've lived in the village all my life, Inspector.'

Callum was sure the brick dust in Conchita's hair and the lead paint related to these bases. He experienced a giddy surge of boyish excitement. He bundled the papers into a heap.

'Keep them,' Daphne said.

He picked them up and went into her hallway. 'Thank you for these, Mrs Smart.' He clutched them to his chest and ducked out into the porch.

'And for the cake,' Daisy said, following close behind him.

'You are very welcome on both counts. Good luck.' The door snapped closed behind them.

Callum's phone pinged as they neared his Sportage, and he paused at his passenger door to read it.

'Nothing at the other houses.' He buckled his seat belt. 'Forest Cottage. And step on it.'

Daisy slid the vehicle smoothly up through the gears and Callum eased back in the passenger seat. His glance in the door mirror showed the fallen leaves twisting like a kite tail flying in their wake.

* * *

The five-bar gate to Paul's cottage was closed across the gravel path. A rising wind stirred the branches and shot a blast of cold air down the back of Callum's neck. There was an eeriness about the darkening pines that creaked and groaned, and he saw Daisy shiver. The dank odour of dying vegetation was a promise of approaching winter and tasted sour on his tongue. As atmospheres went, it did not bother him. If you stripped out each of the elements, individually they held no menace. It was only when they were all lumped together that they started to take on a presence. Some people were more susceptible than others and he knew he could rely on Daisy to comment.

'Spooky,' she said closing the gate behind them. The clash of the metal catch echoed around the trees like cymbals in a concert hall.

Callum took the house key from his pocket and passed it to Daisy. As she fiddled with the door, he glanced at the orchard. The fruit trees moved listlessly as if marking time until the last of their curled leaves joined the decaying apples and foliage amongst the tussocks of cocksfoot grass.

It took her three attempts to get the key to turn the lock. 'God. It's cold in here.' She pushed open the door and snapped on the kitchen light. The room was just as they had left it.

'That is because there's nobody to light the fire.' Callum was struck by how quickly the house had developed an unlived-in feel to it. Even the cooking smells had disappeared. It could have been empty for years.

'Hope you've got proper central heating in your new place or I'm not coming to your housewarming,' she said, picking up letters from the mat and putting them on the table.

'Underfloor. And it is a long way from being finished, as you well know.'

'Just saying.'

'You do upstairs this time and I'll do down,' Callum said. 'Fresh eyes.'

Chapter Twenty-Seven

Callum went into the front room. The afternoon sun was struggling to get through the small panes of the leaded lattice window. The sill was covered by house plants in clay pots sitting on a miscellaneous assortment of saucers. They leaned towards the light. He thought it was counterproductive to partially obscure the only light source, not to mention depressing. His house was designed to let in as much of it as possible.

Two armchairs covered in faded green fabric, one with a sagging seat, squatted each side of the hearth, like a pair of tired toads. The fabric might once have been bright and cheerful. There was a wooden settle against the wall opposite the window. Dark patches, from years of use, stained the hard seat. Sitting there must have felt like a penance.

The walls were papered beige up to the picture rail with white paint above it. Hanging on long hairy strings were dark-framed pictures of austere people dressed in their Sunday best. A rogues' gallery of ancestors haunted the room. Disapproving looks seemed to be a family trait as if they were just waiting to comment on something you were doing wrong. It must have been an unnerving room to sit in for a child. He would have considered turning their sour faces to the wall.

The underside of the mantle was blackened by years of smoking wood fires. The single bulb of the overhead light was reflected in the bevelled glass face of the mantle clock. The mechanism ticked with a soft cluck, like a roosting hen. He checked the time and found it correct. Above his head, the beamed ceiling creaked as Daisy moved across the floorboards. The fire was laid in the grate, screwed-up balls of yellowed newspaper beneath thin kindling wood, with a layer of dry logs on top. Callum recognised the dog-like smell of wet soot, saw the black prills scattered over the wood and knew the fire had not been lit for a long time. Where had Paul spent his evenings? Here in the cold surrounded by his disapproving ancestors, or on a hard chair by the kitchen fire. Neither seemed an attractive proposition nor would have suited him, but then he was not Paul.

The measured tread of Daisy's boots sounded on the thin carpet of the stairs and she joined him in the kitchen.

'Anything?' he asked.

'Nothing. Not that I was expecting to find anything. You?'

He shook his head. 'Let's go outside.'

He heard her lock the door behind them and felt the key pushed into his hand. He went back to the entrance gate.

'I thought you wanted to look round the garden.' She glanced at her watch.

He stood with his back to the gate. 'I do but I want to look at this through fresh eyes.'

'Okay.' Her tone confirmed her doubt that this was a sensible strategy. She was always quick to let him know if she thought he was off track and he could sense her growing resistance to this idea. She glanced at her watch again.

He leaned back against the gate, folded his arms, and closed his eyes. 'Tell me what you see. Describe the property to me.'

'Like in an estate agent's particulars?'

'If that helps you focus, then yes.' She's always so literal, he thought.

'Right,' she said. 'It's a triangular site and the ground rises to the rear of the property. It is approached along a gravel track across a wide grass verge and that track continues along the inside of the east curtilage.' She paused. 'Is that the sort of thing you want?'

'Keep going.'

'The three-bed character cottage faces the road with a small area of lawn in front of it and the kitchen door near the entrance gate. Beyond the house, along the road frontage is an ancient orchard full of the spooky graves of past pets.'

He opened one eye and saw that she was looking up at him and grinning. His tone was firm. 'A child could die. If you can't take this seriously, then I don't want you here, Sergeant.'

'Sorry.' She did not look apologetic. She looked as if she was beginning to enjoy herself, which irritated him.

'Stick to the facts, Daisy,' he said.

'Behind the house, the land rises on a gradual incline to the fenced rear curtilage. Beyond this is a plantation of mature trees under other ownership. At the top end of the property is a closed barn of galvanise construction with a large sliding door accessed from the gravel track. Okay?'

'Keep going.'

'Between this barn and the house and accessed from the same track is a more modern concrete-rendered workshop with a pitched roof. It has Crittall windows along both sides and is entered via double timber doors.' Daisy paused and climbed up to sit on the top bar of the gate close to Callum's shoulder. 'Behind the workshop and on the... west curtilage are a few silver birches in a clump, then a greenhouse with three raised beds on the house side and a large flat cultivated area beyond. It is pretty much rough grass everywhere else. Will that do?' She looked down at him from her perch.

'For now.' He wondered if she read estate agents' particulars for entertainment. 'Now, we have established that there is no access from the house to any hidden hideaway, so if you want to get from the house to the orchard, to hang out the washing, how would you do it?'

'Out the kitchen door to the flagstone path that runs along the back of the house.'

'And the greenhouse or vegetable garden?'

'Same but go up the sloping path that starts halfway along the flagstone one.'

'And the garage workshop building?'

'Walk towards this gate and up the gravel track. Same for the top barn.'

'Hop down off the gate. Now let's go and see if any paths lead to somewhere other than those destinations, or don't seem to go anywhere at all.'

Fifteen minutes of careful examination drew a blank. In the orchard, the flattened grass ended at the washing line. A well-defined path had been trodden to the greenhouse and three raised beds but did not go into the rough tussocky grass beyond.

'Are you going to have a garden at your house?' Daisy asked.

He ignored her attempt at distracting cheerfulness and looked at the stand of silver birch trees. He did not want her to break his focus. An empty bird feeder swung from the lowest branch and the grass below was untrampled. In the other direction, a trodden path fronted the raised beds. A circular patch of crushed grass in front of each showed that Paul regularly attended to the crops growing in the knee-high constructions.

On his last visit to Seil Island, Callum's grandmother had accepted his help in making similar beds for her vegetables. She had told him that gravity was stronger than when she was younger and getting back to her feet after a weeding session was not as easy as it had once been. Her mouth was pursed as if she was stopping further comment from escaping. He had smiled at her, aware that the need was caused by her advancing years, but he had known better than to voice his thoughts aloud.

Paul had a good twenty years on his grandmother. Why then use raised beds? The sides were timber and well-weathered; perhaps they stemmed back to his grandfather's time.

The vegetable patch was just that; a flat area of earth where Paul grew vegetables. Runner beans stood tall at one end, supported by cut hazel sticks, the long green pods dangling like lamb's tails between the fluttering leaves and scarlet flower heads.

Paul had been digging late potatoes, the newly turned earth darker in colour than the weathered surface, and he still had two more rows to harvest. The foliage was dying back, the stalks yellow and woody and soon he would have been lifting them all to store in sacks for winter use. There was hardly a weed to be seen. It was a garden that reflected the many hours of expert care that Paul lavished on it.

'Nothing here; can we go now?' Daisy asked, joining him after her tour around the perimeter of the property.

'Let's do the garage next.' Callum suppressed his surge of impatience. He would not allow it to morph into panic.

They walked up the track to the workshop garage. There was a groove in the gravel from constant use or perhaps from water finding the lowest point when it headed downhill after rainstorms. The double wooden doors were roof-height and well-oiled and swung open noiselessly. Paul seemed to take good care of the things he was responsible for.

A timber workbench sat against one long wall. A vice and lathe were mounted on it, along with a circular saw and other woodworking tools that Callum recognised. Chisels and files, handles upwards, were slotted individually into a shelf above the bench. Everything had its place in this kingdom. Paul was methodical, predictable, a creature of habit who paid great attention to detail. Callum felt a flash of annoyance as his eye slid over the neatly stacked shelves. The place was almost obsessive in its tidiness, unlike the interior of the cottage. The hidden base had to be here. It had to be on his land, under his control. Why the hell, then, couldn't he find it?

An inspection pit was sunk into the garage floor. Paul's box trailer, part-filled with split logs, was neatly positioned over the back of it. It was ready, Callum assumed, for delivery to a winter customer. From habit, he ran an eye over the tyres and found they had plenty of tread.

'Callum.'

He swung round at the excitement in Daisy's voice. She was pulling open a pine door in the opposite wall and he hurried over to join her. The hinges were well-oiled, and he felt anticipation as they looked inside. A row of clothes hung from hooks along the back wall. There were protective trousers for chainsaw use, high-visibility jackets and orange overalls. A pair of steel toe-capped boots on the floor below the empty legs looked as if the wearer had withered away inside the clothes.

'He keeps bees.' Daisy slid a white suit to one side to examine the back of the cupboard. Her hand grazed against the solid block wall, and she pulled it away in disappointment. 'Damn. I thought I was onto something there.'

A muscle in his cheek tightened until the tension made it flutter like a butterfly trying to escape through a closed window. He relaxed his jaw and stopped grinding his teeth together. He wanted to shout with frustration. Where the hell are you, Kim? Why can't we find you? He closed his eyes against the image of Jeanie Cowie.

'Now the barn.'

Chapter Twenty-Eight

Daisy kicked a stone at the edge of the track, and it disappeared into the tall grass with a whispered hiss. Callum knew that she considered this search futile but was wise not to voice her opinion. It was his call, his job on the line and Kim's life. He knew he was right about this; he had to be right. He strode up the incline, hearing her desultory footfalls trailing in his wake.

Paul had a saw bench inside the barn to cut tree trunks into smaller, more manageable sections. An axe was blade-bedded into a chopping block, the long handle laying a fragmented shadow across a pile of split logs.

'Looks as if he uses this for his wood business,' Daisy said.

Callum closed his eyes to suppress his irritation with her for stating the obvious.

The split logs were stacked into chest-high walls to dry out. Callum could imagine the steady rhythm of the axe, the flash of the blade as it arced through the air and the thud of honed metal cleaving timber. It was a job for the self-motivated, the solitary soul who could function without contact with fellow human beings. Callum liked his own company and was not afraid to spend time by himself, but the prospect of living life as a hermit was extreme. It was not for everyone.

'I love the smell of sawn timber, don't you?' Daisy stirred the mound of yellow flakes with her toe.

'Fruitwood and fir.' Callum breathed in the memory of his grandfather's woodshed. He heard the rhythmic plunge of the axe head, the crack of the timber splitting followed by the satisfied grunt of effort. Had Paul stood beside his grandfather and watched the old man at work, learned from him, just as Callum had done? What else had Paul learned that made him choose to live the life of a near recluse?

On the shelf beneath the window, light glinted from the shark teeth of the chainsaws sitting in a predatory row next to red and green petrol cans. It was exactly what you would expect to find. Nothing out of place. No secrets.

'There's nothing here, is there, Callum? We should get back to the office.' Daisy started towards the door without waiting for his confirmation.

Callum counted the hours in his head since Paul had completed his shopping.

'No. There has to be something. We're just not seeing it. Look again.'

'I have looked. And there's nothing to find. Can't you see that?' Daisy lifted her chin, an exasperated glint in her eye.

'You're wrong, Sergeant.' There was an edge to his voice. 'We've missed something. We keep looking.'

He went out onto the gravel track and down the slope, the reluctant scuff of Daisy's boots behind him. Once again, he stepped inside the cool interior of the garage, closed his eyes and stood still. Daisy stopped beside him and took a deep breath. His raised hand stopped her from speaking and he registered the huff of her exhaling breath. It reminded him of the sigh his sister Dolina made when she was fed up with his dreamy dawdling.

All he could hear was the soft *coo-coo* of a wood pigeon in the trees outside and the creak of branches moving against one another. He could detect the scent of a lubricant, oil of some kind, before it was overpowered by the apple scent of Daisy's shampoo as she stepped closer to him. He opened his eyes.

'We've searched in here.' Daisy glanced at her watch again.

'Then we search again. We're out of options and she's nearly out of time. She is here.' Callum thrust his hands in his pockets, pushed away the image of Jeanie and urgently focused on the interior of the building.

'Or she's not here at all. Or she's already dead.'

'If you can't say anything constructive then shut up. Or go back to the station, Donaldson.' His tone was sharp. 'Five more minutes and then I'm calling in the rest of the team.' He turned his back on her and strode towards the trailer parked over the inspection pit. His unguarded reaction annoyed him.

He stopped beside the trailer and unleashed a kick at the tyre with the toe of his new boot. He felt the jolt as his foot slammed against the toecap and the trailer slowly rolled backwards towards the end of the pit.

Daisy had followed him. 'That's funny. Look.' She pointed down into the concrete-sided pit.

The excitement in her voice had him moving to her side.

She was indicating the opposite side wall that was no longer in the shadow of the trailer.

'See, there? It's smoother than the rest. Not as rough.' She seemed anxious not to be misunderstood.

'I know what smooth means, Daisy.' Callum jumped down into the pit. The dull thud of his boots echoed in the enclosed space like a round of applause. It could be something. It could be nothing.

Daisy descended the four narrow concrete steps built tight against the pit end wall and headed towards him.

'Wait.' He held up a hand to stop her approaching and squatted down to examine the floor where it joined the wall.

'What are we looking for?' she asked, crouching beside him.

'Boot impressions. If there is an access door, I want to know where he stood to open it. There's no visible catch, Daisy.'

'Okay. Can you see anything? Would a light help?' She took a small torch from her pocket and shone the beam across the concrete in a slow arc.

'Go back over that last bit,' Callum said. 'Stop.' His heart pounded. 'There. See it?'

'See what?'

He snatched the torch from her fingers and played the beam over a small area of floor on the right. 'There. A boot print in the dirt. See the pattern of the sole?'

'Got it. So that's where he stood to open the door. I can't see a catch though.'

Callum stood, handed the torch to her and moved closer to the footprint. He ran the palm of his hand vertically down the wall where the concrete changed texture. His fingers discerned a slight difference despite it looking almost identical to the section of wall on either side. He remembered Daphne Smart saying Paul should have been an engineer. If this was a door, it was skilfully constructed.

Daisy went back up the steps and walked along the lip of the pit, peering down at him. 'I was expecting a lever sticking out of the wall. Or a knob that you twisted.' She sounded disappointed.

'This is not *Indiana Jones*. If we've found it, and I think we have, then this is a new entrance, built long after the war. This concrete is certainly not seventy years old.'

'*If* you've found it, that means there's another entrance and we missed it.'

Callum agitated the silver earring in his left lobe and scrutinised the grey wall. 'According to Martha, Conchita was well-fed. When Paul brought her food, he would have needed to open that door with one hand, or perhaps none if he was carrying a tray.'

Daisy stood above him, hands on hips, watching. He walked back to the base of the steps, and she scuttled crab-like along the lip of the pit, a fluff of dust marking her progress. Callum held an imaginary tray and returned to stop an arm's length from the wall. He could barely hear his footfalls over the sound of rushing blood in his ears.

'Now what?' She leaned out further over the edge.

Callum turned his shoulder to the door and leaned on it.

The click was audible above a gasp from Daisy, who jumped backwards in a swirl of blonde hair. The concrete wall moved outwards towards Callum for a few inches, paused for a second, and then, with a pneumatic hiss, surged straight up. The top edge stopped where Daisy's head had been. She trotted along to the steps, jumped down two at a time, and stood beside him. They looked into a straight-sided brick passageway with a rounded roof. Callum held up a finger and paused with his bowed head inside the tunnel.

No sweet foetid stench of decay, just a reassuring smell of warm house and dust. He took a cautious step into the darkness as Daisy fumbled for her torch. She didn't need it as a line of motion-sensor lights at knee level suddenly lit the space with cold bright light. It was an incongruous mix of high-tech and Neanderthal. A stride in, he grazed his skull on the roof and speedily dipped his head. Set at the top of the curved ceiling was a round button, the white paint worn away from use. The side walls brushed his shoulders and an irrational fear of being entombed increased his heart rate with a surge. He hoped that button activated the door from the inside. How cavers thought it was fun to creep into small spaces without knowing how they were going to get out again, he would never understand. He concentrated on counting his footsteps.

'Busted,' Daisy muttered behind him.

'What?' In turning his head to question her, he caught the notes of a pop song playing on a radio. The passageway ahead ended at a white door beneath which a narrow threshold of white light escaped.

'The music. Busted. She's listening to them.' Daisy nodded her head at the door. 'Don't frighten her,' she said.

The muted throb of the bass beat was infectious, and Daisy's stride picked up the rhythm.

'Ready?' Callum pushed the door gently and it swung into the room. He stepped to one side and felt Daisy's arm brush against his as she joined him. At the periphery of his mind hovered an image of Jeanie.

Chapter Twenty-Nine

Callum always tried not to have preconceived ideas of what he might encounter in any situation, but the room surprised him. Colourful posters dressed the whitewashed walls, vibrant, bright and inviting. The row of suspended lights reflected pools onto the polished wood floor and warmed the green architrave. It was functionally furnished, warm and homely, and conjured up memories of his student days. It smelled better than his memories.

A rainbow rag rug lay in front of a small sofa pushed back against the wall. A kitchen table with two chairs had small bottles of flavoured water, salt-and-pepper pots and a radio dotting the pine surface. The music playing was not to his taste; he thought it was probably aimed at teenagers. A well-stocked bookcase on the opposite wall displayed spines in barcode neatness.

'Wow. Very organised.' Daisy tilted her head to scan the titles. '*The Hobbit*,' she said.

He should have realised it was missing from Paul's house. A bathroom was visible through an open door next to a bed. The room was cosy, but there were no windows and Callum quelled an urge to sprint back out into the light.

Daisy pointed. 'Look, Callum.'

Beneath the covers of the bed was a slight mound, child-shaped and still. They hurried closer. The girl lay on her back, eyes closed, white face surrounded by a halo of fair hair. Her skin was washed chalk, except for the thumb-smudged grey of her eye sockets and rose-blushed mouth. Three livid red weals criss-crossed the left side of her face, the edges blurring from pink to charcoal and ochre. Daisy gasped a sharp breath.

'Ambulance, Daisy,' he said.

She raced back out through the tunnel, cursing the lack of a phone signal as she ran. Callum leaned over Kim, and gently placed two fingers against her neck. His breath caught in his throat with a sound like fluttering bird wings. Her skin was moist and warm; a pulse bounced strong and rhythmic for a few beats before her eyes flashed open and she drew breath to scream.

He snapped upright. 'Kim. It's okay. You're safe.' He showed her the palms of his hands as he stepped away from her, relief flooding over him like a warm shower. 'My name's Callum and I'm a policeman.'

The scream dissolved into a gulped sob. The covers fell away from her upper body as she pulled herself up into a sitting position. She was still dressed in the sweater she had worn when Kelly had last seen her. Colour was seeping back into her face with every waking breath, and he realised that her corpse-like pallor was due to her being deeply asleep. Her forehead was damp, stands of her hair were stuck to her face and two pink spots blushed her cheeks. She must have been terrified to be woken by fingers on her neck and a stranger with long black hair looming over her. Kim screwed her knuckles into her eyes, removed them and blinked as if she couldn't believe what she was seeing.

'You're safe now, Kim. I'm Callum, I'm a policeman.' He gave her the information again, not sure how much she had understood in her initial moment of panic. His relief was so overwhelming that he felt the prickle of tears at the back of his eyes. He squatted down on his haunches to minimise his height and gave her what he hoped was a reassuring smile. 'We've been looking for you. Are you okay?'

Her brown eyes stared at him as she drew her knees up to her chest and touched a tentative finger to her cheek. 'Where's my mum?' Her sobs had quickly dried to a hiccup. This was not a child in fear of her life, terrified of a captor.

'She'll be here soon. Are you hurt? How did that happen?' He touched his own cheek as a hundred definitions of hurt chased through his brain. It was the question all parents of missing children asked him when what they meant was: had they been sexually assaulted. He had never found an easy way to confirm their fears.

She shook her head. 'Not really. It still stings a bit, but Paul bathed it with some special stuff and gave me some cream to put on it and that helped.'

'Did he?'

Callum shuffled the assumptions in his head. Had Paul caused the injury and then tended to it in a show of

189

remorse? Or had someone else injured her? He couldn't explain why, but he hoped it was the latter.

'Yes. And his hands were all shaky. Where's Paul? He said he was coming back with my mum... and I'm thirsty. My throat's sore and my head still hurts. Can I have a drink please?' She pointed to the table. Callum went to it as she continued. 'I left my phone behind so I don't know the time. I have to wait for the man on the radio. Paul said he wouldn't be very long.'

He picked up an unopened bottle of water and twisted the lid until he heard the seal snap. Kim reached out for it and gulped down several noisy mouthfuls.

Callum pulled up the time on his phone and passed it to her. 'In the afternoon.' He was not sure how long she might have slept. 'How did you hurt your face?'

'I didn't hurt it myself.' She returned his phone, glanced towards the tunnel then pulled up her right sleeve to reveal two raised indigo lines like giant veins along her forearm. 'Or these. Will you stay here until my mum and Paul come back, please?' She gnawed at her bottom lip. 'Paul showed me the button to get out, but I can't reach it.'

'Your mum will be here soon.'

Daisy would have put the wheels in motion, one of which was contacting Louise. He squatted beside her bed, back against the wall, and rested his forearms on the knees of his jeans.

'What caused those, Kim?' The bruises on her arms looked like defence wounds, received as she tried to protect her face from blows.

She shivered a little sigh. 'I was poorly, and Paul said I was asleep all day. He's gone shopping.'

'And what hurt your arm?' Callum asked again. She had been missing longer than that, but he let it pass.

'My riding crop.' She scratched at the back of her hand. 'Something has bitten me. Look.' She stretched towards him, and he saw the cluster of raised red dots. 'They itch.'

'Probably best not to scratch them, if you can manage that.'

'Kelly was cross with me, as usual, and she had the stick in the shelter and was trying to hit Drummer. She doesn't like Drummer.'

'I see.' And he was beginning to. 'But you didn't want her to hit Drummer, so you tried to stop her.'

She nodded. 'And she hit me instead.' She touched her cheek. 'She's never hit my face before.'

Anna Green had been right. Kim was being bullied, but not by someone at school as they had supposed. Her sister was the aggressor, someone who would be expected to love and protect her. Did her parents suspect but were unwilling to acknowledge the true situation? He remembered the hard look Sam had levelled at Kelly, and Louise's assertion that all sisters squabbled. Perhaps they had suspicions that all was not well between their daughters.

'Did you tell your mum and dad, Kim?'

She shook her head. 'Kelly said she would hit me harder if I did. She is always angry with me because she's unhappy.'

He felt a surge of anger towards Kelly.

'Kelly said I was just being a baby because I cried' – she touched her finger to her face – 'but it really hurt.' She took another drink, and the bottle crackled when she squeezed it.

'I'm sure it did. Then what happened?'

'Kelly stopped hitting me and threw the stick at Drummer and he cantered out into the field. I put it on the ledge and went to see if Drummer was okay.'

'And where did Kelly go?' His tone was light.

'I don't know.' She shrugged. 'I caught Drummer, and he had a mark on his leg where she hit him. I didn't see Kelly.'

'Which leg?' If there was still a mark, it would validate her account. He had not noticed one, but he didn't know what to look for.

'Near fore. If you run your hand down his leg, you can feel it just below his shoulder.'

That would be one for Daisy to deal with. He had no intention of getting that close to the pony again.

'Then what did you do?'

'I went to fill Drummer's hay net, but Kelly had used all the hay. Dad says we have to carry a new bale over from the barn together, so I shouted but she didn't answer.'

'Good. So, you went over to the hay barn to get a new bale?'

Kim nodded. 'But it was too heavy for me to carry. I dragged it halfway across the field on my own, but my leg and arm hurt, and my head. I was feeling a bit ill before that, but I didn't tell Mum because she worries and she had to go to work.' Tears threatened and she dashed at them with the back of her hand.

Callum thought her extraordinarily brave.

'I got cross and shouted at the bale and kicked it.' She lowered her eyes to the quilt cover.

His soft chuckle elicited a sheepish grin from her.

'I expect I might have done the same. And then?' His feet were tingling so he adjusted his cramped position. Where had Daisy got to?

'I can't really remember until Paul was picking me up and asking if I was all right. He had the bale in one hand and helped me with the other cos I was all wobbly, and then he did Drummer's net for me.' She touched a finger to her cheek. 'He was staring so I think it might look funny. Is Drummer okay? Have you seen him?'

'Drummer is fine.' He remembered the pony following him around the field. 'I was talking to him yesterday and he blew his nose all over me.'

A bubble of laughter started in Kim's throat and exploded through her nose in a snort.

Callum smiled at her.

'I love Drummer,' she said, smiling back, 'and Drummer loves me too.'

'He is a very nice chap, as ponies go.' He recalled the velvet nose pushing at his pockets for treats. He mulled over the possible answers to his next question and decided to ask it anyway. 'Why did Paul bring you here?'

'Because I wouldn't let him take me home.'

'Why not?'

'Because Kelly was there, and Mum and Dad were at work. I told him I thought they were working all the next day too because lots of people were off sick.' She pushed at the strands of hair stuck to her forehead. 'I can't really remember; I was ever so sleepy. I wanted Paul to let me stay in his cottage. I've ridden past it lots of times and he always waves to me. But he said it wasn't proper. But I was scared to go home, so he said I could stay here. I don't mind because it's nice.'

'And Paul was going to bring your mum to get you?' That explained the chocolates and flowers in the front of the van. Paul had intended to drive down Tethering Drove, stop at the Tanners' house, give Louise the gifts and take her to collect her daughter. His death had thwarted that plan.

'He made me promise to tell Mum what had happened with Kelly. He said being beaten and nobody knowing about it was like being invisible.' She frowned. 'I think I sort of know what he means.' She looked across towards the tunnel as Daisy hurried back into the room. 'Hello, Daisy. How's Moses?'

'Kim!' The relief on Daisy's face told Callum that she had thought Kim was dead. Daisy sneaked a look at him, and her adjustment was swift. 'Moses is fine, thanks, except he's in my bad books.'

Kim leaned forward and rested her elbows on her knees, mirroring Callum. 'Why? What did he do?'

Callum eased himself upright and felt the stab of pins and needles when the blood rushed into his feet. Kim was relaxed and engaged and if he had to listen to a conversation about his least favourite subject then it was worth every syllable.

Daisy sat on the bottom of the bed. 'I was cantering along the back of Mays Firs. He got the wind under his tail; gave the loudest squeal you have ever heard and went into a bucking fit.'

Kim shrieked with laughter.

'It was not funny,' Daisy said, a wounded expression on her face. 'I nearly fell off.'

'If I fall off, my dad always says I need stronger glue on my bottom.'

'That sounds like good advice,' Callum said.

Daisy leaned towards Kim and said in a stage whisper, 'I think he's afraid of horses. But don't tell him I know.'

Kim's mouth opened as she looked at Callum, then back to Daisy. 'You're teasing me.' She giggled. 'No one could be frightened of horses. Especially not of Drummer.'

The pulse of pain was lessening in Callum's feet. He thought Kim still had a fever but was otherwise satisfied with her condition. Soon the small space would be filled with the response team, and he was beginning to feel claustrophobic, like a giant in a cave.

'I'll go and find your mum, Kim.' Callum waited for Daisy's consenting nod before turning away.

Chapter Thirty

Callum went through the tunnel then outside where the gravel chattered beneath his boots. The air had chilled, and he filled his lungs with the cool pine-scented freshness. His phone alerted him to a call, and he realised that as Daisy had thought Kim was dead, the rest of the team would be working on the same assumption and the atmosphere in the office would be sombre, tempers frayed by frustration and failure.

'Bird. Good news. Kim is fine.'

Bird's slow expulsion of breath hissed against his ear and Callum pictured the tightness leach from the craggy features as the information sunk in.

'Thank bloody God, guv. The mother and the family liaison officer are on the way over. I'll give the FLO the heads-up so she can update Louise. Medics en route, ETA update is three minutes. I'll tell Martha to stand down, shall I?'

Callum lifted his head as tyres scrunched onto the gravel outside the gate. 'I'll do that. She's just arrived, and the ambulance is right behind her. Thanks, Bird. Get SOCO out here, will you? See what DNA there is in the bunker, see if we can confirm this is where Conchita was held.'

He reached the gate as Martha climbed out of her car. The suspension groaned and the bodywork lifted a few centimetres.

'False alarm, Martha.' He rested a forearm along the top bar of the gate and waited for her to come to the opposite side.

Martha closed her eyes for a moment and the tension melted from her face.

'Is she hurt, MacLean?' The question in her eyes was more specific.

'She seems fine on that score. She has some superficial wounds from being struck with a riding whip. Not delivered by Paul,' he added when her jaw tightened. 'I left her and Daisy talking horses.'

Two green-clad figures jumped out of the ambulance, bag straps slung over their shoulders, and approached Callum. They nodded to Martha as Callum swung open the five-bar gate to allow them access.

'The child, Kim, appears to have just surface injuries. She's sitting up talking to Sergeant Donaldson, whom she knows. Up that track, into the first building and down into the inspection pit where you will find a tunnel entrance.'

The female medic looked at her colleague and then at Callum. 'That's a better result than we expected.' She smiled up at Callum. 'That's made my day, Inspector.'

'Mine too. Call to Daisy when you get in the tunnel entrance. We don't need to stress Kim more than is necessary. And keep me informed, please.'

One of the figures raised a hand in acknowledgement as they headed up the track.

Martha lifted her foot onto the bottom rail of the gate and continued their conversation as if the interruption had never occurred. 'That will do her the world of good, a bit of a chit-chat about her pony. She must have been very frightened, poor little thing.'

Callum told Martha what Kim had told him.

'What with the Spanish sisters and now these two,' Martha said, 'I feel blessed to have been born into a family of men.'

'Oldest or youngest?'

She gave him what his grandmother labelled 'a straight look'. 'Slap bang in the middle of five, MacLean, as you ask.'

He gained the impression that she did not often divulge personal information, and this signalled a minor shift in their relationship. 'Lucky boys,' he said.

'They didn't think so at the time.' She took her foot from the bottom bar and stood up straight.

Callum recognised her withdrawal. 'This is the closest I could hope for to a happy ending, Martha. Kim seems quite cheerful and composed.'

Martha barked a short laugh. 'You wait till she sees her mum. Then the tears will start. Guaranteed.'

* * *

Daisy pushed open the office door with her bottom and reversed into the room. She was hugging some books to her chest. She heeled the door closed behind her.

'Anyone here speak and read Spanish?'

Cookie waved an idle hand above his head without removing his eyes from his screen. Callum had not pegged Cookie as a linguist but found that the information didn't surprise him.

'Really? Jolly good.' She placed a book on his desk. 'Homework. Have a read through tonight. And they found this mobile. It's a pay-as-you-go and I reckon it's older than you, Cookie. See what you can find on it.' She waited, perhaps anticipating the mention of a prior engagement. When none came, she moved across to stand by Bird's side.

Callum came out of the fishbowl. 'What are those?'

'Conchita's diaries. They were on the bookshelf. You were right about the two cases being connected. I had a poke about while I waited for the powers that be and found them.' Daisy blew a fine grey dust from the cover of the top volume. 'Forensics have finished with them, so I brought them back for a little night-time reading. The first volume is in Spanish and Spinglish.'

'Spanglish,' Cookie corrected. 'A mixture of English and Spanish.'

'Okay,' Daisy said. 'You've got that one. I never knew you spoke Spanish.'

Cookie's curls danced. 'And French and German and a bit of Italian. I'm trying to learn Japanese at the moment. It's fascinating. Did you know—'

Callum halted him with a raised palm. 'How many are there, Daisy?'

'Three. One for every year she was missing. The last entry is the day before she died. And these last two are in English. Do you want to read one?' Daisy held out two pink-covered books and he took one of them.

She followed him into the fishbowl, wrapping her arms around the remaining book.

'How's Kim?' Callum asked.

'She's okay. Look, sorry about earlier. I genuinely thought it was a waste of time to keep searching.' She did not look away, just gave him a rueful grin of apology.

Callum was pleased to hear her acknowledgement that she was wrong. Part of a sergeant's job was to have the inspector's back, to keep them on the right track, and that was the closest Daisy had ever come to challenging his decisions. She had been wrong, but he wouldn't make an issue of it.

'I didn't notice,' he said, and one corner of his mouth lifted in the suggestion of a smile.

'That's all right then.' Her grin widened. 'When Louise walked into the bunker, the floodgates opened but Kim soon recovered and was chatting twenty to the dozen. The medics took her in for the usual checks. They think she's probably had this nasty bug that's been going round flattening people but they aren't keeping her in.'

'That's good news. She's a nice child, despite the fact she likes ponies.'

Daisy laughed. 'I told Louise I'd call round in the morning. I had a quiet word with her while they were checking Kim, and neither she nor Sam had any idea that Kelly was abusing Kim. I believe her.'

'As do I. If they had known, then they wouldn't have left the two girls together. And Sam would have come down on Kelly hard. They are honest, hard-working parents trying to give the girls the best start they can. Did Louise say how Sam is coming along?'

'Oh, didn't you know? He's home. It wasn't a heart attack, thankfully; it was a panic attack. Kelly's out of danger but they're keeping her in for another day. Having Kim home will perk him up a bit.'

'Probably. But every time they look at her, they'll feel guilty for not noticing what was going on under their noses. And Kim is likely to hold back on some things to spare their feelings. She has a generous spirit.'

'Yeah. Kim's a good kid and she loves her parents. That's a good start.' Daisy smiled. 'She insisted on going to see Drummer on the way home. She had me trotting him up and down the field to be sure he wasn't lame. You are lucky she didn't ask you to go with her. She was kissing Drummer and telling him that you are his new best friend.' There was a sparkle in her eye.

Daisy was enjoying this a little too much for Callum's liking. 'And how is my new best friend?' he asked.

'He does have a mark across his near fore just below his shoulder, exactly where Kim said. Her hand went straight to it. I believe her story.' She hugged the book a little tighter.

'As do I. Did you mention the flowers and chocolates to Louise?'

'Kim must have told Paul what to get,' Daisy said. 'Freesias are her favourite. I think Paul tried to do his best for Kim but I don't understand why he didn't take her home the next morning.'

'That was my thought too,' Callum said. 'Kim thinks she remembers telling Paul that her parents were at work the next day which might explain his actions. If he was trying to do his best for her, then he wouldn't want to take her back to her house if it was only her sister there and she was scared of Kelly.'

'Fair enough. I buy that. And I bet Paul was pretty scared about what people would think about him, but it doesn't explain Conchita,' Daisy said.

'No, it doesn't.' Callum placed his volume on his desk. 'Perhaps this will.'

'And remember Conchita was missing a gold earring? SOCO found it under the bed along with a lot of dust and dog hair.'

His phone rang. 'MacLean.' He listened without interrupting before killing the call and addressing Daisy. 'They have found the second entrance to the base.'

'Where? We looked everywhere.' There was a hint of annoyance in her tone.

'Remember the raised vegetable beds by the greenhouse? The one with onions has a solid bottom. It lifts up vertically and has steps beneath it that go down into the shelter. They found it from the inside of the base. The outside trigger was sunk into the raised bed at soil level.'

'I can't think how we missed it,' she said widening her eyes.

He ignored her sarcasm. 'It worked on a cantilever principle, and they are all pretty impressed with Paul's skills on the engineering front.'

'I told you it was against his nature to hurt Kim.'

Bird leaned into the doorway of the fishbowl. 'I was chatting to a PC in the corridor. Is it right that some of those graves in the orchard might not be pet-sized?'

'You're joking, right?' Daisy said.

Callum nodded to Bird.

'Are they going to dig them up, then, guv?' Bird asked.

'The light's going today. They'll make a start in the morning. None of them are recent so I've put in a nightwatchman.'

'Spooky,' said Daisy. 'I told you the orchard felt spooky. Definitely spooky.'

Callum picked up the diary. 'Good work, people,' he said. 'Let's knock it on the head tonight. It's looking like a loaded day tomorrow with Kim, the Fenmans and Jericho. Get a good night's sleep.'

Cookie sprung from his chair. One hand closed down his computer, while the other scooped up the diary and lifted his jacket from his chair with a finger through the loop at the back of the neck.

'Hunky-doodley, guv. See you in the morning. Nighty-night.'

By the time Bird looked up to respond, Cookie had gone.

Bird scrubbed his hand over his tufts of hair. 'Whichever girl takes him on,' he said, 'is going to need eyes in the back of her bleedin' head.'

Chapter Thirty-One

Callum stopped outside his building plot and looked through the closed heras fencing. All the vehicles had gone, and the darkness was lowering the sky like a descending candle snuffer. Cool air chilled his face as he stepped out onto the verge and across to the fence. He curled his fingers over the chain links and rested his forehead against the cold metal. Would the basement terraces provide sufficient natural light to alleviate his earlier feeling of entombment? Could he live in this half-buried house? He certainly hoped so.

A blackbird dived into the thorn hedge where its strident homecoming skirl was greeted by fluttering feathers and a rustle of leaves. A juvenile tawny owl called from the larch tree at the end of his garden before its swooping shadow floated across the site with hardly a wing beat. Bats exhibited their aerial acrobatics, and he fancied he could hear high-pitched chatter accompanying their faultless choreography. The gloaming folded around him, enveloped him, safe and cocooning.

He breathed in the tang of damp peat and horse dung. A pang of guilt stabbed him. How could he feel that this place was so right for him when Grace would not have been happy here? When they had visited his grandparents on Seil Island, she had walked closer to him than she ever did on the streets of Glasgow. She was panicked by the lack of street lights and the vast overarching darkness sprinkled with twinkling stars. He felt disloyal in knowing that if he let himself, he could be happy here.

He closed the car door and drove along Tethering Drove. His phone silenced the trumpet concerto on his radio and flashed "Martha" across the display. It was unusually late for her to call.

'Evening, Martha.'

'I know it is. I omitted to tell you something earlier.'

He noticed she didn't say 'forgot' and grinned to himself. 'Which is?'

'That Paul Barnes died of natural causes. He had a massive heart attack. Dead before his van left the road. Perhaps it was the result of swerving to avoid a pony but we'll never know. Night, MacLean.'

The radio cut back in before he had a chance to respond. No foul play, just one of life's accidents. One that had resulted in the loss of one life and had so nearly cost a second.

The cat wasn't waiting to greet him at the door. He peered into the indigo shadows beneath the shrubs and saw nothing. Perhaps she had gone home to her rightful owner. He should feel pleased; he didn't like cats and didn't want one in his life. Pausing at the open door, he swept his glance across the bushes, but no streak of grey flashed out to dash through into the warmth, so he closed the door.

He flicked on the light and his kitchen leapt out of the darkness. Dropping his keys on the table, he filled the kettle and switched it on. Having missed lunch, hunger grumbled in his stomach, and he belatedly appreciated Grace for always having a meal ready for him when he arrived home. Pulling open the fridge, he peered in at the near-empty shelves. Grace had also made sure there was food in the flat.

He had meant to shop yesterday and again today, but the hours had slipped through his fingers like strands of fine silk. Drinking the remaining fruit juice from the bottle, he put the empty out for recycling. He found a tin of corned beef and made a triple-decker sandwich with tomato. Half a tomato. He dropped the other half on the floor and when he stooped to pick it up, it was speckled with dust, so he threw it in the bin. Sandwich in one hand, he surfed through his contacts and made a call.

'Dave, sorry it's late.' He tipped his head away from the speaker to chew.

'Callum. Problems?' His voice was cautious.

'Nothing to worry about – apart from the state of my house and an empty fridge.' A laugh simmered against his ear. 'So, I was wondering if Anna is still looking for a job? Bit of cleaning? Some shopping?'

'Yeah, I'll check but I'm sure she can fit you in, mate. And I hear you found young Kim, alive and well.'

'We did and both girls will be fine. If Anna could help, that would be grand.' He took another bite of the sandwich.

'What's for supper then? I can hear you eating something.'

Callum hesitated then settled on the truth. 'Corned beef sandwich and black coffee.'

'Ha. Leave her a list on the table with some cash and she'll do you a shop tomorrow. You can discuss the rest with her yourself.'

'Thanks. And thank Anna for me.'

'Yeah, mate.' He chuckled. 'We had home-made steak pie, mash and veg and jam pudding with thick, creamy custard.' His laughter still echoed along the airwaves after the call had ended.

Callum swung round at a movement in his peripheral vision and the cat sauntered in from the hall, tail aloft in welcome. She purred a greeting and rubbed against his legs.

'Fine welcome home, this is. How did you get in?'

The cat worked through a routine of yoga stretches, yawned and went to sit by the empty bowl from last night.

'I forgot to close the cat flap after you left, didn't I? Did you leave? Where have you been all day?'

Blinking lancet eyes at him, the cat yawned again and followed Callum's movements as he crossed the kitchen and returned with a tin.

'Tuna or fresh air, which do you want?'

He forked the fish into a bowl and stroked the cat as she purred in appreciation.

The handwriting in Conchita's diary was neat and sloped to the right. The *k*s looped upwards and the descenders curled downward like rows of monkey tails. The tiny black script hovered just above the line with even-length spaces between words. Her English was good. Occasionally she reverted to continental construction, noting that Paul had eyes brown rather than brown eyes, but not often.

Two mugs of coffee later, he had a feel for both her personality and her sense of humour.

> Today he brought me a new night dress and grey slippers. They are fluffy like a baby flamingo. So soft. *Muy galante*. My *héroe*.

Callum had long since got over the sense that he was invading her privacy, prying into her innermost thoughts and feelings. Conchita presented as honest and thoughtful, caring about what Paul thought and felt. He had imagined a very different stream of text, fraught with angst and frustration, railing at her captor and plotting her escape.

> He brought me some new books, paperbacks, I think when he went to the shopping. He is funny. He gives me the things I ask for but looks away when he puts the tampons on the table. He is so–

Conchita had scribbled out the next word and Callum tilted the page back and forth to see if he could discern any of the letters but without success. He read on.

> Not like Spanish *jóvenes*, grabbing hands and dirty mouths. And he is kind to me, not cruel like María. She is a cow. She frightens me.

She had drawn little cartoon illustrations on the pages and had a good eye for line and perspective. Little vignettes of Spanish villages, nestled on the side of mountains; cascades of tumbling blossoms on the sunny wall of a finca; small fishing boats pulled up on a cliff-backed beach. He wondered if she had sketched them because she felt homesick, as he had done when he drew Fingal's Cave. The bluebell sketch on Paul's kitchen dresser was probably down to her as there had been no suggestion in the cottage that Paul did any drawing.

He turned the page, and the next sketch was the view from the top of Paul's garden looking across the orchard. To have drawn that, she had to have been outside. Perhaps hiding away was her choice, not Paul's.

Reading her diary felt intimate and personal, like carrying on a conversation with a friend. Callum turned over pages with increasing speed, scanning the neat text, and noting the accompanying drawings. Her character was maturing in his mind, and she was not what he had anticipated. He was beginning to understand Conchita and her motivations.

Two fat fingers of single malt sploshed into the tumbler, and he held the glass up to the ceiling light, admiring the amber shards like a shoal of small fish darting around the kitchen walls. In his sitting room, he settled into an armchair. Placing the glass on a side table beneath a lamp, he watched the cat jump onto the sofa and curl up against the cushions. She could stay there for a while. He could move her later. Resting a notepad and pencil on the arm of his chair, he reread the diary.

He made notes, his focus centred within the golden circle beneath the lamp. Outside, the darkness had descended like a watercolour wash, fixing as it fell, until the garden became a tonal study in charcoal. When he reached the end of the diary, he closed it. He wanted to clear his mind, distancing and distracting himself from the list he had made on the lined pad.

He stood, stretched and moved to the window to look out into the garden, at the sculptural plants. He attempted to name the plant silhouettes aided by his daytime memories. It reminded him of Cookie naming the American states. Everything appeared different in the dark. Things that had seemed unimportant, invisible almost, were now defining the shrubs and trees.

He went back to his chair and sat and read through his list one final time. Draining his tumbler, he savoured the heat on his tongue, the peaty richness that rose into his nostrils, the burst of flavour that trickled down his throat. It reminded him of home, of so many things, some of which he would never experience again. A little needle of homesickness stabbed at his heart. The fragrant liquid dried on his lips, and he rose to his feet and gathered up his books. He stroked the cat as he passed the sofa, and she looked up at him and purred like a distant motorcycle. Things always looked different in the daylight.

In his bedroom, he discovered where the cat had spent the day. There was a cat-shaped hollow in the centre of his quilt. Sleep settled easily on him as he looked through the uncurtained window at the silver stars, the same stars that formed a canopy over Kim. He wondered how she was feeling, back in her own bed, coming to terms with the death of Paul and the attack on Kelly. Her sister had become an aggressor, and he hoped there was a chance of reconciliation.

Chapter Thirty-Two

Callum was woken by a sensation of heaviness in his legs. He had slept on his side and the cat was curled up in the crook of his knees.

'Hope you slept well. Made yourself at home?'

The cat extended one front paw towards Callum, yawned, wide-stretched jaws filled with needle teeth, before lowering her head, curling the striped tail over her whiskers and closing her eyes.

'Not a morning person, then.'

She showed no interest in Callum who dressed in running clothes. He envied her ability to effortlessly return to sleep; he should ask for advice.

Once out on the open purlieu, he kept up a steady pace for several miles. He had found a route he liked that offered a good distance on the flat, a sharp descent into a streamed valley followed by a taxing ascent back up to the level. His legs were tanned, a legacy from the warm summer mornings, and, when he felt his shirt sticking to his back, he was pleased that he had opted for shorts.

The early sun sucked misty moisture from the peat, the dampness deadening his footfalls on the track between copper bracken and stands of grey gorse. His hair, tied back, bounced between his shoulder blades with every stride of his final sprint, knees lifted high, and his quads burning. Slowing to a walk, blood racing around his body, he took deep breaths. When his heart rate slowed, he heard another person running and the bald woman sprinted up behind him, then slowed to match his stride.

'Whoooh. Hello.' She was breathing out through her mouth and in through her nose. 'I usually warm down along this track. Mind if I join you?' She wore a pink breast cancer T-shirt that was darkened by sweat between her breasts and under her arms. She looked well-exercised, and Callum judged that she had plenty left in the tank.

'No problem. I'm Callum.' Close up, she did have hair, see-through blonde, cut tight to her head.

'I'm Rain.' She plucked the damp shirt away from her chest. 'And this is not me. It's my younger sister who has breast cancer.'

He put her in her early thirties, so her sister was young to be coping with such an illness. 'What's it short for?' His shirt was sticking to his shoulders, and he pinched the fabric away. 'If you don't mind my asking,' he added.

When she didn't answer straight away, he cursed his policeman's curiosity.

'It's short for Rainbow.' She grinned. 'It's okay to laugh. Most people do.'

He smiled at her. She had very brown eyes flecked with gold, and he thought it would be a pity to make them sad. Names were very personal, and rarely the choice of the person who bore them.

'Unusual, but nice.'

'Thank you. It was my dad's fault.'

The track was narrower now, the leggy spiked gorse pushed into the pathway. His elbow brushed against her arm.

'How was it your dad's fault?'

'They'd given up all hope of having kids and when I was born Dad got a bit overexcited and downed a few too many with his mates. Mum wanted to call me Iris, after the goddess of the rainbow, but Dad was hungover when he went to register me. He could only remember rainbow.'

'Very individual.'

She laughed. 'Thanks. But not when your surname is Waters. No prizes for guessing my nickname at school.'

They stopped when the track split in two.

'I'm this way.' She bobbed her head to the right.

'And I'm that way. I hope we meet again some morning.'

'Me too, Callum. And if you fancy sponsoring me for the 10K run for a good cause' – she tapped her shirt front – 'the info's in the parish mag.'

'Consider it done, Rain.'

She raised a hand and walked away. He watched her for a few strides, then turned for home.

A shortcut from the purlieu back to his cottage followed a gravel path through gorse bushes along the back of the school, and he used it now. At the scrunch of approaching footsteps, a pair of black dogs trotted into view. They stopped and glanced back along the curve of the path until Daphne Smart marched into view too.

Stopping in front of him, she raised a hand to shade her eyes and looked up to his face.

'Good morning, Inspector.'

'Lovely morning, Mrs Smart. Hello, boys.' Dropping a hand on each black head, he felt suddenly self-conscious. He could imagine Daisy smiling at his gesture and the fact that he still couldn't tell Rufus from Paddy.

'I hear you found young Kim. Well done, Inspector.'

'It was a team effort. And she's safe, that's the main thing.'

'I'm surprised at Paul. He seemed such a nice, thoughtful young man. So out of character.' Her eyes were sharp, questioning and focused on his face.

He couldn't disclose details, but she had helped him get information crucial to their finding Kim and he felt he owed her something. Help from the public was not always so forthcoming.

'Sometimes, Mrs Smart,' he said carefully, 'I find, that our first instincts are often the best.'

She nodded, seeming satisfied. 'It can be that way. First impressions are often the most accurate.'

Callum relaxed a fraction, his skin prickling over his cooling limbs. 'Good news all round, then.'

'Not entirely. The major wanted to be the one to find the site. His kitchen is like a military operations room, and he said he thought that's where the base was all along.'

'Pity he didn't share that information with us then.' Callum's tone was light, his disbelief evident.

'Silly man. It's easy to be an expert after the event. But well done.' She dropped her hand to her side and her eyes to his legs. 'Is it true that all Scotsmen are born with shapely knees so they can wear kilts?'

Callum caught the glint in her eye and the lift at the corner of her mouth. 'Och aye.' His accent was pure Glasgow. 'If they've knees like clootie dumplings, we make them wear the trews.'

'Hah! Thought so. Come on, boys.' The sun flashed on the metal rims of her glasses as she chuckled, and he wondered if anything evaded her scrutiny.

Back at his house, he kicked off his damp trainers and went in through the kitchen door. He filled a glass with tap water and drank deeply, the coolness like a waterfall in his chest. Under the shower, he realised that all the observations on the list made from the diary entries had fallen neatly into place. They linked together as snugly as a jigsaw. Smoothing the water out of his hair, he reached for a towel. Why had he not thought of it before? Now *he* was the expert after the event.

The cat watched him dress then curled up on the quilt and closed her eyes. Callum ran a hand down her back and the purr vibrated through her striped body. Her eyes stayed closed.

'No bringing in mice, mind.'

She ignored him.

He gathered up the diary and his notes, placed a shopping list on the kitchen table, and anchored banknotes beneath a marmalade jar. He found his copy of the parish magazine. Car keys in hand, he opened the back door, paused, then went back to the table. "Or similar", he wrote on the bottom of his shopping list, then added his phone number and "text only, please" beside it. He went back a second time and wrote "CAT FOOD".

* * *

There was a noticeable shift in the atmosphere of the office. He glanced around and thought they were sitting up straighter than the previous day. He knew the team would like to down tools and celebrate finding Kim alive. It was the sort of result that brought tears of emotion and relief to the most hard-nosed detective. Days like this made the job worthwhile.

'Right, people. Let's see what we have found out about Paul and Conchita. Cookie, you had the earliest diary,' Callum said.

Cookie swivelled his chair around to face the room. 'The first entry starts about a week after she disappeared. Paul had found her with her wrists bleeding along the coast in Christchurch and made her get in his van. She doesn't say how she got there, but he had been buying spare parts for mowers.'

'She was bloody lucky,' Bird said gruffly. 'Any pervert could have come along.'

'She told him she didn't want to go to hospital and he took her to a cave and bandaged her cuts. Her arms made him cry.' Cookie looked from one face to the other. '*Cueva* is cave. She really didn't care what happened to her. How sad is that? I think communicating was difficult because her English was not good, and Paul didn't understand Spanish.'

'Not then he didn't,' Daisy said, 'but she says in my diary that she taught him Spanish.'

'Some of his shopping list on the kitchen board was written in Spanish,' Callum said, remembering "*cosas*" on the initial list.

'Well, anyway,' Cookie continued, 'she was pretty miserable at the outset. She says she slept a lot and cried and was quite happy to have him look after her. I can understand, if she felt like that. It's easier to stay in bed and hide than it is to get up and face people sometimes. And then it starts to get weird.' Cookie had been sitting still but now his left toe began tapping a beat against the leg of his desk. 'Her arms were healing, and he wanted to take her back to her sister. She refused to go. She didn't want to go back home because her parents didn't believe her that María was hurting her. She told him she had run away before and she thinks he was concerned for her.'

'That explains some of the entries in my book,' Daisy said. 'Conchita seems to have shared interests with Paul like plants and gardening. Do you think she said she liked the things that Paul liked so he would let her stay?'

'Could be,' Cookie said. 'He bought her the diaries, by the way.'

'There was a sketch of bluebells on the dresser in Paul's kitchen,' Callum said. 'I think she drew it. The diary I have is full of good sketches, like views in his garden or flowers. There's one of him in the orchard picking apples.'

'My diaries are full of drawings, too,' Cookie said. 'And they are really good. All the calls on her mobile were only to Paul's mobile. She thought Paul was pretty cool.'

'So do I. He had hidden depths,' Daisy said. 'But it's a bit weird that he didn't turn her over to the police when he found her.'

'He must have known we were looking for her from the news,' Cookie said.

'It was a fortnight before anyone knew she was missing,' Callum said.

'And we are out of the local news area,' Bird pointed out.

'Plus,' Daisy said, 'he might have been concerned that he would be accused of abducting her. Which we now know he didn't, but I think it would have worried him.' She was still fighting his corner. 'He wouldn't let Kim stay in his house because he didn't think it was right. He's not a lawbreaker. He even kept to the speed limit every time he got behind the wheel.'

'We get it. You see Paul as a victim, too,' Callum said.

'Conchita had boyfriends in Spain.' Cookie's pink cheeks deepened to madder. 'She was a bit adventurous in her sex life.' He turned over a couple of pages of his notes as if searching for a particular sentence. It was an old trick, and he was just giving himself time to compose his thoughts because he looked up without locating it. 'She wanted a sexual relationship with Paul, but he wasn't interested. He asked her to leave then agreed to let her stay a bit longer, but sex was a step too far. Amongst other comments she made about him, she thought he was still a virgin.'

'He might well have been.' Daisy frowned. 'He was very old-fashioned, with a sort of chivalry about him you don't see these days.'

'Thanks very much,' Bird said.

Daisy flicked her fingers at him. 'You know what I mean,' she added. 'Holding open doors for women, carrying their bags. No sex before marriage. Conchita thought he was caught in a sort of time warp. An English gentleman.'

'He was brought up by his grandfather,' Callum said, 'who would have had different social standards from today.'

'He was frightened of his grandfather, according to Conchita.' Daisy turned to a page she had bookmarked. 'Says he didn't like some of the things the old man did.'

'That's another thing, guv, while we're on the subject of Jim Barnes,' Bird said. 'I looked up Esther's death and it's not registered. Neither here nor in Hereford where she was supposed to have died visiting her sister.'

'Must still be alive then,' Cookie said.

'She'd be a medical miracle then,' Bird grunted. 'She'd be a hundred and twenty-one years old. And she's not drawing her pension.'

Callum thought about the graves in the orchard. 'Is the daughter, Susan's death registered, Bird?'

'Not that I've managed to find. I don't think she was married; both the children had her maiden name. The little girl is buried in the churchyard. I checked with the reverend.'

'Any headstones marked Susan and Esther?' Cookie laughed at the absurdity of his comment. 'Only joking.'

Many a theory had started as a joke. Perhaps Daphne Smart had been right to be scared by Jim Barnes.

'In my book,' Daisy said, 'and this is going to sound odd, Conchita seems to have been on a mission to "save" Paul. She developed an emotional attachment to him. I think the sketches she did were for him, to foster that relationship.'

'Agreed—' Callum was interrupted by Cookie.

'What I don't get, guv, is why she stayed there when she had the chance to leave. I wouldn't want to stay cooped up in a bunker in the dark if I could escape.'

Daisy laughed. 'That's because you can't sit still for five minutes, and you make her sound like a chicken. But actually, the base was quite nice, cosy and warm. She had personalised it, made it into her own little nest.'

'It's a good point,' Callum said. 'She stayed because Paul saved her life. She saw him in a positive light.'

'Some sort of saviour?' Cookie shook his head. 'I still don't get it.'

'Okay.' Callum counted off points on the fingers of his left hand. 'One, she sees him as saving her life. She was self-harming, miserable and ready to give up on herself. Two, he provided her with a good living environment. She had decorated the base to her taste. Three, she's isolated from the outside world, so she begins to see things from his viewpoint. Four, she develops an emotional attachment to Paul, and they start sharing common interests.'

'Like the flowers?' Cookie asked.

'Exactly. She wanted to please Paul, and she developed a dependence on him.'

'Got it, guv,' Bird said. 'Classic Stockholm syndrome, isn't it? I wasn't expecting that. But it's so bleedin' obvious when you put it all together. Paul wasn't using her; she was using him. He asked her to leave, and she refused. She wanted to stay with him.'

'I think they used each other, to some extent. Conchita used Paul as a protector, he gave her a haven. She felt safe and secure, valued even, and it took her away from her uncomfortable life with her sister and the expectations of her parents. Paul respected her, and he found a friend, and he was probably short of those. Conchita was someone who needed him, provided company, and cared for him. It was a win–win for both of them. We were just looking at it from the wrong perspective.' It also went some way to explaining where Paul spent his evenings if not in his austere front room or sitting on a hard chair by the kitchen fire.

Bird scrubbed his hand over his stubbly head. 'Well, I'll be chased by a bull with a bundle tied to me arse.'

They all looked at him as the words tripped off his tongue.

He grinned sheepishly. 'Sorry. Private joke.'

'What you get up to in your spare time is your affair, Bird.' Humour glinted in Callum's eye and Daisy laughed aloud.

* * *

Mid-morning, Daisy joined Callum in the fishbowl.

'You asked for an update on Kim, and she's doing fine. Her wounds are superficial. This morning, she was up at the crack of sparrows and down the field to see Drummer. She's convinced he's been missing her.'

Callum looked disbelieving. 'If you say so.'

Daisy pulled a face, mocking him. 'I thought he was your new best friend, or were you lying to Kim?'

'Let's settle for reassuring her, shall we? She's a resilient girl and for her, the world is pretty much back to normal.'

'Sam doesn't want to let her out of his sight. He went to the field with her this morning "at an ungodly hour", but he was smiling from ear to ear. He looks much better now his daughters are safe.'

Callum closed his eyes against the memory of how he had felt when Grace died.

When he looked back to Daisy, she was holding her head tilted to the side, her blue eyes questioning. The corner of his mouth lifted in a wry smile.

'Another lifetime, Daisy.' His voice was low and gentle.

'If you say so.' She looked sceptical. 'I think all our lives are joined together like Christmas tree lights on a long wire.'

'You may be right,' he said.

And if she was, there was no escaping from past events. He would remain connected to them, however far he travelled from Glasgow. It also meant that Grace would never leave his side until he took his last breath. Should he feel saddened or comforted? For now, he was happy with the status quo.

'I am right. Are you trying to shut me up, end the discussion?' she said.

'Me to know, you—'

'Yeah, yeah, I get it.' She went back into the outer office and sat behind her desk.

* * *

The promised Indian summer was following the script from the meteorologist and threw a bright quilt of gold over his team. Anna sent him a text and he responded with a thumbs up before going into the outer office. She had purchased everything on his list. He and the cat now had food.

'Well done, people. That was good work all round, and a great result finding Kim safe and well. Her parents have asked that I pass on their appreciation for your efforts.'

Murmurs of satisfaction were shared.

'You found her,' Daisy said. 'It was down to you.'

'It was down to excellent teamwork. Thank you, all.'

Cookie tapped a drum roll on the surface of his desk with two pens accompanied by a falsetto screech of 'Simply the best!'

'Can it, Cookie,' Bird shouted good-naturedly.

Cookie laughed aloud, unsuccessfully attempting to dodge a paper clip launched by Daisy, then teased it out of his hair and tossed it back at her.

'Good shot, Deedee,' Cookie said.

'And now,' Callum said, 'if you are free this evening, there is a barbecue at mine to show my appreciation. Bring a friend.'

Cookie whooped and spun his chair round on its axis, an arm raised above his head like a cowboy with a lasso.

'Yes, please,' Bird said. 'Helen'll be delighted not to have to cook. Count us in.'

Murmurs of affirmation floated across the office.

'Count me in too,' Daisy said.

'Good.' Callum looked around at the smiling faces before adding, 'But sorry, no dogs.'

'Why no dogs? We'll keep them away from you,' Daisy teased.

'Because…' he said, 'I have a cat.'

Character List

Jimmy Eastwood – local agister

Kelly Tanner – older sister of Kim Tanner

Kim Tanner – a missing child

Louise Tanner – mother of Kelly and Kim

Sam Tanner – father of Kelly and Kim

Paul Barnes – lives alone, raised by his grandparents

Anna Green – daughter of Dave Green

Bryony Osbourne – a friend of Callum

Eileen – supermarket employee

Ester Barnes – Paul's grandmother

James Barnes – Paul's grandfather

Susan Barnes – Paul's mother

Freya – one of Callum's sisters

Susan Eastwood – Jimmy's wife

Sheena Hatcher – Jericho's wife

Acknowledgements

I want to thank two groups of writers who have provided critique and encouragement in equal measures. The first are Lisa, Sandra, Valerie, Penny and Jan, and the second are Emma, Sam, Zab, Veronica, Tracy and Caroline. They are all writers, and I am privileged to have their support. Thanks also to beta reader Helen, and Hugh Bond for all things medical.

This would have been a very different book without the input of all these people, and I cannot overestimate the importance of them all to the finished novel.

My gratitude goes to the team at The Book Folks who have been all-round amazing and a pleasure to work with, and especially Arianna for her extreme patience.

My special thanks go to my husband and son for their endless enthusiasm, unstinting support and their belief in me.

I hope you enjoy this crime novel and that reading about the New Forest will encourage you to come and visit us. There is much to explore, from historic sites to open heaths and grassy lawns. Come and see the herds of wild ponies, donkeys and deer in a setting that dates back to William the Conqueror.

If you enjoyed this book, please let others know by leaving a quick review on Amazon. Also, if you spot anything untoward in the paperback, get in touch. We strive for the best quality and appreciate reader feedback.

editor@thebookfolks.com

www.thebookfolks.com

Also in this series

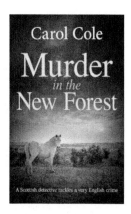

MURDER IN THE NEW FOREST (Book 1)

When a woman's body is found on the ground next to her horse, it seems an unfortunate accident had occurred. However, DI Callum MacLean, newly arrived in the picturesque New Forest from Glasgow, suspects differently. But hunting a killer in this close-knit community, suspicious of outsiders, will be tough. Especially when not everyone in his team is on side.

FREE with Kindle Unlimited and available in paperback!

Other titles of interest

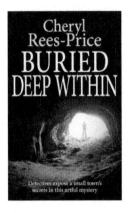

BURIED DEEP WITHIN
by Cheryl Rees-Price

When a baby goes missing during her christening party, the local community come out in force to help the search. Some of them were at the do, and are considerably worse for wear. Detective Winter Meadows tries to make sense out of the chaos and prevent people from jumping to conclusions about the likely culprit. But tempers are flaring. Enough to test the patience of this cool-headed cop.

FREE with Kindle Unlimited and available in paperback!

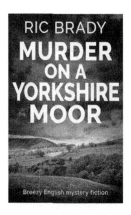

MURDER ON A YORKSHIRE MOOR
by Ric Brady

Ex-detective Henry Ward is settling awkwardly into
retirement in a quiet corner of Yorkshire when during a
walk on the moor he stumbles upon the body of a young
man. Suspecting foul play and somewhat relishing the return
to a bit of detective work, he resolves to find out who killed
him. But will the local force appreciate him meddling?

FREE with Kindle Unlimited and available in paperback!

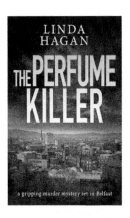

THE PERFUME KILLER
by **Linda Hagan**

Stumped in a multiple murder investigation, with the only clue being a perfume bottle top left at a crime scene, Belfast cop DCI Gawn Girvin must wait for a serial killer to make a wrong move. Unless she puts herself in the firing line…

FREE with Kindle Unlimited and available in paperback!

As a thank-you to our readers, we regularly run free book promotions and discounted deals for a limited time. To hear about these and about new fiction releases, just sign up to our newsletter.

www.thebookfolks.com